A Crossroad to Love by Lauralee Blis
True to the Quaker tradition of
family transform their home into ar
one guest challenges their resolve mo.e than any other. Silas Jones scorns the Halls' lifestyle even as he continues to stay with them. But as the Christmas season approaches—and the story behind Silas's headstrong ways comes to light—the Halls have a new holiday mission to heal a hurting soul.

Simple Gifts by Ramona Cecil
Following her husband's death, Lucinda Hughes struggles with her faith. And Will Davis struggles with his guilt, believing he should have been in her husband's place at the mill that fateful day. Will's wish is to help Lucinda, though he soon wants only to be near her. But will Lucinda's own dwindling faith—and the truth surrounding her husband's death—keep them from discovering the true joy of the Christmas season?

Pirate of My Heart by Rachael Phillips
Keturah Wilkes loves God. She just struggles with the excitement her sedate Quaker upbringing denies—including celebrating Christmas. Then she meets Henry Mangun, a young man thirsting for a quiet escape from his rowdy family. But although Keturah's drawn to Henry, it's his devil-may-care brother, Charlie, who truly captures her interest. . .until she's trapped in one of Charlie's hijacking schemes with seemingly no way out.

Equally Yoked by Claire Sanders
Barely five months after her wedding, Susanna Griffith faces a lonely Christmas without her husband. Nathan has gone to help a fellow conductor on the Underground Railroad with Susanna, never more than a bystander, left holding the reins of uncertainty in his absence. When a pregnant runaway slave arrives at Susanna's door, she knows she must help this young woman gain her freedom . . .while trusting her faith to see her through.

A QUAKER CHRISTMAS

FOUR-IN-ONE COLLECTION

LAURALEE BLISS
RAMONA CECIL
RACHAEL PHILLIPS
CLAIRE SANDERS

BARBOUR
PUBLISHING

Cover design: Kirk DouPonce, DogEared Design

Published by Barbour Publishing, Inc., P.O. Box 719, Uhrichsville, Ohio 44683, www.barbourbooks.com

Our mission is to publish and distribute inspirational products offering exceptional value and biblical encouragement to the masses.

 Member of the
Evangelical Christian
Publishers Association

Printed in the United States of America.

A CROSSROAD TO LOVE

Lauralee Bliss

Dedication

To my hosts, the McCormacks, who displayed
the essence of hospitality while I was hiking the
Appalachian Trail in New York and who furnished a
computer so I could work on this idea. My thanks.

Chapter 1

1846
A crossroad near Waynesville, Ohio

"Christ's cross is Christ's way to Christ's crown."
WILLIAM PENN

The limp had become too pronounced to ignore any longer. Silas Jones grimaced as he dismounted, patting his mount on the muzzle even though frustration built within him. Examining the hoof, he found strange fluid oozing out, accompanied by the horse's nicker of pain. He grimaced at the ugly conclusion. They could go no farther.

"Sorry, Barzillai," he said softly to the mare. "I shouldn't have kept riding you after you threw the shoe." But he had, thinking the animal was as strong as iron, like the biblical name implied. Now he would pay the price of a lame animal, without the means to continue.

Perhaps it was for the better. Why did he feel the urgency to press this journey? He'd wanted to make it to Independence before the snows became too deep. That would set him up to join a wagon train next spring. But now that plan might be in jeopardy, all because of his hasty heart in desperate need of healing, like Barzillai's hoof. Silas knew the reason for his haste, but the poor animal shouldn't be made to suffer. He must give her time to heal. And hope the delay wouldn't be too long.

Silas looked up then and saw a rider approaching. The man was simply dressed in a plain black frock coat and hat. Silas frowned and shook his head, refusing to compare the image with his past. He was in Ohio after all. That is, until the man spoke.

"Does thee require assistance?"

Silas's hands froze. His heart jumped. "No!" The reply came out so harshly, even Silas was startled by it. He turned away, unwilling to have the man's appearance and holy nature penetrate his soul. He'd left it all behind, all the pain and more, to embrace a new future.

But looking at his wounded horse, Silas realized he did have a need. He must accept the man's help if he was to continue this journey. "Yes, I do need assistance. I'm looking for a place to stay. My horse went lame, and I need to find good care for her."

"Just up the road a bit is the home of the Hall family. They take in weary travelers. And the son there, George, is a wonder with horses. They will care for thy needs, most assuredly."

Silas nodded while avoiding the man's steady gaze. He was thankful the man said nothing further but only offered a handshake farewell before continuing up the road. The methodic *clip-clop* of hooves faded into the distance.

Think nothing of the encounter, he told himself. *The appearance. The manner of speech. It's only a coincidence.* But he had to wonder if God had sent the man from Philadelphia, as ludicrous as it sounded. The past had followed him, even if he wished it hundreds of miles away, where it belonged.

Silas wrapped his fingers tightly around the horse's reins and led the mare down the dirt road, hoping this place of refuge wasn't too far. His shoes had already worn thin from miles of walking to allow Barzillai needed rest. He should find a town to lay in some supplies, a good blacksmith for Barzillai's needs, and a cobbler to mend his own shoes. But at this moment, just the thought of a comfortable bed, plenty of food, and perhaps a strong drink to deaden the pain of the past sent his hopes soaring and the reminder wrought by the man in black to some distant realm.

Barzillai shook her head and neighed, limping from the wound on her hoof, until Silas arrived at a large manor house made of stone. It looked rather wealthy compared to the log cabins he had passed in his travels, and even those cabins that also welcomed travelers. The house reminded him of Philadelphia. It could have been set on a busy city street there rather than on its own small rise of ground, surrounded by brown grass long since withered from the change of season and a few hearty oak trees sporting their bare limbs. It did prove a pleasing sight to his weary and downtrodden soul, even if it held another reminder of a city he still tried desperately to forget.

A man about his age strode out of the barn and down the small hill. His face turned to a picture of a warm greeting, with a broad smile and large eyes that glinted in the sun's light. "Welcome!"

11

Silas removed his hat. "Sorry to bother you, but my horse is injured and—"

"I will gladly tend thy horse. I have a way with horses, or so people have told me." He held out his hand. "I'm George Hall. My father owns this place. We have many travelers come and stay, and I hope thee will decide to stay as well."

"I'm Silas Jones. Thank you for the kind offer."

George took the reins from Silas, and Barzillai ambled after the man as if they had known each other a long time. Assured his mount was in good hands, Silas headed for the main house, only to stop short when a young woman walked across the yard, carrying a woven basket of folded clothes. She wore a dark linen dress and a heavy wool cloak about her shoulders to protect her from the biting wind. Her dark bonnet hid most of her face from view until she turned to offer him a curious glance. She did not acknowledge his presence but instead opened the front door to the house and called for her father.

A short man with graying hair, dressed in dark clothes, came to the door. "Welcome to our inn!" he said with enthusiasm, much like the young man named George. "Is thee in need of a place to stay?"

"Yes, thank you. My horse went lame."

"George can help thee with thy horse. Please, come in and be comfortable."

Silas stepped inside the home. The interior held an aura of simplicity but was far richer than the rustic places he'd come to inhabit on his journey. Finely crafted wood chairs with attractive fan backs, a large drop-front desk, and a

library of books met his curious gaze. There were no gran-
diose paintings or other fabrics of decorations but plenty
of paned windows, allowing the sunlight to brighten each
room. Fires burned cheerily in several fireplaces to warm
the cold day. In the dining area, a long wooden table with
benches on either side stood ready to receive a multitude of
guests.

"There's talk of snow," the man said as Silas surveyed the
warmth of the home. "Thee has surely arrived in time. God
has guided thy footsteps."

Silas turned. He wondered if the family had anything
to do with the Society of Friends, hearing all the thees and
thys. Just like the talk he'd heard earlier on the road. Surely
he didn't happen upon a village of Quakers. He dismissed his
disturbing thoughts and took a seat in one of the fine chairs.

Mr. Hall disappeared into another room but soon
returned with a steaming mug in hand. Silas licked his lips in
anticipation of the mug's contents. Just what he needed—a
nice mulled wine to deaden his senses and liven his situation.
He took a large swallow of the contents and nearly choked,
both on the hot liquid and on the realization it was apple
cider in his mug. "This is not mulled wine," he sputtered.
"Have you no brew at your inn? I've had the privilege of
indulging many times on my journey so far."

"Brew? I don't understand."

"Liquor. Spirits, my good man."

"I'm sorry, but we don't serve spirits here. A good drink of
the earth, like this apple cider, does well for one's soul. It will
warm thee better than anything else. I trust thee will enjoy it."

There it was again. *Thee.* Wording he could not ignore. *They must be of the Friends' persuasion....* Between the Hall family and the man he'd met earlier on the road, he must have inadvertently stumbled upon a Quaker settlement in the middle of Ohio. And just when he was looking to escape it. Was this God's way of forcing redemption when he wanted no part of it?

Silas stood, wishing now he had the means to leave this place, but he couldn't. Snow was coming. Barzillai was lame in the hoof. And his shoes were mere scraps of flapping leather with barely a nail attaching them to the soles. He sat back down with his mug of apple cider, feeling more and more like a small lad with his childhood drink. He wanted to spout his frustrations to Mr. Hall—that this was no inn, that the man had no business taking in travelers if he could not fulfill their requirement for fine spirits to warm a winter's night. And he didn't care to hear pious people uttering thees for the rest of the evening as if they reigned on some mountaintop while he lay snared in the valley's trap.

All of this weighed on Silas until he became distracted by the young woman he'd seen earlier. She now stood in the doorway, staring at him. With her dark bonnet replaced by a cap of thin white, he saw fine brown hair fixed in a bun. The color of the cap matched the creamy paleness of her skin, and her cheeks were tinted a dusty rose from being outdoors in the cold wind. But he saw a look of fire in her blue eyes and lips turned downward in distaste. Then with a rustle of her skirt, she left.

Silas folded his arms in dismay, knowing she must have

witnessed the interaction with her father over the matter of spirits. But why should her reaction bother him? He certainly wasn't here to win her heart or any other, especially if this was a family of Quakers. Heaven knew he could not nor would he ever associate with such people again. He gritted his teeth. The Society of Friends in Philadelphia had purposely left the door open to evil. Evil came stalking like a predator and killed like one, too. And that, to him, was a grievous wound that nothing could heal.

Silas shook his head and drank the cider, feeling its soothing effects in his stomach, just as the proprietor had promised. And then something filled him. Not some false peace born out of liquor that fooled with men's minds. Rather, he felt comfort. Refreshment to a weary soul and spirit. A sense of spiritual peace, as strange as it seemed, when he'd experienced no such peace for many weeks.

Another woman walked in then, older, plainly dressed, with a brown kerchief about her shoulders for warmth and the simple white cap on her head. She carried a platter of biscuits. "I'm Mrs. Hall. Thee must be hungry, Mister. . ."

"Silas Jones, madam. You may call me Silas, if you wish." He took two flaky biscuits and hungrily consumed them. He hadn't tasted anything that good in a long time.

"My goodness, he is quite a hungry man, my husband," she said with a laugh to Mr. Hall as he entered the room. "I fear he would eat the platter if he could."

The husband told his wife of Silas's circumstances and Barzillai's misfortune.

Silas then lifted his foot to show them his worn shoe. "Is

there a cobbler in town?"

"Oh dear. Look at his shoes! Simply dreadful. We can mend them, can't we, husband? He cannot go like this with the snows coming. Or perhaps our neighbor, Mr. Warren, can help. He makes shoes."

The wife then pointed at her shoe, gesturing for Silas to remove his. When he did, his feet also revealed his wool socks, full of holes. Again Mrs. Hall shook her head and talked of knitting him some new socks as soon as possible. Silas sat in amazement, though he knew the Friends possessed a generosity of spirit. They cared for all people, believing God's Light lay within each. But that simple faith in humanity and a belief in equality among all also brought trouble.

Silas felt his fist clench then at a painful memory and fought to relax it for fear of observing eyes. Like those of the young woman who returned to the doorway with a look that bespoke a thousand questions on her mind. He would refuse any inquisition, even if the young woman was a beauty to behold.

He stood now and inquired about his room.

"Of course. Mary will show thee to thy room," Mrs. Hall acknowledged. "Mary?"

"Follow me, please," Mary said.

So the beauty with eyes like the deep-blue skies above had a name, and a nice name, too. The name of the Savior's mother. He took his mug and followed Mary as she swiftly swept up the flight of stairs to a row of rooms on the second floor. "Thee may have the room on the far left," she directed.

"Don't you grow tired of your thees?" Silas suddenly remarked.

She faced him, centering her large blue eyes framed by arched eyebrows on him. "No, I do not."

"Why not, pray tell?"

"One man is not better than another, as scripture says. We are all equal."

"It's all foolishness. It brings you nothing. Nothing at all, you know. It only makes you appear vain and haughty. Or rather it makes *thee* appear that way." He ended with a scornful chortle.

"I'm sorry thee believes such things. Perhaps the description of vanity is better meant for those who believe they know what's best in life, though their hearts are dark with lies." She wheeled around.

Silas laughed. "Look at you. Haughty in your opinions, wouldn't you say? Maybe *thee* needs a little more humility and less pride."

"And maybe thee needs to show more respect for the household in which thee has found lodging." She strode down the hall and down the stairs.

So it appeared a black sheep resided in the flock; a sheep with eyes of blue fire and a sharp tongue to match. It left him speechless, he admitted, but also intrigued. No woman from the Society of Friends in Philadelphia held to such brazenness. They were all respectful and dignified. They wore the mark of a Friend as if it were a symbol for all to see and bear witness. A Light in a dark world, or so they believed. But this woman, Mary Hall, met his challenge face to face, word for word. No demureness or humility was evident on her part. Only fierce determination, and he feared what such determination could do to someone like him in the days ahead.

Silas rested in his room, thinking about his life and what the future might bring, until he heard the dinner bell. The pit of his stomach churned with thoughts of a hearty meal. He hastened down the stairs to see two other gents had arrived and stood in the hallway, eager to partake of the Hall family's evening meal and lodging. They were boisterous fellows, dressed in dusty travel garments, with conversation flowing readily from their lips. One sported a silver flask of spirits. Silas wondered what the family would think of the flask as the men made introductions.

"I'm Abe," the man with the flask said to Silas. "So how do you feel about our hosts? Strange folk, eh? But friendly." Abe laughed at his own pun, took a swallow out of the flask, and passed it to Silas.

"I had no choice. I was in need of a place to stay because my horse went lame." Silas took the flask and drank. He nearly choked as the potent liquid singed his throat. Then he thought of Mary Hall. She would be glad the liquor scorched him. She would tell him he deserved it and more. *It will never quench thy true thirst in life*, he imagined her saying.

Abe grinned and took back his flask. "We know they don't like liquor, but it will make the evening a bit warmer and friendlier, wouldn't you say?"

"Quite," Silas sputtered. "And do you know why they are called Quakers?"

Abe shook his head.

"Because they think they are so close to God that they visibly tremble in His sight." Glancing behind him, Silas saw Mary in the doorway, with her arms folded and her lips pressed tight. He waited for some rebuke from her, how he lacked good manners. He would meet her challenge with one of his own.

Instead she rang the dinner bell once more and invited them into the dining room. Silas ignored the look on Mary's face and, laughing with the men, sauntered inside. Mrs. Hall had placed an abundance of food on the table. Already seated at the table was the son, George, and Mr. Hall, who greeted each of them. Mary and the mother hastened about, serving them. He caught sight of Mary's wide eyes traveling to the flask Abe had in his possession, its shiny metal reflecting the candlelight. She opened her mouth as if to say something and then looked to her father. Mr. Hall said nothing of the liquor in their presence but only sat at the head of the table and smiled.

Silas was enjoying this all very much. The food was good, but the spirits were even better. It wasn't long before the contents of the flask passed to him under the table had loosened his tongue. "Did I tell you about the Friends I met in Philadelphia?" he said to Abe.

"So thee once dwelt in the City of Brotherly Love?" Mr. Hall inquired.

"Brotherly love, sir? Ha! There is no such love to speak of. The city breathes evil, my good man. And the so-called Friends do nothing but speak their pious babble, which means little and does even less."

Mary gasped. George stared. Mr. Hall's smile never wavered as he lifted the platter to offer them more meat.

When little came of his remark, Silas grew silent. It was as if the wax had been stripped from his candle of discontent. Nothing remained to fuel the flame. Except Mary, who continued to stare at him with her narrow set of blue eyes, her nose slightly lifted in the air, and her arms crossed. He sensed no satisfaction over her reaction, just disappointment. Perhaps rightly so. This family had nothing to do with Philadelphia, except that they were Quakers. He should not brand them with his past.

Silas excused himself to wander out into the sitting room with the fancy wooden chairs. He no longer wanted to associate with anyone or drink of any flask. None of it brought the peace he sought. Instead he only wished he could ride out of here in the morning. He glanced out the window to see a few flakes of snow drifting down from the skies. The storm foretold by Mr. Hall. Between his horse and the storm, God Himself had decided that Silas should remain here for now, perhaps to face what he could not. And that fact irritated him to no end.

"Oh, Mr. Jones, thee has not had thy dessert!" Mrs. Hall called to him. "I made a good pumpkin pie. Come join us."

He offered her a small smile before quietly entering the room and occupying his place once more at the long table. He made no eye contact with anyone, least of all Mary. In his heart he wanted to apologize to the Hall family for what was said. Or alluded to. But pride locked the words in his throat, where they remained.

Abe and the other gentleman, Thomas, made light-hearted comments as they feasted on thick slices of pie. Silas remained silent, eating the delicious pie, knowing that those around him likely wondered what ailed him. No matter. He would leave this place as soon as he could. Pray the snow-storm would amount to nothing and Barzillai would have a miraculous recovery. Anything, so long as he could abandon this Quaker home and be on his way, continuing a journey of the soul, with no real conclusion in sight.

Chapter 2

He's inconsiderate of our ways. He's conceited. He's like a wolf in sheep's clothing. We must send him away as soon as possible." Mary tried in vain to add a sense of urgency to her words. She could not ignore the feelings that rose each day Silas Jones remained under the roof of their home.

But Father would not hear of it no matter how much she ranted. "Mary, must I read to thee what scripture says? That like the Mary of old, thee must choose a wiser course, such as love and mercy and truth. Thee must sit at our Master's feet to hear His bidding. And take in a lost sheep like Mr. Jones. Thee should not dismiss opportunity. Only God knows the time of his departure, and I am glad he is here and told him so."

"But he's not of the brethren, Father. Opportunities are only for those in fellowship. We have taken in a wolf among us. I'm certain of it. I've seen it in his eyes. And we've seen and heard what he's said and done in our presence. Drinking spirits at dinner. Mocking our beliefs." She looked around. "And have we taken stock of our goods? The money jar? We ought to find a new place for the money."

"Come, come, Mary. Does thee truly believe Mr. Jones is here to steal from us? He is not the evil one. And who are we to judge his condition? Certainly not thee. Or myself. Or anyone. He has done nothing ill since he's been among us. He is but a lost soul in great need. His heart, I believe, is already accepting of God's mercy and light. And so we, too, should be merciful."

But Mary refused. No matter what Father said, she would not trust Silas Jones. Any man under the influence of strong drink, with contempt for others, mocking even the most sacred things, such as the trembling brought forth by the Spirit of God, should be cast out from among them. Her family could be poisoned by it. Surely the elders would agree with her.

Just the mere thought of Silas laughing at them made anger flow through her. Anger that neither Father nor the elders would approve of, she knew. But she couldn't help how she felt. If only they could see the eyes of Silas Jones that revealed the man's inner self. They were a delightful deep, dark brown, but they concealed mischief. Eyes that taunted and challenged the very fabric of her family's existence—of who and what they were.

Mary took up her basket in a huff and hurried outside. Frustration built within her. Did no one see the signs? Were they all blinded by simple trust—a trust that could turn disastrous if they were not careful? Oh, if she must remain silent for days she would, to confirm what she believed in her heart.

She spent the next hour digging in the cold, dark-brown soil and the bit of snow that lay from the storm several days ago. A few vegetables still remained from the harvest many weeks back. Mother asked that the remainder of the vegetables be taken up from the ground if possible. The soil felt as hard and cold as the chunks of ice Father sometimes purchased in sawdust during the summer. *Not very different from the hardness of men's hearts*, she mused. *Like the heart of Silas Jones.*

She then considered Father's response of thankfulness for the stranger with them. Perhaps it would do well for her to think on the man's lost nature as Father did. The darkness where he hid. His wandering soul in need of God's Light to guide him back. But she could not dismiss his outright blasphemy of their ways. Or how he addressed her and the brethren's way of communicating, even going so far as to call her haughty and vain. With each aggravating thought, she dug deeper into the earth to free the potatoes before plopping them into the basket. She grabbed up the load to take back to the house.

Suddenly she felt something bump into her. Her basket sailed into the air, scattering root vegetables on the ground. She stood there, stunned, until she heard a voice exclaim an apology and saw a man's large hands gathering up the vegetables now frosted by flakes of snow.

"I didn't see you, Miss Hall. My humble apologies. I hope you aren't hurt."

She looked up then to see eyes of the deepest brown. Were they really the eyes of mischief, as she believed? Right now the eyes of Silas Jones seemed to display a look of genuine concern. Perhaps even compassion, though she had no idea why. Silas cared only for his opinions. She sucked in her breath, remembering her own words, of the wolf in sheep's clothing, prowling about, looking to devour the innocent like her family. And now this supposed sheep was trying to grab other things. Like her heart, perhaps?

She took back the basket of vegetables, brushing away the bits of snow mixed with brown grass and soil from her skirt. "Thank you, but I must go." She bit her lip, realizing she had misstepped the Friends' language. *How could that have happened?*

All at once the basket was back in his hands. His swift action surprised her. "What are you doing?" she demanded.

"At least let me carry this back to the kitchen. It's heavy."

"I can handle it quite well. I thank thee."

"Yes, I'm sure you can. Or shall I say *thee* can?" His lips turned up into a faint smile.

She grabbed the basket's woven handle. "Please, I grow tired of your mockery. I know you. I mean, I know thee. It's quite easy to see what thee is doing. But it won't work." She felt her face burn with her continued slip of the tongue. She wondered if this man was somehow causing her to stumble. What else could it be? She had never found her spirit in such disarray. Unless there was more working here to disrupt her heart than she realized.

His large hand released the basket into her possession. He took a step back. "So what is it about me you know? I thought only God could search out the depths of one's heart. Unless you all have made up your mind what ails me. And what a sinner I am in your eyes." When she didn't answer, he took a step forward. In haste she retreated. "You have no reply?"

"Only that I have seen men like thee before. Men who

prefer to walk in their cloud of darkness rather than embrace God's Light. And His Light is in thee, Mr. Jones, if thee would open thy eyes and heart to it."

"I need no reminders of the Light. I have seen it. And all it has done is blind those who embrace it. And they end up seeing nothing and doing less. Not even when death takes one of their own." He turned then and strode to the door leading to the kitchen.

Gripped by his words, Mary couldn't help but follow. Now she wondered about the secret he concealed and if she could draw it out. "What do you mean? God's Light causes no such hurt. God is life and love."

He stopped abruptly, whirled, and gazed at her so intently that she felt warmth tease her cheeks and her hands tremble in response. "Please don't force me to tell you any more," he mumbled. "I won't say it. I can't." He bumped through the doorway and into the house.

Mary thought on the words uttered by a desperate voice that fought to conceal the truth. What was that truth in the heart of the man, closed over by pain? Mary wasn't certain she wanted to bear such a burden, even if the Friends taught her to do such things. Perhaps that burden was better left to others. Like Father. Or even her brother, George, whom she'd seen talking to Silas in the barn. Then again, George had taken over the task of nursing Silas's mare, and he seemed quite happy with the horse's progress. Silas might be comfortable confiding in another man his age. Or perhaps even speaking to one of the elders like Friend Daniel Gray.

Mary gathered her shawl about her shoulders and cautiously approached the kitchen. Inside she saw Mother talking with Silas. From the way they conversed, it seemed the man was also trying to win Mother's heart. She frowned in dismay. Mother seemed to respond favorably to him as she smiled and nodded. But Mary knew the truth. The man's anger toward the Quakers. The unrequited things stored in his heart.

Mary tried to scurry past the kitchen, but Mother's voice caught her short. "Mary, would you be so kind as to fetch Mr. Jones a mug of apple cider? I have some warming on the stove."

Indeed I do mind, she thought but took a clean mug from a hook on the wall. "Surely thee wishes it weren't cider," she remarked to him in a low voice, dipping out the fragrant brew teeming with spices.

He calmly took the beverage and said nothing until they entered the sitting room. "Please tell me what it is I'm eager to drink, Miss Hall, as you seem to know everything. Though I don't understand where such wisdom comes from, since I've only been here a few days."

"You would drink that poison that clouds men's judgment. How you could drink from that flask in our home . . .and at the table. . ." She didn't care that her words were directed at him without the common Friends' language. He'd disgraced their family with the drinking and the comments about their faith. He'd disgraced her.

"If I were to apologize for my conduct that first evening, would you accept it?" He took a long drink and waited for her answer. She stayed silent. "So you wouldn't."

"Why should I? You've given me no reason to believe you

mean it. I mean, thee." Warmth again teased her face. She turned aside.

Silas laughed. He then approached her in a manner that sent tingles shooting through her. Only they were not tingles of concern but of some strange attraction she dared not even entertain. *He—he's an outsider. An insolent man of the world.*

"Put aside your humble speech, Mary. You trip over the words like they were stones. God isn't a respecter of persons or of the language they speak."

The words surprised her. He was not a heathen. He did know something of scripture. And using it to trap her, perhaps? Or maybe to teach her. But how could it be the latter? "I—I don't know what thee means."

"A woman of the friendly persuasion doesn't need to hide behind a bonnet or rules to be who she is. Let go, and live in freedom."

"And become like thee? No, I'd rather be at peace than be miserable." She hurried away to her room to find her embroidery, anything to rid her mind of Silas Jones. How he could suggest such things went beyond her sense of reasoning. Why couldn't she convince Father of the man's disturbing ways? That Silas Jones sought to strip them of their faith. Take away all that brought them close to God by trusting in Him for everything in their lives. *I have warned them of this man's ways*, she thought in despair, even as her fingers fumbled to thread the needle. *But they won't take heed.*

She puzzled over it until she remembered Friend Daniel Gray, one of the elders. Surely he would listen to her complaint and bring the matter to Father. After all, Friend

Daniel once voiced concern over her family opening this inn. While he agreed with their wish to provide hospitality to outsiders, he cautioned it would also open them to the ways of the outside world. And Silas Jones had proved him right.

❄

"Thee has come here unescorted?" Daniel Gray inquired when Mary arrived at his doorstep, chilled by the cold air. He looked beyond her as if expecting her father or George to be sitting in a wagon. She knew it was inappropriate to come alone to a man's home, but her anxiety demanded it. The sooner her family rid themselves of Silas Jones, the better she would feel.

"I'm sorry, Friend Gray. I—I had to come right away. It's very important."

"It must be." He stepped aside. "My cousins are visiting from South Carolina. We are not alone."

It was well they weren't, for Mary knew Daniel was widowed, having lost his wife in childbirth a year ago. She hadn't considered what she would do if she arrived to find him alone in his home. Now she wondered what drove her heart to do such things and if she would be rebuked. But after she greeted Daniel's cousin and his wife, Daniel lit a few extra oil lamps in the sitting room and gestured her to a chair.

Mary wasted no time telling him about the guest in their home and how she believed him to be of ill repute in soul and spirit.

Daniel stirred. "I see. In what manner has he brought ill upon thee and thy family?"

"His words and mannerisms are like thorns. He—he

29

mocks our ways and our beliefs."

Daniel chuckled. "And why is that so strange to us? Does thee recall the persecution of those who came before us? Friend William Penn even found himself falsely arrested and a prisoner many times. Newgate Prison twice, even the Tower itself."

"Yes, I know the stories." She had been told many times of the forbearance of the Quaker William Penn, who met with grave persecutions before Friend William founded Philadelphia, Pennsylvania. The place the people call the City of Brotherly Love. And even the state of Pennsylvania was named after William Penn's father, to whom the king of England owed a great debt.

"Then thee shouldn't trouble thyself with one who doesn't know the Light of God in his heart. Rest in God's protection and His will." Daniel hesitated, looking over to the adjacent room where the cousins were. His voice lowered. "Actually, I am glad thee stopped by, Mary. I've been thinking of thee and have been meaning to come by thy father's house."

Mary caught her breath. "I—I can surely use thy prayers," she managed to say.

"Prayers, yes. But perhaps thee would consider going riding with me?"

She hadn't expected this kind of attention from a man of the Word and the Faith, looking at her with more than the simple interest of an elder to his flock. "It is kind of thee to ask."

"Actually I blame the cousins," he said with a chuckle.

"They wonder when this lonely heart of mine will seek another. And I believe it's time. I've mourned a year for Elizabeth. One must live for Christ and not the grave."

Mary paused, thinking of Silas, though she didn't know why, and said quickly, "Yes, I would like to go riding with thee."

His face erupted into a smile of pleasure. "Next Thursday then?"

Mary nodded. They conversed a bit longer, about the short winter days, the past meetings among the Friends, and what he might speak about at First Meeting. He began to share more of his thoughts, as if he dearly wanted her to be a part of them. When she finally bid him good day, she inhaled quick breaths of cold air that sent pangs of pain fluttering in her chest. Nothing was turning out the way she'd expected. Here she had come asking for protection and prayer against an outsider and came away with a proposal of courting. Was God indeed guiding her heart? Was this what His Light did, shine in ways she never considered?

Mary mounted her horse, Whisper, and made for home, certain she would be rebuked if she did not arrive back soon to help with the daily baking. How she wished she could ride forever with the cold breeze filling her and its unseen tendrils brushing her face. If not for the unpleasant winter days, filled with cold and snow, she wouldn't mind seeing other places. Again her thoughts drifted to Silas. He talked of his desire to journey west. She shook her head, unwilling to compare his goals with her own. They were like night to day. And she could not forget how he belittled her and the family.

When Mary neared home, she saw several people gathered outside as if waiting for her arrival. Father, George, and Silas Jones of all people. "Where has thee been this day?" Father asked, his voice laced with concern.

"I. . ." She paused, glancing at Silas, who looked at her with what appeared to be equal concern. "I went to confide in Friend Daniel Gray of a matter, Father. But I have returned, as thee can see. There is no need to worry."

"Thee went to see Friend Gray? Without an escort?"

She felt her cheeks warm, even as she noticed Silas gazing at her intently. "His cousins were there." She nearly spoke of the invitation to go riding with Daniel but kept silent. Right now she must calm the rising tide of anxiety. "I'm sorry, Father. I should have told thee of my intentions."

"So thee should, taking off without a word." Father took hold of the bridle to steady Whisper. Silas was at her side, offering his hand to help her dismount. Mary wanted to ignore the gesture, but with George and Father looking on, she reluctantly gave him her hand. She refused to acknowledge his dark eyes surveying her or the warmth of his large hand around hers. She did not care to entertain any misconceptions now that she had accepted Daniel's invitation. Silas would be gone in a matter of days anyway, and that would be the end of it. Or so she thought, even as his hand tightened around hers. *Help me, dearest Lord!*

Chapter 3

Silas tried not to think about Mary's abrupt visitation to an elder of the Friends, but he couldn't help thinking she had gone on his account. After their initial encounter, he'd tried to calm the rising tide of animosity between them. He knew, of course, that an explanation for his opinions concerning the Society of Friends would set things at ease. But he was not of a mind to share that part of his life. Why he left Philadelphia so abruptly. Or why he was journeying across the country, as far away from the East as possible. Or why the Quaker mannerisms shown by the Hall family tested him beyond his ability to reason.

He did, though, find his irritation with them calming as the days passed. George Hall proved a wonder with Barzillai, who was making a rapid recovery from the injured hoof. Mr. Hall had shown him the workings of the inn, and his acceptance of Silas comforted him. And Mrs. Hall slipped him freshly baked desserts, bread, or biscuits hot from the hearth. Despite his irritating ways when he first arrived, the family had been forgiving and patient. All but Mary, who viewed him as a thorn in their heel. Or as she had once said, some predator out to destroy the family. The connotation proved unsettling, and he vowed to somehow change her opinion.

But this day, Mary seemed in another world. She walked around humming a joyful tune. Her face appeared sunny like the bright day as she went about her chores. He wondered what spawned such happiness—certain he had nothing to do with it. He took up the ax to split firewood over Mr. Hall's protest. Silas preferred work and not idleness while waiting for Barzillai to make a full recovery. After roaming about the house, bored with the library of books that espoused the works of George Fox and other notable Friends, he decided physical labor would do his mind well.

Silas brought the ax to bear, neatly splitting the log into quarters that were then thrown into the ever-increasing woodpile. He glanced over to where Mary stood in the yard, and suddenly she rose up on tiptoe, clutching her raven-black bonnet. He heard the nicker of horses. A buggy rolled up the dirt road, driven by a man in a black hat and dark coat.

"Good day," said the man. "Thee is the visitor from the city of Brotherly Love?"

Silas blinked and heaved the ax into another waiting log. And how would a stranger know that? "I have been there," he admitted cautiously.

"Friend Mary told me of thy sojourn here at her family's inn. I'm Daniel Gray, an elder of the Friends in Waynesville." He offered his hand, a common act of greeting with the Quakers. Silas reluctantly shook it. "I'm here to take Mary for a ride."

"I'm sure she will enjoy it." Silas hefted the ax and drove the blade deep into another log. Now he knew why Mary was so happy. She had a suitor. And a fine gent he appeared, outfitted in humble clothing, conveying the mannerism of a pious Friend and an elder at that. A perfect man for her, without a spot or wrinkle. The ax flew into the wood, sending a spray of wood chips into the air.

"How long does thee plan to stay among us?" Daniel asked.

"Not much longer. I hope to be in Independence before the snow gets deep. That is, if my horse is well enough to make the journey. I won't go without her. As it is, I walked part of the way and wore my shoes through."

Daniel Gray smiled then turned his attention to the fair Mary, who ventured forward in her cloak and dark bonnet, the smile ever broadening on her pale face. Silas tried to ignore the scene but couldn't help watching her take the man's hand and climb onto the seat. She smiled warmly in the man's direction and settled in, tucking the corners of the lap robe around her. Silas thought then how he would like to take her in his rig and drive her around, that is, if he had a rig. And if he weren't plagued, too, by nagging thoughts of their previous conversation. He and Mary were more akin to iron sharpening iron than feeling any love and devotion like this couple who shared smiles and warm conversation. He grimaced, wishing he and Mary had been introduced differently when he arrived. Wishing, too, he hadn't allowed the past to infect the present or the future. But what was his future? And where? California, perhaps? Certainly not with the Quakers.

He couldn't help his conflicting emotions at hearing the laughter on the wind as the buggy containing Mary and this Friend Daniel rolled down the road. No doubt they were speaking in humble language while espousing the Light shining within. Silas considered God's Light and how Grandfather had spoken of it when Silas was a mere lad and still a stranger in many ways to its principles. The older man spoke of his affections for the writings of George Fox, the founder of Quakerism, and William Penn, the founder of Philadelphia, whom he esteemed a great man of wisdom despite his rough beginnings.

"Thee is much like Friend William Penn, young Silas," Grandfather told him as they fished in the river near Philadelphia.

"How is that?" young Silas wanted to know.

"Like thyself, William struggled with his newfound faith. He desired to find justice among the unjust. And like thee, he found it difficult submitting to God's will in such matters. He wanted to take justice into his own hands."

It was as if Grandfather had a foretelling of future events. For the very thing he spoke of came to pass when Silas confronted the pain of injustice: that terrible struggle to right the wrong and his inability to do anything about it.

"It will not go away, either," he said, squeezing his eyes shut to ward off the images. Of his beaten and bloodied grandfather lying on a cobblestone street. The man's labored breathing as he struggled to live. The glazed eyes and silent heartbeat that followed. The criminals who had taken away a man's life but still roamed the streets of the City of Brotherly Love without paying for their crimes.

"I will not accept it!" he shouted aloud and then turned about, wondering if anyone had overheard. He hoped God

Himself had. If He had ears to hear, that is. If He cared at all to act on Silas's behalf.

"Silas?"

A soft voice spoke like one eager to reach him, though he wanted to turn a deaf ear. George had emerged from the barn. "Is thee well?"

Silas shook his head, his complaint lodged in his throat.

"What troubles thee?"

"I—I was thinking of the past. And seeing how it affects my future."

"Like how it affects my sister? Thee does have affections for her, right?"

Silas's mouth dropped in stunned amazement. He thought for a moment but decided not to pursue his actual pain-filled memory of Philadelphia. "Even if I did, I am not of the Friends' persuasion. Certainly not like the elder who is escorting her."

George shrugged. "Mary has little difficulty making up her mind. But I wanted to tell thee, also, that if thee still wishes to leave on thy journey, thy horse is nearly healed."

Silas straightened. "Really? She's well?"

"A fine animal with a strong heart. I can see thee has cared for her."

Silas relished the comment as he followed the young man into the barn. Barzillai greeted him with a soft whinny. "Why, she does look well enough to ride. You've done a splendid job." And he meant it. As much as the Quaker family had irritated him at the outset, far be it from him not to give noteworthy praise. And plenty of well-deserved coins, too. But really, he owed more than he could pay for the tender care given, not only to his animal but also to himself.

"A fine horse," George acknowledged, stroking the horse's muzzle. He found a carrot and fed Barzillai, who munched it with pleasure. "A horse is one of God's great creatures, to help a man in his pursuits. I'm certain this horse has done much for thee, bringing thee here from so far."

"Yes. She was a gift from my grandfather. That's why when she took lame, I wanted. . ." He paused. "I wanted her made well. If she continues on, a part of my grandfather does as well."

"He no longer lives?"

Silas shook his head and slowly retreated inside himself where no one could see, or so he thought. Into a realm of anger and injustice and an overwhelming desire to right the wrongs committed. He looked up then to see George staring at him. Silas flinched.

"It's hard to see death come to those we care about. I'm not without understanding, Friend Silas. A good friend of mine drowned last year in the Ohio while carrying supplies on his bateau. I asked God the reason why. It seemed senseless to me."

"Did you get an answer?" Silas couldn't help the eagerness in his voice.

"Friend Gray, the elder of our meeting, told me that God knows best. That He sees beyond our mortal minds. And we must have faith in His providence. With God there is more than this life. Those departed are with Him in eternity. We're here for a moment. Like the grass that fades or the flower that withers and dies. We must do what we can now for His glory. And leave eternity and its timing to God."

Silas said nothing more as he watched George feed Barzillai another carrot. While the words seemed good and true, they brought him little satisfaction. Nor a calming of the torrid waters stirring him. There would be no peace until justice was served.

❄

"Thee has said little on this trip," Daniel observed. "Aren't thee well?"

"Oh, I'm fine. Just enjoying the lovely day. There is so much to see." Mary didn't realize how silent she'd been, with her sights set on the beautiful Ohio countryside. On this cold December day, the land appeared ready to receive whatever the winter planned to bring, though they had already seen some snow. Along the way they passed several farmhouses of families that were outsiders, preparing for the Christmas holiday. Pine boughs decorated porches, and fruited arrangements hung above the doors. Mary remembered several guests who had stayed at their inn last year and asked her family what they did to celebrate the holiday. Father announced privately to the family that they would have a day of remembrance while the outsiders in their midst celebrated the Christmas holiday. And Father honored his guests by having a special meal prepared for them and allowing them to exchange gifts at the table.

Now Mary wondered what this season would bring as she sat huddled beneath the blanket. Then she thought of Silas Jones. Why, she didn't know, even as Daniel cast her another glance.

"Actually, I'm also thinking," she added.

"About what? The outsider staying at thy father's place? This Silas Jones?"

Mary straightened, hoping Daniel didn't notice the flush of her cheeks as a positive answer to his inquiry. Why would he say such a thing? Unless he perceived that she and Silas had shared words earlier that day. God could whisper such things to an elder like Daniel. But now was not the time to bring out the secrets of the heart. Besides, she felt right in her dealings with Silas and his ill regard for their faith.

Now she'd rather change the subject. "I—I only wonder who we may have during this Christmas season. I'm certain Silas Jones will not be there. He plans to leave for Independence as soon as his horse has recovered."

Daniel nodded. "It's strange that people feel they must have a special day to remember our Lord's birth. We know that every day is a day of remembrance. But I know, too, we must show understanding. And the Lord's love and light."

"Last year we exchanged gifts. Father thought it proper but then told everyone at the table that each day is a gift from God, that we only did it in our guests' honor to remember the occasion they celebrate."

"As is right. For thee knows one occasion isn't better than another. Each day is a gift to be shared." He took Mary's hand, covered in the warmth of a mitten, and held it in his hand. "Just as thee is also a gift."

"Friend Daniel, it—it's kind of thee to say." But she didn't feel much like a gift these past few days, especially during the confrontations with Silas Jones. Why the man bothered her, she didn't know. Or she feared knowing. She must instead focus her thoughts on this fine man before her. Daniel Gray was an honorable man and a gift in his own right. An elder and a man Father would be proud to have court his only daughter. If it was the right thing to do. But now she remained uncertain.

Daniel guided the buggy down another road leading toward home. She was glad he'd taken a more country route and not one through the town of Waynesville. Quaint as it was, and even with the Friends' meetinghouse there, she instead felt closer to God among the great fields and forest He'd created. And they also avoided the curious eyes of the townsfolk.

When they arrived back, Silas was in the yard with his horse, looking as if he were about ready to take his leave.

"Thank thee, Friend Daniel," Mary said swiftly, her gaze falling on Silas. "I enjoyed the ride very much."

Before departing, Daniel offered his hand once more to Silas, who shook it. Then Daniel left. Mary stood in her place, uncertain what to say or what might unfold between them.

"Barzillai is much better," Silas finally said. "Your brother did a fine job caring for her."

"I'm glad. George is a wonder with animals. God has given him a great gift of healing." She paused. "So thee is leaving?"

"Yes. I'm certain things will be better here if I do. I know you're unhappy with me."

Mary inhaled a sharp breath, recalling Daniel's words

that she was a gift to others. She had hardly represented herself as a gift to Silas in her words and thoughts. Nor did she allow for God's Light to pierce the darkness in his heart through her. "Silas Jones, I beg forgiveness if my tone with thee these past days has not been pleasant. I felt I needed to come to the defense of my brethren. But I should remember that God is our defender."

"I admire someone who stands for justice."

His words took her by surprise. "But surely it is the Lord who justifies and who brings forth fruit from what is sown. It is not for me to judge. And I did judge thee severely."

Silas was silent for a minute. "I accept your apology, but I do have reasons for what I say. Even if I'm at fault for having harsh opinions."

"A man is right in his own eyes until he is corrected."

"True. All I've had the last few weeks on my journey is a lame horse to tell me right from wrong until I came here. A horse doesn't speak too well to one's condition."

Mary couldn't help but chuckle, which brought a smile to Silas's face.

"But Barzillai's limp did speak in other ways," he continued. "It told me to stop and take notice. To not let my ideas affect everything I see and do. And so I think I will stay through Christmas, which is not far away, and then leave."

"We don't celebrate Christmas. . . ," she began then caught herself. "Rather, we have different ways of celebrating among the Friends. We believe every day is a celebration of our Lord and His coming."

"I know. I'm Quaker also."

Mary stepped back, stunned by the revelation. "You're a Friend? But I thought..." She knew her mouth had dropped open, but she could barely close it. "I—I don't understand. After all that's been said between us and..."

Silas turned away. "Now I see I've said too much." He led his horse back into the barn, as Mary stood fast in place, unable to believe what she'd heard. *Silas is a Friend?* The man who had mocked their language and their manner of keeping? What was it, then, that had turned him from the Light? What had sent him into darkness? Curiosity over-whelmed her. She hoped and prayed the man would not take his leave until all had been revealed. Even with that, she wasn't sure how she would react or what she would say.

But right now it looked as if Silas didn't wish to reveal anything more. "Lord, I pray Thee will keep him here until his heart's condition lays open," she whispered. "Do not let him leave with a troubled heart and a wandering soul. Keep him in Thy tender care. And our care, too, until he finds healing for his soul." With that prayer, Mary found her thoughts about Silas changing. A heart of compassion began to emerge, to help one in need. Silas Jones was in desperate need, whether he believed it or not.

Chapter 4

Silas chastised himself for allowing part of the past to slip out. Why he told Mary he was once a Quaker was beyond him. He'd wanted to avoid it. Disown the mere fact out of his choosing. But since his arrival here at the Hall home—watching the tender care given to his horse and the warmth of a true Quaker family who helped each other and greeted strangers with kindness and smiles of joy—his heart had softened. If only that warmth could change what had happened. But even with the Halls' displays of kindness and generosity, nothing could take away a past that still left a deep wound in his spirit.

Now with the revelation of his ties to the Friends, Mary looked at him oddly for the remainder of the day. That evening over a fine meal of chicken and dumplings in savory gravy, he noted Mary's fiery blue eyes observing him as if desiring to know why he'd left the Society of Friends. What led him away from the Light? Why had he run from Philadelphia? But the questions remained unspoken, and for that he was grateful.

After a dessert of fresh apple cake, Silas cleared his throat and looked around the table. "I wanted to thank you very much for your kindness. I've decided to leave tomorrow."

The cups of evening tea were set down on the table. Every member of the Hall family gazed at him, except for the two guests in for the night.

"But I thought thee was staying until...," Mary began.

"I'm sorry to hear this," Mr. Hall said. "We do thank thee for gracing our home with thy presence and for helping chop wood. We enjoy having others come and stay, but we also know the road beckons to thee. May thee find a satisfactory ending to thy wanderings."

Silas was both happy and unhappy. Thankful Barzillai was well and he could continue his journey westward. But sad, too, that he would leave a family who appeared ready to have him be on his way, despite their friendly attentions. Did Mary feel the same, he wondered? He cast a glance at her, but she said nothing. It was fitting. Elder Daniel stood poised to court her. They would enjoy many a fine sleigh ride when the winter snows piled high. She would have a fine Quaker gentleman who did not suffer like he did. Oh, but he did wish he no longer suffered in his soul. It would be good to have lasting joy and peace in embracing the Light of God.

If only he could.

After dinner Silas returned to his room to begin packing his satchel of meager belongings. He heard a rustling in the hallway and looked out of his room to see Mary standing there, clutching a small cloth bag. She looked lovelier than he'd ever seen her. Maybe it was her hair, which had loosened and fallen around her shoulders, though she still wore the modest white cap atop her head. Or maybe it was the innocent look on her face.

"There were a few biscuits left over from the meal. I—I thought thee might want them for thy journey."

"Thank you." He took them, and when he did, their hands brushed. And for an instant he had the overwhelming desire to take her lovely form in his arms. He inhaled a quick breath. She would feel so good in his arms, too. Warm and soft and sweet. The fragrant scents from the day's baking still lingered on her. He would slowly take off her white cap and let his fingers drift through her luxurious brown hair. Her blue eyes would look up into his, so trusting, seeking his protection and his love. . . .

Silas gulped and turned away, feeling a bit too warm by these thoughts. He expected her to leave. But when he looked back, she was still standing there.

"Are you really a Quaker, Silas?" Mary caught herself. "I mean, are thee. . ."

"Yes, I was. I may still be. I don't know who I am. Or really, where I stand with God."

Mary took a step forward. "There is no need to leave now. Friend Daniel Gray can help," she added, the eagerness lacing her voice. "He can show thee thy condition, show God's Light within thee and. . ."

"Mary, I know you want to help, but no one can. What I suffer goes too deep for any kind of understanding."

"Nothing is too deep that God is not in it." She drew even closer, and her warmth filled him. They stood but two feet apart. Her blue eyes held no fire as they had in the past but a measure of questioning and even compassion. Her lips appeared moist and inviting. Silas took hold of her arm and led her gently into his embrace. She did not resist. He enjoyed the taste of her fair lips until finally she struggled out of his grasp, her breathing rapid.

"Please. . . ," she managed to say, her face flushed like a strawberry. "I—I was trying to help."

"Yes, you were. And I was letting you know that you're a beautiful woman. Did you ever stop to consider there might be better plans for your life than just the small life you live here as a servant in your inn? That we may have been brought together for a reason?"

She grew rigid, and the compassion that had softened her features rapidly changed to a fire of indignation. "I'm glad to be here. There is nowhere else I wish to be. And. . .perhaps it is better thee is going away after all." She began to retreat.

"As you wish." He stood his ground, only to see her turn and scurry away. Yet the warmth of the encounter remained, especially the touch of her lips on his. But he must force it away and ready himself for the journey, now marred by another haunting memory.

❄

Oh, why did I ever allow myself to be kissed by him?

Mary thought about what had happened in the upper hallway, wishing she'd had enough strength to ward off temptation. But Silas Jones crept in when she was most vulnerable to the hurt in his heart. And worst of all, she'd allowed him! She shuddered, wondering if she should confess to the elders her troubled state and ask for their prayer. But if she did, Daniel would know she had kissed another man, and a fallen one of the brethren at that. What would he say? After all, she knew Daniel's intent was to court her.

He would suffer hurt, and he'd already endured so much hurt after the loss of his wife. She couldn't bring that kind of pain upon him.

But why was my heart so quick to respond to Silas? Did she find him that appealing, out of all the men God had put in her path? Silas had mocked them. Abandoned the Friends. Then he used the moment when she wanted to help to trap her. The wolf in sheep's clothing, as she once described him, had swooped down with stolen kisses, looking to take full residence in the confines of her heart. She felt weak in spirit, as if suffering the ravages of a fever. Without direction. Thoughts trapped in a fog. Her only hope was that he'd be gone by dawn, and she could wait upon God to cleanse her and make her whole in mind and emotion. But did she want to be cleansed? Did she really want Silas to be gone forever?

Mary hurried outside to find her brother handling his new acquisition to the herd—a fine stallion in desperate need of breaking. He looked at her as she approached. "Mary? Why so downcast?"

Was it that apparent in her features? Mary tried to smile then, but it felt forced. "Oh, it's nothing, George. Nothing at all." Nothing that hasty abandonment couldn't cure. But her lips still tingled from his kiss, and her arms still remembered the warmth of his strong embrace. *Dearest Lord, help my feelings.*

"There *is* something wrong. I can see it." He strode over to the fence and leaned against it. "Is it Silas?"

"I. . ." She hesitated.

"I know he has feelings for thee. He told me as much."

"I—I'm glad he's leaving," she blurted. "It will be better for all of us. He's done little but stir trouble among us. And did thee realize he was once of the Friends' persuasion but abandoned the Light?"

George's eyes widened. "No, I didn't. But I knew something had happened with regards to the Friends. If only he could find his burden lifted. Perhaps a meeting with Friend Daniel would help."

Mary felt her face heat at the suggestion. "No, no, that will never do. The only choice is for him to find the Light for himself. I've heard his words." *And felt his lips on mine. And the strength of his arms.* She shivered at the memory. "He—he really must go."

George looked at her with a strange expression, almost as if he knew what had transpired in the house. She turned quickly, lest her expressions give away anything. George returned to training the young horse with a short pole, giving commands. She thought of the Friends, the beliefs they held to, the ways in which she was to guard her heart and her thoughts, focusing them solely on the One who loved her and held her in His hands. Of the full devotion she must give. Until she saw it all thrust in a whirlwind by the man with deep-set brown eyes and an overpowering will to take hold of her when she least expected it.

Suddenly she caught sight of a tall figure exiting the house. Silas, carrying a satchel as he walked toward the corral, stopped short when he saw her. He opened his mouth as if to speak but instead went to the door of the barn. Mary edged closer so she could hear the conversation.

"So thee is truly going," George remarked to him.

"Yes, I need to go before the snows get too deep. I want to be settled in Independence, maybe by Christmas if all goes well."

"Thee has a long way to travel. Why not stay until spring? Father could use the extra help, I'm sure."

Silas glanced in the direction of the house. "I can't, George. But thank you for inviting me. Your father does have an excellent place. Even if. . ." He hesitated. "Even if I was not appreciative of it when I first arrived."

George smiled. "Thee has seen the Light, Friend Silas."

"I don't think so. But maybe I will once I find out where I'm supposed to go." He entered the barn. Mary waited, watching until Silas returned, leading Barzillai by her bridle. She inhaled a sharp breath as his tall, sturdy figure mounted the mare with his large hands gripping the reins.

"I pray God will keep thee in thy journey, Friend Silas," George said, offering a handshake of farewell.

Silas shook her brother's hand. He looked at Mary then tipped his hat to her. He appeared strong and command-ing on his mount, ready to face whatever the world gave. At that moment it brought him little but disappointment, as he had conveyed to her. But that was not for her or the family to heal. Only Silas could find the healing he needed, through God's mercy and guidance.

Just then Mary heard a loud neigh then a thump, fol-lowed by a groan. She whirled to find George a crumpled heap on the ground. The horse he had been training nosed him with its muzzle. "George! George, are you all right?" She ran and knelt before him, shaking him. His eyes were closed, his breathing ragged. One look at his contorted lower leg and bloodied trousers told her something terrible had happened. "Oh, dearest God!" she cried, the tears burning in her eyes. She looked around to see the dust of Silas's departure. Or rather a cloud of dust stirring as someone came galloping up in a frenzy.

"What happened?" It was Silas. Mary had never felt more relieved to see him. He dismounted and hurried to her side, kneeling next to George.

"I—I don't know. I was. . ." *I was looking at you, wondering why you were leaving.* . . . She paused. "I didn't see what happened until I heard a loud noise." She pointed with a trembling finger. "Look at his leg. It looks terrible!"

"I'll go for the doctor. Where is your village?"

Mary gave him directions to the doctor's residence with a wavering voice. Then she felt a strong hand take hers and give a gentle squeeze. "It's going to be all right," he said.

Mary wiped away the tears so she could see better and composed herself with a few quick breaths. George began to stir then and moan in pain as his hand fumbled for his leg. "Just lie still, George. Silas is going for the doctor. You have broken your leg."

"It hurts," he moaned. "It hurts badly. Oh, Mary. Pray. . .pray for me. Please. Oh."

"Yes, yes, I will labor with thee, dear brother. Thee knows I will, with all my heart." And she did, for many long minutes, thankful to see George calming under the prayerful words.

Father and Mother came rushing out when they heard the commotion. Even the two visitors who had been inside the house followed. Mary told them all what happened and that Silas had gone for the doctor.

"We can't leave George lying in the dirt," Mother said. "And we have trusted his well-being to some outsider? What if he doesn't return? He was leaving, after all."

"George shouldn't be moved, Mother. And Silas will return with the doctor. He said he would," Mary added in confidence.

Father agreed, and together they tried to make George as comfortable as possible. But the leg wound was grievous, with the white of bone protruding. Mary knew he would be bedridden a long time. The elders and Friends would help in their time of need. They would be all right, she felt certain. If only she didn't feel so helpless.

George moaned again and struggled to sit up. He saw his leg, groaned, and looked to heaven. "Why? Why did this happen?"

Why indeed? Mary thought. No one was more faithful and protective; no one was a better man than her brother. Mary could only stay by his side with the others and wait.

At last they heard the sounds of horses. Silas arrived, bringing the doctor, and to her surprise, Friend Daniel. Mary wasn't about to ask how Daniel discovered their misfortune—if Silas had gone to fetch him, also. She laid aside her questions with the physician here to tend to George, and Daniel here to give spiritual guidance.

The men gathered to hoist George up on a litter made from a blanket and bring him into the house. They placed him on the bed, where the doctor examined the extent of the injury.

"Thank thee so much for fetching the doctor," Mary said softly to Silas, who stood by her side, watching as the doctor cut away the pant leg to expose the open wound. George groaned and shook violently. Mary trembled and turned away. Silas winced, also. They looked at each other rather than at what the doctor was doing. Finally Silas stepped outside the room, and Mary followed.

"This is terrible," she said, and suddenly the tears came fast and furious.

"I'm sorry, Mary. Truly I am. George is a fine man. He cared for my horse, and he cares about others. He doesn't deserve this. I don't understand the ways of God or why good men must suffer so."

She wiped her eyes. "Sometimes it isn't for us to understand. We have to trust and believe in God's goodness, no matter what happens." But little did he know that she, too, struggled with the reason why. And with the terrible pain her brother endured as the doctor worked to fix the leg.

Mother rushed out then, her face pale. "The doctor says he must try to straighten the leg." She wrung her hands in despair. "He. . .he needs men to help hold George down. Silas, will thee help?"

Silas immediately went inside the room. Mary took Mother into the kitchen area at the back of the house, but even there they could still hear the awful screams. A fresh round of tears came forth as they held each other and murmured prayers. When it was over, they returned to find the doctor had splinted the leg and wrapped it in heavy linen. George lay still, having fainted from the pain and the effects of the laudanum the doctor had given him to ease his suffering.

The doctor gestured the family to the sitting room. "I will not lie to you. It is a bad break. With an open wound, fever is likely and could be severe. Even if he survives the fever, he could very well be crippled."

If he survives? Mary gasped. It was as if the heavens had fallen. She might have collapsed in despair if not for Silas supporting her.

Chapter 5

For the next week a cloud of somberness hung over the Hall home. While Mr. Hall insisted they keep the inn running despite George's accident, the family found themselves further and further behind in their work. Mary and Mrs. Hall ran ragged trying to keep the inn's guests entertained and well-fed while caring for George. Mr. Hall was away on the supply runs that George normally did and struggled with the upkeep of the house and grounds.

Silas could hardly turn his back on a family so in need, especially when they had helped both him and Barzillai. He did what he could to help, but he maintained his distance from Mary. Since the kiss, he'd decided to stay away, not wishing to cause her further discomfort. But still, a yearning rose within him to be with her, to hold her, to offer comfort for the trials she was facing, like he had when George was first injured.

Silas was busy hitching the horses to the supply wagon when Mary came around the side of the house, toting the usual basket filled with the weekly wash. He offered a smile, which she returned.

"How's George today?" he asked.

A frown appeared, and likewise his good cheer disappeared. The news must not be good. "He still has a fever. I don't know what else to do for him but bear his burden in prayer and give him tea made from herbs."

"The fever will break soon," Silas tried to reassure her, though he didn't know the future. He'd seen a loved one injured beyond the ability of medicine and even beyond God's ability to heal, it seemed. He prayed that would not be George's lot.

"Where is thee off to today?" she asked.

He waved a piece of paper. "I have a list of supplies from your father that I need to buy from the store in town."

To his surprise, Mary hastily put down the basket of clothes and came forward, her face bright with excitement. "I would very much like to go to town." She gazed back at the house. "Thee will go and return quickly? I shouldn't be gone long."

"Yes, but doesn't thee think thee should ask?" He waited, hoping she would notice his use of the Friends' language.

The response was not what he expected. "There is no need." She climbed into the wagon beside him without asking for help or even inquiring if she might go along. Her boldness surprised him. "I need this trip, and I'm quite able to decide for myself if it's reasonable. There are no new guests in for the night. George is resting. All that can be done has been done." She settled herself on the wagon seat, with her hands folded in her lap and her gaze focused directly ahead.

Silas said nothing further, only flicked the reins and guided the wagon to the rutted dirt road. He'd been careful to keep his distance from the attractive Mary, but all determination to do so melted away with her close proximity and her aroma reminiscent of spring wildflowers. Her bright face and blue eyes reflected the clear sky above. He nearly reached for her hand but kept a firm grip on the reins instead.

"Ah, such a lovely day for a ride," she said with a sigh.

"I'm sure thee had a nice ride with Friend Daniel that one day." He cringed then, wishing he hadn't brought up the subject. Now the talk would steer Mary into thinking about the fine Quaker gent.

"He is kind and wise. But. . ." She paused. "I would only be in conflict with a memory if we were to court."

"I don't understand."

"His wife died in childbirth a year ago. I don't want to be compared to her in matters of marriage. Who she was. What they did together." Her hands trembled, and she looked off into the distance to the farmlands surrounding their travel. "I'm sorry. I've said too much about this. It isn't proper."

"Thee has shared thy heart, Mary. If one can't do that, what good are the brethren? Or the cause of helping one another in times of need?" Despite the joy he felt over her reservations concerning Daniel, Silas was uncertain her words proved the man held no interest in her eyes. Or that a door now lay open to him. She'd shown little interest in him except in his past. They had shared the one kiss, but it might as well have been a kiss farewell, as he'd planned to leave until George's injury. But things were changing day by day. Could this conversation mean that she did hold some affection for him?

He inhaled a quick breath, hoping it were so, as the wagon approached the outskirts of town. Dropping Mary off at the general store, Silas went to see about a shovel and to have the ax head sharpened. Several people asked about George, having heard about the accident. Silas told them what he knew and what the future might hold.

"Very sad," several said.

"He trained my horse," said another.

Silas, too, felt remorse for the situation. He would do what he could to help while he remained there. Later he'd decide what would become of his journey westward or if Almighty God had other plans.

He stopped the wagon before the general store to await Mary's return. She soon came out of the shop carrying several parcels. She never looked prettier, even if her clothing was a bit drab with the black skirt and matching cape, and the black bonnet concealing her fine hair. He helped her with the packages, which included a pie, and put them in the wagon bed. He offered her a hand up. "The townsfolk shared their condolences over George's accident," he told her.

"Several of the Friends asked about him, too. And one gave me the pie. The brethren are so sweet and giving."

Silas didn't comment, though his thoughts buzzed as they headed out of town. While his opinion of the Quakers had changed since coming here to Ohio, he still couldn't rid himself of what had happened in Philadelphia. How a roving gang of rogues came upon his grandfather on the road and beat him. The Friends who warned Silas not to take matters into his own hands. Then they forgave his grandfather's murderers, allowing them to go unpunished, while he was cast off from among the Friends for harboring thoughts of revenge.

"Thee is quiet all of a sudden," Mary observed.

Silas wanted to confess the inner workings of his heart, as she had done concerning Daniel Gray. But her advice would be like that of all the Friends. Treat everyone with respect, even the murderers. Do not give evil for evil. Allow God to deal in judgment.

But Silas could not accept it right now. Instead he made small talk, inquiring about the work that still needed to be done and what they would do about the holidays should any travelers arrive.

"Mother will make her famous gingerbread cookies, I'm sure," Mary said. "It's a very old recipe but delicious. Last year Father allowed us to give gifts to each other. We had a nice dinner for those who came. And Father lit candles in the windows for each person present to symbolize God's Light in all of us." She paused. "I'm certain in Philadelphia thee did not celebrate Christmas."

"A few friends I know did. Not 'Friends' as in the Quakers," he added, "but friends among strangers. I was invited to one such gathering over my father's objections. It was a grand time. They had a feast, a Yule log, warm cider, and even a tree."

"A tree inside the house?"

"They cut down a small tree in the woods, brought it inside, and decorated it with candles and paper trimmings. I had never seen anything like that before."

Mary shook her head. "Such grave idolatry. Worshipping a tree as if it could grant one Light. How foolish."

"They didn't worship it. It was only a decoration, and many liked it. It was as if a bit of creation was brought inside.

They said the candles on the branches bore witness to God's Light in each of us. Which the Friends themselves believe, of course."

Mary paused and dropped her head, folding her hands tightly in her lap. "I'm sorry. I shouldn't be so judgmental."

Silas couldn't help but chuckle. "Thee has a mind of thy own. And a mind God can surely use. He used it well with me." Out of the corner of his eye he saw Mary smile. And again his heart leapt in hope. If only the past didn't hover over them like a storm cloud.

Silas sensed nervousness when he was called into Mr. Hall's study one afternoon. The man sat in one of his fine chairs, his Bible spread open in his lap. He glanced up through wire-rimmed spectacles, which he slowly removed and folded. "Please come in."

Silas slipped inside the room and into a chair opposite the fatherly figure, wondering why he had been summoned. Had he been improper with Mary since the day of George's accident? True, he did try to comfort her. He'd held her hand a few times. Whispered soothing words. And brought her to town on an errand. But surely those incidents shouldn't bring about a rebuke.

"I wanted to thank thee for all thy help these many days," said Mr. Hall.

"I'm happy to do whatever I can."

"I wish, especially with the approaching season, to keep my establishment open to all who travel," Mr. Hall continued. "But I fear without George's help, I will be unable to do so. I know it isn't right to ask thee to remain any longer, as I know thee has other plans. . . ." The man hesitated and looked down at the Bible. "I wonder if thee might consider staying on to help."

Silas sat still, absorbing this.

"I would pay thee fairly. And we expect more visitors wishing to celebrate Christmas, as I'm sure thee does."

"I do not celebrate it, Mr. Hall."

"Oh? I would have thought a man of the world would." He hesitated. "Not that God doesn't abide in all of us, for He surely does. But anyway, I would be most happy to have thy presence at the inn. Please consider it."

"I will. Thank you." Silas shook the man's hand, stood, and wandered out. He saw the open door leading to the bedroom where George had been since the accident. He walked over and peeked in. George lay in bed, staring up at the ceiling, his wounded leg a mass of bandages and resting on a feather pillow.

George's gaze fell on him. "Silas." He tried to shift in bed and grimaced.

"Please, don't move on my account. How does thee feel?"

"In pain. And frustration. The horse I was training will falter if the training isn't continued. Father wanted to shoot the horse for attacking me." His face twisted at the thought. "I told him no. The horse didn't know any better. It was an accident."

"I'm sorry thee is hurt." Silas was glad to use the Friends' language. A wounded Friend lay before him, one who struggled with a terrible injury, who might even be crippled.

Using the wording was wholly fitting and honoring of the man and his beliefs, the one who had tried his best to help him and Barzillai.

"Thanks. I don't know how long I must stay in bed. No one will tell me." He tried once more to sit up and muttered in pain. "Has thee heard any news?"

"Only that it's a severe break. And how sick thee has been with the wound where the leg bone pierced through."

George winced. "I may never be the same, will I, Silas?"

The voice of desperation tugged at the core of Silas. "I—I don't know, George. I will pray." And he meant it. Pray he must, but restoring fellowship with God he must do first. If he could reconcile the past.

He walked out, his head down, scuffing along the wooden floor, when he noticed a pair of leather shoes before him and a brown skirt. He looked up to see Mary, carrying a pitcher. "Did thee see George?" she asked. "His fever has broken. I'm so thankful."

"He looks much better. And he's asking questions about his condition. How long he might be in bed. He fears being crippled."

Mary's hands trembled at the words, and for a moment Silas thought she might drop the pitcher. He thrust out his hand to steady the vessel, which she placed on a nearby table. "The doctor comes again today. I fear what he will say. But we must remain hopeful in God."

"I told him I would pray."

Mary stared at Silas in appreciation when he said these words, as if they had unlocked another door between them.

During the past week he'd already sensed a door opening. The other day she'd thanked him for helping her father with the chores around the house. What would she say now if she learned that her father wanted to hire him? Would she welcome it? Or would she wish him gone, as she did before the accident and after the kiss they'd shared?

Silas decided not to say anything just yet. Instead he went to the woodpile to make certain the wood box was filled. He then walked to the corral and George's precious herd of horses, including the rambunctious stallion that had been the cause of the young man's misfortune. He knew a little about training horses from helping with Barzillai. What a surprise it would be for George if he could train the animal not to rear up and kick. It was a small price to pay for the way the young man had nursed Barzillai back to health.

Silas picked up the pole George had used with the animal and began gently rubbing the tail. At first the horse neighed and backed away. Ever so slowly Silas worked with the animal. A gentle prod there. A poke here. And then he was able to lead the horse to one side of the corral. Excitement built within him, even more so when he noticed Mary coming over to the corral to watch.

"Wherever did thee learn to do that?"

"My grandfather. Barzillai was actually his horse. He gave her to me." Silas allowed the horse to rest and met Mary where she stood by the fence. "I thought it might be a nice surprise for George if I could continue at least some of the training."

"It's kind of thee."

He stared at the horse as it gathered grass from a hay bale.

"So does thee plan to stay here?"

Silas glanced at their fine home and then at Mary. "Does thee want me to stay?"

She looked at him in surprise. "It's not for me to decide. I know Father asked if thee might be able to help him. He needs an extra hand, what with all the work that must be done." She paused. "I would be grateful if thee did stay."

"Then I will stay, Mary, if thee wants me to." He saw her face brighten and even the teasing of a smile form on her delicate lips. Inwardly his heart sang. Not for their circumstances, but that those circumstances could be used in good ways. Like being with Mary.

Mary turned and made for the house. Then he heard the rumble of a wagon from the road. Friend Daniel Gray. Silas blew out a sigh. The pious Quaker had come for a visit and maybe more. So much for his good intentions where Mary was concerned. He feared he would be forever lost in the elder Friend's holy shadow.

Chapter 6

Mary sat still in her chair, her hands folded demurely, her gaze focused on the wooden flooring beneath her shoes as Friend Daniel sat opposite her. He had come to pay a call, first to check on George's progress and then to be with her. She'd heard the elder and Father conversing in the sitting room and wished she were a mouse scurrying about so she could overhear their words. But afterward Daniel came out, his thin lips curved into a crooked smile, and inquired if she would like to sit with him. She knew then the result of the meeting. He'd asked Father's permission for visits between them in their home, and Father had agreed.

But now her gaze drifted to the window and Silas outside in the front yard, hard at work splitting wood. From the swiftness of his work with the ax, she wondered if he wrestled with some internal struggle. He turned back to the house with his face contorted in a grimace. Her cheeks felt warm at the sight. What might he be thinking? Was he dismayed over Friend Daniel's visit? Did he have a desire to be inside talking to her rather than her conversing with the elder?

She heard Daniel clear his throat, and her gaze turned to him. He stared at her. "Once again thee appears preoccupied during our visit. Is thee upset to be with me?"

"Of course not. I'm glad thee is here. George is thankful

to have an elder come bear his burden. Thee brings the joy of God's Light into our home." She hoped she didn't sound too zealous, even as her sights once more drifted to the window and Silas attacking the logs as though the chunks were some enemy he wished to conquer. She considered the last few days. George's accident and how Silas had rushed to help. The trip into town. His decision to stay and help Father. She spoke up then. "Does thee know that Friend Silas is staying to help us?"

"I did ask thy father if he required help, and he said that Silas Jones agreed to stay and assist. I was very glad to hear it." He paused. "I was wondering—would thee consider accompanying me to Meeting this Friday?"

"Go to Meeting with you?" Her mind was a blank.

"We are having a special gathering. I thought thee might want to attend with me."

"I. . ." She found herself twisting her fingers. "Oh, I do love Meetings, Friend Daniel. It's just. . ." She paused. "George may still need help. If we have guests also, Father and Mother need help serving them."

Daniel looked at her rather somberly. "Why do I feel as if thee is avoiding me? Have I done something wrong?"

Mary straightened and looked into his dark-blue eyes that displayed his concern, along with the rigid lines criss-crossing his face. "Oh no, certainly not. It's just. . ." Mary didn't even know why she stumbled over such an important invitation. Surely it couldn't be the man behind the ax outside their window. She felt strange even considering it. There was, too, the other reason she had confessed to Silas during their journey to town. "I know that with thy loss of thy wife, Elizabeth. . . ," she began.

"Is that what this is about? Mary, please don't think that my previous affection for Elizabeth means I cannot love and care for another woman. It has been over a year since her passage to glory. She is in a better place. God is the healer of our wounds and the giver of life and love."

Her gaze fell once more to the window. To her startled surprise, Silas was staring straight at the window at the same moment, as if they shared some secret communication of the heart and soul. She wondered if God would heal Silas's wounds and be the giver of life and love in their circumstances. *Oh dear, what am I thinking?*

She stirred in her seat, again feeling the warm flush in her cheeks. Then she sensed Daniel's stark perusal, as if he could read every thought and feeling passing through her. She stood quickly. The wrap around her shoulders fell to the floor. "Let me fetch us some tea, Friend Daniel. Please excuse me." She grabbed the shawl off the ground and hurried into the kitchen, thankful for the respite. "Dearest God, what am I going to do?" she said aloud, looking for the kettle. "I don't know what to do."

"Is something wrong, Mary?" Mother entered the kitchen, clad in her apron dusted white with flour from the morning's baking.

"I—I was only praying, Mother."

"A good thing to do, dear one." Mother gave her a kiss on the cheek. "But thee does seem troubled these days. I must say I'm not sure why. George is feeling stronger every day. I believe we will soon see a miracle with his leg."

Mary sighed, thankful Mother didn't realize her inner turmoil had nothing to do with George, though she did care for him. It had everything to do with the two men outside the walls of the kitchen, each playing with her heart in different ways. "Mother, did thee always know Father would be thy intended?"

"Of course. Our parents agreed to it. And so did the eldership. There was no mistaking it."

"I don't want to make a mistake, either."

"Oh, dear one." Mother reached out to take Mary's hand in hers. "Is it Friend Gray? I know he has asked to court you."

"He is a nice man. A good man of God. But. . ." She hesitated. "I don't know if he's the man for me. I fear thee and Father will both agree that he is, and then my heart will be forever troubled, wondering if it was truly God's will."

"Mary, thee must trust God in these things. He guides us in matters of the heart. He will guide thee and help thee see His will with regards to the perfect man and husband." The kettle began to steam, and Mary fetched a cup. Mother poured hot water over the tea leaves. "I believe thee will be happy and content with God's choice."

Mary nodded and carried the tea to Friend Daniel who, to her surprise, stood with his back to her, staring out the window to witness Silas in his labor. He whirled as she entered. "Thank thee," he said quietly as she set the cup on a table. "Is this outsider, Mr. Jones, still affecting thee?"

"Affecting me? I don't understand."

He picked up the teacup. "I know thee was deeply

troubled by his difficult mannerisms when thee came to see me awhile ago."

Mary remembered it well and now wished she had never made the visit. Perhaps if she had given her fears over to God and allowed Him to correct them as He saw fit, she wouldn't be in this predicament of the heart. "He did apologize."

Daniel grimaced. "Does thee realize the man was once a Quaker and then disowned by the Friends in Philadelphia?"

Mary stared wide-eyed. "Silas told me he was a Friend. But I. . .I didn't know he was disowned. What did he do so wrong among the brethren?"

"Awhile ago I met with a visiting Friend in Waynesville who was once associated with the Friends in Philadelphia. It seems Silas Jones had a grandfather who was mistreated by outsiders. The man eventually died from his wounds. Instead of embracing the Light in this grave situation, Silas wanted revenge. That, of course, is not the Friends' way. When he became a disorderly walker, looking to take matters into his own hands, he was asked to leave."

Mary continued to stare at Daniel until she realized what she was doing and shifted her gaze to the floorboards. "I didn't know this. I knew he was troubled by some matter. I knew he'd suffered loss."

"He didn't just lose a loved one, but I fear he has also lost his soul and spirit. Thee would do well to allow others to deal with his condition, Mary. Thee isn't meant to have this brought upon thyself, nor is thee meant to correct it. He must bear witness to the truth."

Mary listened to the elder's advice. Instead of yielding,

she yearned to help Silas even more now that she understood why he reacted the way he did. She realized how the previous disagreements they had were spurred by events in his life. Loss can sometimes cause one to do things one wouldn't normally do. Driven by grief, in deep mourning, some must act out their feelings. She recalled his struggle with injustice. How the Friends had seemingly turned a deaf ear to the things that weighed him down. The shattered glass of life could be mended still. All was not lost.

Friend Daniel placed his hat on his head. "I hope thee understands that we must release Friend Jones to the elders and to God. And thee must take care to keep separate from this situation."

Mary struggled with this pronouncement as she watched Daniel stride toward the door. Of course she wanted to humble herself and agree with the elder. Instead she returned to the window to see that Silas had just finished his task at the woodpile. Outside, Friend Daniel stopped before him to offer his hand, which Silas shook. They exchanged words that Mary could not hear but wished she could. Then Daniel left in his wagon.

At dinner that night Mary couldn't help but watch Silas eat as he sat opposite her. He'd said little at the table, which didn't matter since the three guests who had arrived made plenty of conversation for them all. But his stark silence weighed heavily on her. What thoughts were roaming about in his mind? Torturous thoughts, no doubt. Thoughts of grave loss and then chastisement for being human when he needed a loving touch and firm guidance. All the things the Friends normally did in times of trouble. But he did not receive such love, only chastisement. No wonder he disliked the brethren and was eager to find a new life elsewhere. A new life in a new place seemed much more appealing, but it would not heal what he'd left behind. The past would continue to haunt him until he made peace with it.

After the dishes were done, Mary wandered into the library to find Silas reading a book. To her surprise, it was an older work by Friend William Penn. He seemed so engaged; he never even glanced up until she sat down in a nearby chair and cleared her throat.

"Mary." In an instant he put down the book.

"Friend Silas. I'm surprised thee has chosen to read a work by a Quaker."

Silas shrugged. "Grandfather once told me how the man suffered injustice and wanted retribution. But he found the strength of God to stay his hand and his spirit."

"He suffered like thee."

His eyebrows drew together. "And how would thee know what I feel?"

"Oh, come now, Silas. It wasn't hard to see that thee was troubled the moment thee came to find rest in our home. How thee scorned the Friends when thee first came here. And then thee talked of trouble in Philadelphia, which was confirmed by Friend Daniel on his visit."

Silas blinked, silent for a moment before he straightened, as if tense. "I don't understand. How does your Daniel know anything about me or what happened in Philadelphia? Is he so enraptured by the Light that God came and spoke to him in a vision?"

Mary felt her cheeks warm, and she turned aside to gaze at the lone flame flickering within the lamp on the table. "I shouldn't have brought it up."

"Yes, you should. You know things. Things about me. Things you obviously don't understand."

"Yes, there are things I do know. How your, I mean, thy grandfather was mistreated in the streets by outsiders and died from his wounds. And yet the Friends would not oblige thee by making retribution but sought forgiveness instead. And when thee found thyself unable to bridle the passion that demanded an eye for an eye, thee was forced out of fellowship." She watched his fingers tighten around the book he held.

"So you know now I didn't leave Philadelphia peaceably. What they did was wrong. My grandfather loved the brethren with all his heart and soul. They punished me and showed mercy to those who murdered him."

"Oh, dearest Silas." Mary looked at him and extended her hand. "If thee could only know God's true heart. His understanding. His compassion for those in His Light and for those who only look in. And His justice."

In an instant her words drove him to his feet. "I saw no such compassion or justice. My grandfather is still dead and my name tarnished when I have done nothing to deserve it."

"It isn't tarnished here. You are accepted. In fact I will show thee. Come to Meeting with me." She paused. "There is one this Friday."

Silas shook his head. "I can't."

"Why? Thee is not banished from us. Or from our home. Or from me."

Silas sat back down, his gaze never leaving her. Mary realized now the strength found in the words she spoke that bordered on a commitment to him in her heart. What was it about Silas Jones that drew her? She wasn't sure, yet during the past week she had seen the true essence of the man buried beneath the wound. The Light shone quite brightly, even if it was sometimes covered by a basket of disappointment. He was a man who helped in their time of great need. A man of commitment. A man who could love with great depth. And a man whose heart needed only to receive the healing balm of God to make him whole. But Silas must choose whether to embrace God's love and the care of others, like herself. Or live life in misery.

She saw then his internal struggle with the way he shifted about, his fingers clenching and unclenching. He stood once more and began to pace, until they heard a shuffle in the nearby hall. George struggled into the library, limping along on the pair of wooden crutches Silas and Father had made for him.

"George! Why is thee out of bed?" Mary cried, racing to his side.

His pinched, drawn face revealed his pain, yet he looked at Silas with unmistakable compassion. "I couldn't help but hear what thee were saying. And Mary is right, Silas. In thy heart thee must know she speaks the truth."

Silas looked at him but said nothing. Mary saw his taut face begin to relax, as if George's opinion meant something to him. Especially now, as Silas watched him teeter on a pair of crutches with a fractured leg. How similar to a wounded soul, crippled by the heartrending things that happen in life. But George came forward in determination to walk through his suffering. She wondered if Silas could see it and be encouraged.

"Mary told me about Meeting this Friday," Silas began.

"I hope to go," George said. "I already missed First Day Meeting. And I hope thee will be able to help me. I need a strong arm to support me. As we all do, I should say."

"Of course I will help in any way I can. But I don't agree to attend the meeting itself, thee understands."

Mary couldn't help but smile, seeing George wink. A clever man, her brother. *Thank Thee, O Lord. Thou has made the way for Silas to seek the help he needs. How I pray he will see Thy glorious Light where he might find rest for his soul.* She inhaled a nervous breath, and her heart began to flutter furiously. *And maybe a path of Light for us both, Lord, if it be Thy will.*

Chapter 7

Silas didn't know what guided his footsteps as he helped George from the wagon that carried them all to the white brick meetinghouse. If he didn't know better, he'd think that George had purposely injured himself so Silas would need to help the man attend Meeting. Of course that wasn't so, but Silas could see the scripture coming to pass that speaks of all things working together for good.

After he'd guided George to the steps of the building, where the Friends warmly greeted each other, he decided to find a seat in the rear of the humble building. He didn't care that Mary was at the front of the gathering with Friend Daniel sitting across the aisle from her. Instead, his heart and soul were on the words shared and the sense of belonging that replaced the abandonment he'd once felt.

Silas could picture his grandfather then. The man's sturdy frame and shining blue eyes. His strong faith that refused to surrender even in the midst of persecution and death. A faith that surpassed it all to stand in eternal glory. Silas felt his soul stir. Perhaps he'd disappointed Grandfather. He hadn't allowed Christ to triumph over his enemies but met the enemy with anger, an enemy that eventually became one of Silas's own making. Everything Grandfather had taught him would be for naught if Silas allowed his anger to continue.

At the conclusion of the meeting Silas still sat in his place on the bench, not even hearing his name until he looked up to see Friend Daniel Gray standing above him. "I'm pleased to see thee here, Friend Silas. And what did thee think of Meeting? Has thee seen a change in thy condition?"

Silas waited, listening. Then his gaze caught Mary's as she walked up the center of the meetinghouse, her lips forming a faint smile, her cheeks flushed with excitement—a pure vision of holy beauty in his eyes. "Yes, a change, Friend Daniel. I will let the darkness out."

"Praise be." The man patted him on the shoulder. "I'm very glad to hear this."

"Really? I should think with thy heart on a certain young lady, it would be difficult."

Friend Daniel flushed and looked around as if expecting someone to be eavesdropping on their conversation. "It is not proper to. . ." He paused. "I will allow our gracious Lord to deal with the matters of the heart, Friend Silas. But thee has no fear. I understand that both thee and Mary have affection for each other. Thy name was on her lips today as she announced that thee was coming to Meeting. So be of good cheer." He smiled.

Silas sat in amazement as the elder left. His name had been on Mary's lips? She had been speaking about him to others? And then suddenly she stood before him, the radiant beauty of God's true Light burning inside her heart and beaming from her soft features. She had physical beauty, to be sure, but spiritual beauty as well. He came to his feet and faced her.

"Is something wrong?" she asked. "Thee is looking at me strangely."

"Nothing is wrong. Everything is good. More than good, I must say. There is peace once again in my heart."

"Oh, I'm so glad, Silas." She threw her arms around him as several Friends gasped and stared. She withdrew, looking sheepishly about as if expecting a rebuke for such an outward display. But smiles were on the faces of the brethren as well as their own as they left the meetinghouse together.

George waited for them, having already been helped to the wagon by some other Friends. He reclined in the wagon bed on some blankets, observing Silas and Mary with interest as they walked over. "I see it was a prosperous Meeting, Friend Silas. In more than just the Light? Perhaps also in love?"

"Yes, it was indeed prosperous." Silas said it with such passion that it drew a gleeful chuckle from Mary. "I only fear, Friend George, that thee had wished this injury upon thyself just to drag a lowly one like me to Meeting."

George shook his head. "I'm not *that* fond of thee! If God had another way, I'd much prefer it, but I trust in His wisdom. And I'm grateful that everything does work together for good, according to the blessed scripture. If the suffering of one can bring healing to others, then it's good suffering to bear."

Silas marveled at his words. How could suffering ever be good? But looking at Mary, so fair and lovely at his side— if his own personal suffering came about just so he could meet her, then it was well for his soul, too. He could find the same measure of peace in it as George had.

On the ride home they said little, but the unspoken

words conveyed much. With no one observing, Silas's fingers found Mary's hand beneath the woolen lap robe and gave a squeeze of reassurance, and he prayed a symbol of his affection. To his delight, she returned the favor. So she was thinking of him, too. He also thought about other things. What it would be like to marry a true Friend of the faith. Though he did hope on occasion they could dispense with the Quakers' formal language. He would love to simply say—

You have the most wonderful smile, my love. And your lips are like clover honey that I would very much like to consume.

"Thee hasn't heard a word spoken," Mary murmured, poking him playfully in the arm. "What is thee thinking?"

He saw her scrutinize him. "If I told thee, thee would blush."

She blushed anyway. "So did thee hear George's question? He asked if thee will be leaving anytime soon."

Silas glanced at her and then to the wagon bed to consider the young man who had been a help to him in more ways than he could say. "No matter how many times I wanted to leave, God has kept me here. And for very good reasons."

"And not because of my injury," George reminded him.

"Because He knows our hearts. He knew I wouldn't leave all of thee in thy time of need."

Mary snuggled beside him. "Does thee see his heart, George?"

"I always knew Silas had a heart full of God's Light. But he didn't, and maybe neither did others. Everyone was mistaken."

Silas hoped he did have a proper heart, even though he'd made mistakes. If he could be even a fraction of what Grandfather had been to so many in Philadelphia, he would thankfully carry the Jones' name. He settled on doing all that he could to help here in this place. Any thought of removing himself to go west lay as a forgotten dream while he embraced a hopeful future.

❄

A few days later, several visitors arrived to share in the Christmas holiday. While the Halls did not celebrate themselves, they prepared to host their guests with a celebration that included a fine meal, prayers, and lighting candles. Mrs. Hall baked gingerbread cookies, wrapped in paper, for each to have as a remembrance. But one of the visitors at the table, a young man, stared at Silas in a way that made him feel uncomfortable. He tried to place the man, with his medium frame and sandy-colored hair, but could not.

After the meal, the man motioned to Silas to come join him in the sitting room.

"What can I do for thee?" Silas asked, taking a seat opposite him.

The man sighed numerous times, wiping his hands together as his feet thumped the floor. "I–I'm not sure how to say this. . . ," he began. "But I needed to come here. If it weren't for that Quaker in Waynesville. . ."

Silas stared. "I don't understand. Have we met?"

"No, not really. You see, I come from Philadelphia."

Silas straightened. His muscles tightened, but he forced himself to relax when he saw Mary standing in the open doorway of the room. He hoped she was praying for him. He feared what was about to happen, and he would need all the strength he could muster to face it. "Oh?" he managed to say.

"I found out where you were staying from the letter sent by the Quaker in Waynesville to the Quakers in Philadelphia. I—I came as soon as I heard of your whereabouts."

Silas wondered if something had happened in his family. To his father. Or his brother, though he had never mentioned them to Mary or anyone else. He felt convicted.

"I went and talked to your father about what happened." He paused. "He has forgiven me. He showed me the letter and said I should see you as soon as possible."

Silas sensed the heat filling his ears. He wasn't sure he had the strength for this. "Forgiven thee for what?"

"For what I did to the old man. I—I didn't know he was your grandfather. No one did. We—we thought he was just a crazy old man no one cared about. I wasn't the one that injured him. Th–that was Paul. But I know. . ." He hesitated. Silas saw him begin to tremble, and he tried his best not to tremble, too. "But I helped hold the old man along with others while Paul beat him. Please, I have nightmares about it. What we did in the street. And. . .and I know he didn't live. I am so sorry. I live with the guilt of it every day. I realized from your father how much the man meant to you. How what we had done drove you away. When I learned where you were, I had to come beg for your forgiveness."

The news shook Silas to the core. He looked over to where Mary once stood. The spot was vacant, but she was undoubtedly close enough to overhear the confession. And she would look at him with her clear blue eyes, accompanied by her soothing voice. *Oh, dearest Silas. Thee must forgive and let it go. Thy grandfather is at peace with God. And so must thee be.*

Silas heard himself say to the man, "Grandfather is at peace. But I know thee is not. The only way thee can find true peace is through the Prince of Peace, who thee celebrates this Christmas Day. He must dwell in thee to make thee whole." Silas hesitated. "It's true I was angry about what happened. I lost someone I dearly loved. I wanted to see thee hurt because I was hurt. But I see now what it has done to me, thee, and others. That true forgiveness is the only path to peace."

The young man's eyes glistened with tears. "I could not go through Christmas with this in my heart. That's why I came as quickly as I could. I prayed you would still be here. Rumors were you were headed west to California."

"I've found my place and purpose here. And thee must find thy place." Silas saw the man's face quiver.

"I don't know. There is no peace for me on this earth."

"Yes, there is. While forgiveness can take time, I trust in my God that He will supply this free gift and supply thy need as well."

"That is all I can hope for. Now I can leave."

Silas held out his hand. "There is no need. Stay as long as thee wishes. And did thee receive the gift of gingerbread cookies from Mrs. Hall?"

"Yes, and I must say I ate mine already. They were the

best cookies I've ever had." He smiled cautiously.

Silas waved to Mary, who had ducked into the doorway once more. "Please, may we have another gift of cookies for my new friend here, Friend Mary? And a friend, not of the Society, but a friend in need and of the kind we will not turn away. No matter what hurt has been caused."

With those words, Silas found what he had been longing for. Peace at last with Grandfather's passing. And perhaps even an affirmation the older man would have given had he been alive. *"Yes indeed, Grandson. Thee has truly seen and felt the Light! Just as our elder William Penn once said: 'Christ's cross is Christ's way to Christ's crown.'"*

❄

That evening Silas sat in front of the fireplace, looking at the flames dancing before him. Everyone else had already gone to their rooms for the night, but he couldn't sleep after what happened. He marveled at God's hand that could take a situation many miles away and arrange for healing to occur even in a remote place in the middle of Ohio, and at an inn of all things.

He heard a sigh then and saw Mary approach. He stood to his feet, watching the golden firelight cast a holy aura across her face. She came forward without hesitation. "God indeed worked miracles this night," she said softly, smiling. "With the guest."

"Yes," he agreed. "Who would have thought?"

"God cares about our pain and our healing. But most of all, He cares that we draw close to Him in our time of need. Just as we also need each other."

"I care for thee," Silas said quickly. "I care what happens to thee. How you feel. Or how thee feels, that is. I hope thee has need of me."

"More than just a need, Friend Silas. I wonder if thee might be in a dream for my life."

"I do dream of you," he said, drawing her gently to him. She submitted, and they shared a sweet kiss before the snapping of the fire as the flames consumed the wood.

"Dream no longer," she said softly.

"I have no need, if I can ask thy father to court thee."

"He already suspects."

Silas stepped back. "But how can he? I haven't spoken of it and—"

She laughed. "Father doesn't live on the roof. He knows quite well what is happening in his household. He will be most glad to have thee as my suitor. And I must say, I'm glad as well."

Silas took her in his arms, with a peace that surpassed all his understanding, thankful for these precious gifts from God above.

Lauralee Bliss has always liked to dream big dreams. Part of that dream was writing, and after several years of hard work, her dream of publishing was realized in 1997 with the publication of her first romance novel, *Mountaintop*, through Barbour Publishing. Since then she's had twenty books published, both historical and contemporary. Lauralee is also an avid hiker, completing the entire length of the Appalachian Trail both north and south. Lauralee makes her home in Virginia in the foothills of the Blue Ridge Mountains with her family. Visit her website at www.lauraleebliss.com

SIMPLE GIFTS

Ramona K. Cecil

Thanks be unto God for his unspeakable gift.
2 CORINTHIANS 9:15

Chapter 1

S hoo!"

Lucinda Hughes gently nudged the Rhode Island Red hen off its straw-filled nest.

Puck, puck, puck, puckaaw! The plump bird angled its rust-colored head and gave Lucinda an amber-eyed glare. But the hen moved away from the nest and, with a flurry of wings that sent dust flying in the dim chicken coop, jumped to the dirt floor.

Coughing, Lucinda wrinkled her nose and fought the urge to sneeze. "Well, thank thee, Miss Red. Thee took long enough." The fowl strutted into the next room as if proud of what she'd accomplished. A giggle bubbled from Lucinda's throat. The sound surprised her. Her laugh faded as she reached into the indention in the moldy straw, wrapping her fingers around the warm, brown egg.

When had she regained the ability to laugh? Not so long ago she'd thought she would never laugh again.

She and Alan used to laugh all the time. She remembered how they'd laughed that day last March when he brought home the crate of pullets and young roosters. He might have brought her a crate of gold, for the jubilation it evoked.

She tucked the egg into the basket along with the eight she'd already gathered—fruits of the now-mature hens.

Alan had caught her up in his strong arms, lifting her feet off the ground as he'd loved to do. "Thee is a Quaker farm wife now," he'd said. "Thee should have thy own chickens."

Old Mercy Cox said love didn't just happen. That real love grew slowly over time. But Lucinda had known she loved Alan from that first moment sixteen months ago, when she first saw him at a Gurneyite Quaker revival meeting in Kentucky. Could all that had happened since been stuffed into the short span of sixteen months?

Blinking back hot tears, she passed through the roosting area of the coop where several of the chickens already clung to the stair-stepped sapling poles, their eyelids drooping. She emitted a small groan as she bent over her expanded middle to exit the coop's low doorway.

Outside, a cool gust of November wind dried the wetness on her cheeks and sent a shiver through her. Gripping the handle of her egg basket, she gazed at the two-story cabin that sat on the rise in front of her. How proud Alan had been that day last December when he brought her, a new bride, to the hewn-log cabin his grandfather had built sixty years before.

Her gaze drifted to the back of the cabin where a small frame structure jutted out from the old log building. A bittersweet feeling twanged in her chest. Alan had completed half of their new kitchen by the middle of June, when the explosion happened at the grain mill where he worked. So great was the blast that even from a mile away, the cabin had shaken, sending a stoneware pitcher flying from the mantel above the fireplace.

She remembered wondering if the loud boom and shaking was an earth tremor and then grieving over the loss of the pitcher, a wedding present from Mercy. She would soon learn that she'd suffered a far greater loss than any keepsake. For the same instant the pitcher smashed against the puncheon floor, the explosion had killed Alan, shattering Lucinda's life.

The babe within her kicked, as if flailing against the injustice of never knowing his father.

She'd never felt as alone as she did the day of Alan's funeral when she walked away from the little Quaker graveyard, leaving her young husband beneath the mound of dirt. Only the thought of her coming child had saved her mind and spirit from crushing despair.

The congregation of Serenity Friends Meeting had gathered around her, seeing to her immediate needs. The men had even worked together to finish the kitchen. But when Lucinda stopped attending Meeting, the helping hands had become fewer. Only Mercy Cox and Will Davis came regularly now.

At the thought of her late husband's best friend, warmth filled Lucinda. Since the accident, not a week passed without Will stopping by to bring her milk and groceries, take care of some chore, or make a repair to the cabin.

Her face turned unbidden toward the dirt road running past the front of her property. Earlier, when she'd stepped out of the cabin to head for the chicken coop, the mill's whistle had sounded, signaling the end of the work day. Will's mule and wagon would appear soon if he planned to stop by on his way home.

Squinting against the setting sun's bright rays, she gazed through the nearly barren branches of the old poplar tree that partially obscured her view of the road. But the only movement on the dirt thoroughfare was a shower of brown and yellow leaves caught up by a gust of wind.

Though she had no need for provisions or Will's assistance, a feeling akin to disappointment pushed a sigh from her lips and dragged down her shoulders. When had she started looking forward to Will's visits?

She brushed aside the unexpected pang of melancholy along with a strand of hair that had blown across her face. Tucking the errant lock back into her bonnet, she started for the cabin. Maybe Mercy was right when she warned that spending too much time alone in the cabin would shrivel Lucinda's mind and spirit.

The *clip-clop* of hooves and the rumble of a conveyance drew her attention to the road. For a moment her heart quickened but then slowed at the sight of a one-horse shay in the distance instead of a mule-drawn wagon.

When the buggy turned into the lane that wound up to her cabin, she groaned in dismay and immediately felt guilty. Mercy had hinted during her visit yesterday that Levi Braddock and his wife, Charity, might stop by this week. Though Lucinda knew the elder and his wife meant well, she'd begun to dread their calls. Lately, their visits focused less on inquiring about her welfare and more on encouraging her to attend Meeting. But she refused to sit in Meeting and pretend to pray to a God with whom she no longer felt a connection.

The buggy rounded the curve in the lane, and Lucinda saw that it carried only one person. A man. He lifted his head, and she recognized not Levi Braddock's but Will Davis's face beneath the wide-brimmed black hat.

Her heart began to prance like the young black horse pulling the buggy.

It's just because I'm glad it's not the Braddocks wanting to pressure me into attending Meeting tonight.

Then why had her thumping heart not slowed its pace? She ignored the troublesome thought and stepped toward the buggy.

"Lucinda." Smiling, Will raised his hand in greeting and reined the horse to a stop. In one continuous motion, he wrapped the reins around the brake's handle and stepped to the ground. His lanky frame moved with grace as he came around to the horse's head to pet the skittish animal and murmur reassurances.

"Is there somethin' the matter with Bob?" She nodded at the young horse.

"Naw, the mule's in fine fettle." He ambled toward her, giving her that shy, little-boy smile that seemed somehow odd on a grown man. "Simeon just bought this two-year-old colt." He glanced over his shoulder. "He asked me to get him used to the buggy before Naomi takes it out."

Lucinda nodded, her smile fading. Cold and sharp-tongued, Will's sister-in-law, Naomi, was not one of her favorite members at Serenity Friends Meeting.

Will took the egg basket from Lucinda's hands and headed toward the cabin. "I just came from visiting Mercy Cox."

Lucinda fell in step beside him, and it struck her how, without being asked, he was always doing little kindnesses. "I pray Mercy is well."

He nodded and gave her a reassuring smile. "Yes, she is well and holds thee in the Light."

Lucinda loved the Quaker expression for keeping someone in one's thoughts and prayers.

When they reached the kitchen door, he stopped and glanced upward. "Mercy mentioned that thy kitchen roof is leaking."

"Yes. It is just a small drip, but when it rained the day before yesterday, I had to put a pan under it to keep the floor dry." Had Will visited Mercy this evening in hopes of finding a reason to stop by here on his way home? Shame filled Lucinda for both the thought and the spark of joy Will's visit ignited inside her.

He held the egg basket out to her. She took it, and their hands touched, sending a pleasant ripple of warmth up her arm. "It will be winter soon. And a hole that will let in rain will let in cold air. I would be happy to fix it if I wouldn't be a bother."

"Yes—I mean no." Heat flooded Lucinda's face. She must look like a ninny with her words tripping over her tongue. Her laugh, the second one today, came out in a nervous-sounding warble, sending another burst of heat to her face. "Yes, I would like the roof fixed. And no, of course thee is not a bother." That was a flat-out lie. Will's presence bothered her greatly. She wrapped her arms around the egg basket to calm her discomposure. "I'm afraid I'm the bother."

For an instant, a shadow passed across his face before turning serious. She could almost feel the warm caress of his gray eyes on her face. "Thee is not a bother to me, Lucinda."

Somehow Lucinda managed to escape his gaze and stumble into the kitchen on legs that felt like they'd turned to jelly. With unsteady hands, she set the basket on the table then slumped to a chair. Will was like an older brother to Alan. Of course he wanted to help her. Just like all the other times he'd helped her since June.

He only meant that doing God's work is not a bother.

Yet she didn't believe a word of it. She'd heard Will's voice and seen his face. The look in his eyes snatched the breath right out of her lungs.

But Will was Alan's best friend!

That fact, however, didn't calm the tumult in her chest. Her heart beat like the wings of a gaggle of geese about to take flight. Something had changed between her and Will. And that change both excited and terrified her.

Chapter 2

Perched high on the ladder, Will slipped the top edge of a new red cedar shingle beneath the bottom edge of the weathered one above it. The wood's rich scent filled his nostrils and whisked him back to last spring when he had helped Alan cut the shingles for the new kitchen's roof.

He paused to gaze over the roof. As always, thoughts of his late friend sent tentacles of guilt throughout his chest—guilt that gnarled painfully around his heart. The feeling had become a constant companion.

Alan should be doing this. Alan should be here. . . .

But he wasn't here. And the blame for that lay squarely on Will's shoulders. Over the past five months, the weight of that blame had become a ponderous mantle that grew heavier each day.

If only he had refused Alan's request to switch jobs that day at the mill. *If only. . .*

Balancing on the ladder's rung, he shoved his hand into his trouser pocket and pulled out a nail. Two sharp blows of his hammer drove it deep into the shingle. The aggressive movement relieved a measure of pent-up emotion building inside him, and he quickly added two more nails to the shingle.

He reached for a fourth nail but let it fall back into his pocket with a clink against its fellows. The job was done.

And no amount of hammering would expel the anger and regret that dwelt inside him. Sometimes he wished Quakers were not so peace-loving. Once in a while, it would feel good to plow his fist into. . .something.

"*Cease from anger, and forsake wrath.*" The words from Psalm 37:8 convicted him. He would need to spend much time in prayer at Meeting this evening.

But anger was the least of his sins. He breathed out a ragged breath and began to back down the ladder. All day he'd tried without success to think of a reason—any reason—to stop by Lucinda's cabin. So this afternoon when Mercy told him about the leak in Lucinda's roof, his heart had leapt inside his chest.

Another wave of shame and guilt washed through him. When had his vow to see to the needs of Alan's widow become more than a simple act of Christian charity?

He remembered the first time he saw Lucinda sitting beside Mercy Cox, with whom she'd resided, at Meeting nearly a year and a half ago. A group from the congregation had just returned from a revival trip to Kentucky where the preaching of Friend John Henry Douglas had convinced many, including Lucinda, to join the Quakers. For a brief time, he had even considered courting her. Then he learned that she and Alan—his best friend and foster brother—had become attached to one another. After that, he'd thought of her only as a sister. Until now.

He hoisted the ladder onto his shoulder and headed to the tool shed. When he opened the door, its rusty hinges creaked in protest. Perhaps he should oil them.

"Tomorrow," he promised the dim interior of the shed as he slid the ladder along the floor lengthwise and leaned it against the wall. Yes, tomorrow would be a good day to see to the hinges.

His heart quickened as he strode through the lengthening shadows toward the cabin. Only an amber wedge of waning sunlight caressed the west side of the log building. Through the poplar tree's skeletal fingers he could make out streaks of pink and gold smeared across the slate-gray sky.

A cold gust of wind lifted a pile of dried leaves in front of him. Despite his wide-brimmed hat and canvas coat, the wind sent a chill through him. The light from the kitchen window beckoned. How easy to imagine walking into the warm embrace of the cabin. *And that of the woman inside it.*

But those things could never be his. Even if by some miracle God blessed him with Lucinda's affection—affection beyond that of a sister—his abiding guilt surely would throw up a barrier thicker than the log walls of the old cabin to separate them.

He knocked at the kitchen door, his heartbeats matching the quick tempo of his raps. At his summons the door opened, drenching him in a comforting rush of warmth. The tempting scents of sassafras and cinnamon met him, teasing his nose. Lucinda stood framed in the doorway. Her black bonnet was gone now. A few wisps of her hair had pulled loose from the bun at the back of her head and curled appealingly against her temples. The sun's dying rays caught them, burnishing the locks to the rich color of clover honey.

He had seen her at least once a week over the past year and a half, but he couldn't remember her looking lovelier than she did at this moment.

His throat went dry. He cleared it. Twice. "Thee only lost one shingle. Probably during that storm last week." Needing to shift his gaze from her face, he looked up at the roof. How stupid she must think him. His face turned back to hers as if pulled by a magnet. "There were extra in the shed, so I replaced it."

"Thank thee, Will. Now I can keep the dishpan in the sink instead of on the floor." Smiling, she glanced down almost shyly. "Good night to thee," she murmured, then turned and started to close the door.

"Lucinda." Desperate for one last glimpse of her, he blurted her name without thinking.

She turned back at his summons. Her light-brown eyes, which always reminded him of sassafras wood, grew rounder, questioning.

"Meeting is tonight, thee knows." Every week he asked, and every week she turned him down. But he had to try. Without regular Christian fellowship, he feared her young faith might wither. And besides, when her babe came, she would need the support of the congregation even more. "With Christmas coming, the women are planning food baskets for the needy. Mercy may have told thee. I'd be happy to take—"

Dismay filled her features. "No." The word felt like a slap. She blew out a ragged sigh. "Please don't ask me anymore, Will. I just can't go."

"But why?" His breath exploded in a huff of exasperation. "Thee needs to be in Meeting among those of thy faith, hearing God's Word preached and listening for God's voice." In light of her condition and the shock of Alan's death, the elders as well as the congregation in general had exercised unusual restraint and leniency concerning Lucinda's long absence from Meeting. But after five months, Will had begun to notice signs of fraying patience among the elders of Serenity Friends Meeting.

The frown drawing her delicate brows together didn't bode hopeful. "If God cares to speak to me, He can surely speak to me in my own home."

Will heaved a sigh of surrender. "Of course He can, but. . ." How could he get through to her the importance of gathering with those of like faith without sounding judgmental?

Within the cabin, a tea kettle set up a shrill whistle.

"Oh, I forgot I left the kettle on." She whirled toward the sound. As she turned, the rag rug beneath her feet slipped, and she tilted sideways with a gasp.

At the last instant, Will reached out and grasped her around the waist, saving her from the fall. For one blissful moment he stood holding her, safe and warm against him.

"Ahem!"

At the sound of a voice, Will's head jerked around, and he found himself staring into the shocked faces of Levi and Charity Braddock.

Chapter 3

Thank thee for savin' me from fallin', Will." Heat filled Lucinda's face as she quickly stepped out of Will's embrace. "This rug is always slippin'." Hopefully, the Braddocks would attribute any redness in her face to her near accident. She only wished she didn't sound so breathless.

Levi and Charity Braddock's stunned expressions quickly turned to looks of concern.

"Thee should tack down that rug, Lucinda," Charity said in hushed tones that held a definite reproach. "A fall at this time could be very dangerous for thee and the baby."

"Yes, Charity, thee is right. I will do that." Lucinda pressed her hand against her chest as if to muffle the sound of her pounding heart.

Charity looked at Will, and tiny lines of disapproval etched the corners of her tightly pursed lips. Lucinda knew that Will's ruddy complexion had little to do with the chilly air. "It was truly a blessing that thee was here to prevent such an accident, Will." Despite her complimentary words, Charity's voice held a disapproving tone.

Will's hand fisted at his side, and the muscles moved in his jaw. "We should all be thankful that Mercy Cox sent me here to see about a leak in Lucinda's roof." The cold tone of his voice broached no further conjecture about anything the Braddocks might have witnessed.

Remembering her manners, Lucinda forced a bright smile.

"Please come in, Charity, Levi. I was about to brew some tea."

"Thank thee, but we cannot stay." Charity clasped her hand on Lucinda's. "Levi and I are on our way to Meeting and felt led to stop by and offer thee a ride this evening."

Lucinda wished she didn't recoil inside every time someone mentioned attending Meeting. In truth, it was becoming increasingly difficult to come up with both credible and at least partially true reasons to avoid Meeting. But if she blurted out the real reason—that she and God were no longer on speaking terms—she'd invite a sermon from Levi right here on her doorstep. "I—I don't know. I don't feel—"

"I'm sure thee will understand that Lucinda needs to rest after her fright." Will stepped between Lucinda and Charity. "I'm of a mind to fetch Mercy Cox to stay with her this evening."

"Of course," Levi and Charity Braddock said in near chorus. "We will hold thee in the Light, Lucinda." Levi's smile held genuine kindness, twisting the thread of guilt wriggling in Lucinda's chest.

Lucinda watched Levi guide his wife toward the front of the cabin, hating the thought of appearing frail to the Braddocks. Lucinda knew she was fully capable of hitching her horse, Star, to the buggy and driving the three miles to the meetinghouse in Serenity. After the couple had gone, Will hammered a tack in each corner of the offending rag rug.

"There. That should give thee no more trouble," he said as he stood.

"Thank thee, Will. For. . .everything." Gratitude filled Lucinda. He had come to her rescue twice today.

"I meant what I said. I shall fetch Mercy if thee thinks—"

"No." Although she would enjoy Mercy's company, Lucinda needed time alone to sort through the tangle of disquieting feelings she was experiencing regarding Will. Besides, she wouldn't deny Mercy the opportunity of attending midweek Meeting unnecessarily. She managed a smile. "As thee told Levi and Charity, I just need some rest."

Will nodded, but he continued to study her face as if reluctant to leave until reassured that she meant her words.

"Rest well, Lucinda," he finally said in a near whisper. For a long moment, his gaze caressed her face. Then in a sudden movement he turned and, taking long-legged strides, headed toward the front of the cabin.

Five days later, swathed in her wool shawl, Lucinda ambled along the dirt road toward Mercy's house. She still struggled to make sense of her unexpected reaction to Will the previous week. Her mind flew back to the moment when she'd slipped on the rug and he'd caught her in his arms and held her warmly against him. Despite the chilly wind that buffeted her bonnet and snatched at her shawl, a rush of heat rolled through her. A part of her was relieved that he had not stopped by again, while another part nursed a niggling disappointment that he had not.

Mercy was right. Loneliness did strange things to a person's mind. And Mercy should know. Though widowed five years ago, the older woman scarcely spent a full day alone between selling her rag rugs and tending to the needy. If Lucinda followed her friend's example and became more sociable and less dependent upon Will, surely these unsettling feelings and thoughts about him would go away. And once again she would view him as she had before Alan's death—a dear friend and nothing more.

She looked down at the basket full of woolen strips sewn together and wound into balls that bounced against her hip. Since she'd first known Mercy, the older woman had pestered Lucinda to let her instruct her in the skill of rug weaving. Today, she would accept Mercy's offer.

Lucinda couldn't expect to live off the charity of her neighbors for the rest of her life. She would need a way to provide for herself and her child. Many times, Mercy had commented on how thankful she was for her loom, how rug weaving provided her with an enjoyable occupation, as well as a comfortable living since the death of her husband. Lucinda saw no reason why it shouldn't do the same for her. And as Mercy seemed to always have more work than she could keep up with, Lucinda wouldn't be taking anything away from her teacher. But perhaps most importantly, weaving lessons would give Lucinda a reason to spend afternoons away from her cabin, lessening the chance of another unsettling incident with Will.

She rounded the bend in the road, and Mercy's pale-yellow house came into view. Always an inviting sight, the building, with its sunny color and white-railed porch, looked especially warm and welcoming on this raw autumn day. She cast an upward glance at the pewter-colored sky. Hopefully, any snow would hold off until tonight. The thought of walking the mile home in a snow storm didn't appeal.

Quickening her steps, she made her way up to the front porch. She'd scarcely rapped twice at the door when Mercy opened it.

"Child, come in." Stepping back, the older woman ushered Lucinda into the front room. When she turned from closing the door, Mercy's smile faded and she eyed Lucinda, worry lines etching her forehead. "Is anything the matter?"

"No, I am very well." Lucinda gave her friend a reassuring smile.

"I praise the Lord for that." Her smile back in place, Mercy took Lucinda's wool shawl and hung it on a peg by the door.

Inside, Lucinda scanned the familiar space that smelled of cotton, vanilla, and cinnamon. Before her marriage to Alan, she'd spent many enjoyable hours here as Mercy's houseguest. With its white-painted walls, large, denim rag rug that centered the floor, and black potbellied stove tucked in one corner, the room was at once inviting and functional. But the object that dominated the room and drew her eye was the giant floor loom situated near the south window.

"It looks like thee has brought me more work." Linking her fingers over her apron-clad middle, Mercy glanced at the basket of woolen balls on Lucinda's arm.

"I've actually brought *me* some work." Lucinda walked to the loom and set the basket down beside it. "That is, if thee will teach me to weave."

"Of course I will teach thee." Mercy's round face practically glowed. Yet her smile didn't show the least hint of smugness at having finally coaxd Lucinda to the loom. She cocked her head, and her delicate gray brows rose. "Thee was never interested in learnin' before. Why now?"

Fleeing Mercy's studying look, Lucinda's gaze slid to the loom. "I—I don't have the book learnin' to be a teacher, and I'll need a way to make a livin' for me and my young'un." She preferred to keep the part about avoiding Will to herself.

Mercy motioned for Lucinda to sit on the bench in front of the loom then pulled up a ladder-back chair and sat next to her. Fixing Lucinda with an intent gaze, she crossed her arms over her chest. "Which brings us to what I've been harpin' on since the accident that took Alan."

Lucinda stifled a groan. She hadn't come here to argue with Mercy about moving back into this house. She blew out a weary sigh. "I would love to stay here with thee, Mercy. But thee knows how it pleased Alan to think that his child would be born in the cabin his grandpa built. I have to stay in the cabin. It's what Alan wanted."

Mercy reached over and gripped Lucinda's hand. "Child, thee knows Alan would want what is best for thee and the babe." She sat back and gave her head an emphatic nod. "But if thee won't come here, then after Christmas, when my rug weavin' slacks off, I'll go stay with thee. The babe could come any time durin' the last month, and we can't risk thee bein' alone."

"Thank thee, Mercy." At the thought of having Mercy near during her last weeks of confinement, relief washed through Lucinda. But despite the older woman's comment about less work after Christmas, guilt pricked. It bothered Lucinda to think she'd be taking Mercy away from her home and loom. "Is thee sure thee can afford to be away from thy loom for a month?"

Mercy's grin widened. "With thee helpin' me, I should be more than a month ahead in my orders." She patted Lucinda's hand. "God is the Master Weaver. See how He weaves everything together for good for them who love Him?"

Lucinda didn't answer. Once, she'd believed that. When there seemed no escape from Pa's drunken cruelty, she'd believed that God had sent the Quakers with their revival tent to the town near her family's tenant farm to save her. Coming to Serenity, finding a second mother in Mercy and a loving husband in Alan, had all seemed like miracles to Lucinda. But when Alan died, her belief in miracles dimmed along with God's Light within her.

Mercy stood. "Since I already have the warp threads strung, we shall begin a rug, usin' thy material." She glanced down at Lucinda's basketful of woolen balls. "I'd say thee has the makin's of a nice-sized rug, maybe two feet wide and three feet long."

Though she had watched Mercy weave rugs for hours on end, Lucinda was surprised at how much she'd absorbed and how quickly she picked up the steps. And aside from her protruding abdomen impeding her reach for the beater beam, she actually enjoyed the work.

When Lucinda had woven two lines of woolen weft, Mercy plucked at the material, checking the tightness of the weave. "Oh, thee is doing well, Lucinda." With a critical eye, she appraised the beginnings of the brown, green, and blue rug and smiled her approval. "At this pace, thee will have a new rug in no time. Where does thee plan to put it?"

Lucinda paused as she stepped on the treadle to raise the harness for the next row. She hadn't considered what she might do with the rug. "Christmas is coming, so maybe I'll give it away." People were always helping her. She liked the idea of doing something for someone else for a change. "Does thee know of someone who could use a rug?"

Mercy reached up and ran her fingers through warp threads that, to Lucinda, didn't look tangled. "Perhaps thee could give it to Will Davis." Mercy's voice held a touch of hesitancy, as if she were testing the air with her words. "I've never known a kinder, more giving person than Will, and he has done much for thee."

At Will's name, warmth flooded Lucinda's face. Keeping her head down to hide any telltale redness, she focused on her work. "Yes, Will has been very kind to me. Maybe I should give him the rug," she murmured, hoping to put an end to the subject.

Mercy stood at Lucinda's side and instructed while Lucinda wove a couple dozen rows. Then, pronouncing the work excellent, she headed to the kitchen to start supper.

Gradually, Lucinda's motions became smooth and rhythmic, her speed at the loom growing with her confidence. When she finally looked up at the clock on the mantel, two more hours had passed. Two more rows and she would have a three-foot-long finished rug. As she again passed the shuttle through the space between the warp threads, which Mercy had called the "shed," three quick knocks sounded at the front door.

Lucinda rose to answer it.

"Prob'ly somebody wantin' a rug made." Mercy strode into the front room, drying her hands on a dish towel.

Lucinda reached the door first and opened it to find Will Davis standing in the blue-gray gloaming amid a swirl of snowflakes. Her heart jumped then raced like a scared rabbit. "Will." His name came out in a breathless puff of air, snatched away by a gust of wind that whistled past the porch.

"Lucinda." Only a slight widening of his gray eyes hinted at his surprise. She thought she detected his face reddening beneath his hat's wide brim. But more likely, the cold wind had simply whipped extra color into his features. After a long moment, his gaze shifted from Lucinda to Mercy. "I just stopped by to add some wood to the rick on thy porch, Mercy. Does thee need any brought into the house?"

"Yes. Thank thee, Will." Mercy's scrutinizing gaze bounced between Will and Lucinda. "I could use more beside the heat stove and some willow or birch, if thee has it, for the kitchen stove."

"Yes, I have some nice pieces of willow." His smiling gaze drifted from Mercy to Lucinda before he turned and headed back to his wagon.

Her heart pounding, Lucinda returned to the loom. She picked up the wood shuttle and tried to pass it through the shed, but her hand trembled so that the shuttle kept getting caught in the warp strings. She'd thought her odd reaction to Will last Wednesday was nothing more than a symptom of her loneliness. But if so, then why should his presence still affect her in the same jarring way after she'd spent an afternoon with Mercy? Whatever the cause of her strange malady, she remained resolute as to the cure. Until this disquieting feeling went away, she must try her best to avoid him.

Mercy came up behind Lucinda and put her hand on her shoulder. "For a beginner weaver, thy work is excellent, Lucinda." She ran her hand over the woven rug wound on the cloth beam. "I'd say thy rug is at least three feet long."

Basking in her teacher's praise, Lucinda gave a little laugh. "Thank thee, Mercy. I'm blessed to have such a good teacher."

Using a pair of scissors, Mercy showed Lucinda how to cut the rug from the loom and knot the ends of the warp threads to finish it.

"Does thee want to leave the rug here and finish knotting the fringe tomorrow, or take it home and finish it there?" Mercy asked as she rolled up the rug.

"I think I'd better leave it here," Lucinda said. The thought of lugging the bulky bundle a mile through wind and snow didn't appeal. "I'm not sure I could carry it all the way home."

Mercy pressed her hand to her chest and chuckled. "Oh child, I'd never allow thee to carry this home." At that moment the front door opened, and Will entered with a bundle of kindling in his arms. Smiling, Mercy glanced at him. "Will has agreed to stay and have supper with us. Then he will take thee and thy rug home."

Chapter 4

Will strode to his wagon and bounded to the seat, his foot barely touching the wagon tongue. Frustration surged through him, firing every nerve. Grabbing the reins, he slapped them down on the mule's back with a sharper-than-intended snap. The normally placid animal jumped, sending a wave of guilt through Will. "Sorry there, Bob. Didn't mean to whack thee so hard."

For the third evening in a row, he had stopped at Mercy's only to learn that Lucinda had headed home on foot an hour earlier. It hurt to think that she was avoiding him on purpose. But things certainly looked that way, especially considering her oddly reticent attitude when he drove her home from Mercy's last Monday.

A queasy feeling welled up in the pit of his stomach. Could Lucinda have somehow learned the details of what had transpired between Alan and him the day of the accident? He dismissed the thought the second it formed in his mind. Even if she had found out—though he couldn't imagine how—Lucinda was not one to brood. She doubtless would have confronted him with what she'd learned.

But regardless of why she'd chosen to leave Mercy's each day before he could take her home in his wagon, his concern for her health and safety remained. The thought of her making the mile trek twice a day through inclement winter weather filled him with dread. And despite their best efforts to do so, both Mercy and he had failed to convince Lucinda to either move back in with Mercy or give up rug weaving until spring.

Will blew out a long sigh. "Lord, just help me find a way to keep her safe." Why did women have to be so hard-headed? With that thought, his sister-in-law's stern visage flashed in his mind. He groaned, remembering that Naomi had asked him to stop by the mercantile and purchase a tin of baking powder on his way home from work. With the mercantile a block down from the grain mill where he worked, such errands often fell to Will.

Sending up a prayer for patience, he clicked his tongue, turned the mule around, and headed back to town.

Inside the mercantile, Will continued his silent petition for patience as he waited his turn in line behind several other customers. Spying a *Farm Journal* magazine on an up-ended crate, he picked it up and began to thumb through it to pass the time.

Suddenly a black-and-white image on a page caught his eye, and he flipped back to it. Beneath the picture of a home rug loom, the manufacturer promised that for the price of twenty dollars, their product could provide a handsome living for any industrious soul.

Of course! If Lucinda had her own loom, she wouldn't have to walk to and from Mercy's house each day.

When it was finally Will's turn at the counter, he asked for the baking powder and then held up the magazine. "How much for this magazine, Zeke?"

Zeke Reeves scratched his head, mussing the thin

strands of gray hair he'd combed over his balding pate. "Aw, I reckon you can have it at no charge." He shrugged. "It's last month's issue. I should get a new one in another day or two."

"Thank thee, Zeke." Will plopped a quarter on the counter to pay for the baking powder and then hurried out of the store with the powder and the magazine in hand. Whispering a prayer of thanks for God's direction, he could hardly wait to get home and write out an order for the loom.

A half hour later, he'd just sat down at Simeon's desk in the living room when he felt a hand on his shoulder.

"I hope thee does not plan to be long at the desk, little brother." The mingled scents of sweat, chalk, and Simeon's shaving soap filled Will's nostrils as his brother hunched over the desk. "I have a satchel full of test papers to grade this evening."

"No, I won't be long." Will stiffened beneath Simeon's touch, rankling at the absurd term his brother insisted on using to address him. Though seven years Will's senior, Simeon stood a good six inches shorter.

"What has thee here?" Simeon craned his neck, poking his head farther over Will's shoulder as if checking the work of one of his students.

Shrugging away from his brother's hand, Will slid his arm over the magazine's cover. Though Simeon didn't lack in Christian charity, he, like his wife, possessed a strong frugal streak. Will wasn't at all sure how his brother might react to Will spending the substantial sum of twenty dollars on a gift.

"I found something in the magazine I thought might

be useful and wanted to read more about it." Will hoped his evasive answer didn't stray too far from the truth.

Grinning, Simeon stood and backed away with his palms held forward. "Thee need say no more, little brother. My students are constantly reminding me that with Christmas only weeks away, this is the season for secrets." With that he retreated to the sofa and picked up the newspaper, leaving Will alone to write the order for the loom.

When he finished, Will stuffed the letter into the envelope and tucked it into the magazine. Thankfully, for the past several months, he'd been setting aside money to buy a new saddle. Tomorrow, he would use some of his savings to purchase a money order at the post office to pay for the loom.

"Simeon. Will. Thy supper is on the table." Naomi stepped into the living room, smoothing back her jet-black hair that looked to Will as prim as ever.

Smiling, Simeon set the paper aside and rose from the sofa. "Thank thee, my dear. Sausages and cabbage, if my nose tells me right."

"And fried potatoes," Naomi added, turning her attention to Will. "Has thee washed up?" She trained her green eyes on his hands.

Will forced a stiff smile. "Thee knows I would not bring dirty hands to thy table, sister." Still childless after five years of marriage, Naomi tended to treat Will more as an errant child than a brother.

After they gathered round the table and Simeon said grace, Naomi passed Will the fried potatoes. "At least thee is on time for supper this evening. I never know whether to cook for two or three." She lifted her chin a smidgen, and the shadows cast by the kerosene lamplight accentuated her sharp features.

Will dished out a portion of potatoes, ignoring the censure in Naomi's voice. "I am sorry, sister. But thee knows I often stop to do chores for our widowed friends, Lucinda and Mercy."

"Of course thee should help Mercy." Naomi's voice lowered to a near whisper. "But does thee think it is wise to spend so much time alone with Lucinda?"

Will gritted his teeth as he slid his knife through the link of sausage on his plate. "I am only doing as the scripture commands—to see to the widows in their affliction."

Naomi fixed Will with a green glare. "'But the younger widows refuse: for when they have begun to wax wanton against Christ, they will marry.' First Timothy, chapter five, verse eleven."

Will dropped his knife and fork to his plate with a clatter. It took every ounce of his strength to stay in his chair. How dare Naomi use the scriptures to scold him for helping Lucinda. "I know the passage as well as thee does, sister." He fought to keep the anger from his voice. "In that same chapter, Paul preaches that widows of a congregation should first be cared for by family. Alan was like a brother to me. I'm the closest thing to family Lucinda has here."

"Brother. Wife." Simeon's voice held a weary plea. He breathed a heavy sigh. "I spend all day settling arguments between my students. Is a peaceful meal at home too much for a man to ask?"

At Simeon's words, regret drove the anger out of Will. The last thing he wanted was to cause discord in his family. "I'm sorry, Simeon, Naomi. I meant no disrespect."

For the next few minutes everyone ate in silence, which was only disturbed by the clinking of utensils against plates.

At length, Naomi took a sip of water and then delicately cleared her throat. When she spoke, her measured voice held the barest hint of contrition. "Please forgive me, Will, if I spoke too harshly. But as thy elder sister, I feel it is my place to guide thee." She took another sip of water. "I must admit it pains me to see my dear husband shoulder more of the work here at home because of thy absence." She reached over and placed her hand on Simeon's arm. His mouth full, Simeon answered her wifely concern with a grateful smile and a pat on her hand.

As if emboldened by Simeon's support, Naomi's voice grew stronger. "I worry that thy well-meaning acts of charity might be...misconstrued." On the last word, she lowered her voice to a near whisper and then gained strength again. "Lucinda has not attended Meeting for almost six months now. I am concerned that she did not experience true sanctification. Levi and Charity Braddock have attempted to labor with her and bring her back into the Light, but she refuses to hear them. So unless she shows in some way that her sanctification was genuine—"

Struggling to keep his voice even, Will pushed back from the table, scraping the chair's legs against the wood floor, and stood. "If thee both will excuse me, there is something I need to work on in the woodshop before it gets too late." He had quietly listened to Naomi's admonishment of his conduct. But to hear her casually suggest that Lucinda had not experienced true sanctification was more than he could bear in silence. If he stayed another moment, he'd be putting himself in danger of sinning by saying something he would regret.

Will looked at Naomi but couldn't force his lips into even the semblance of a smile. "I thank thee for the fine supper, sister," he mumbled and fled the kitchen. As he passed through the living room, he snatched the *Farm Journal* off the desk and took it to his bedroom where he slid it under his pillow and then headed to the barn.

Five minutes later, he stood in a corner of the barn he'd avoided since Alan's death. Here, years earlier, he and Alan had built a small woodworking shop.

He picked up a rasp from the dusty workbench and hefted it in his hands. The words he'd said to Alan when he first handed him the tool nearly eight years ago echoed in his ears. *We are brothers now. Everything that is mine is thine, too.*

At nineteen, Will had simply tried to make the sixteen-year-old orphaned Alan feel welcome after he'd come to live with Will's family. And indeed for the better part of seven years—with the exception of clothes that rarely fit both Will's tall, lanky frame and Alan's shorter, stockier build—the two had shared most everything.

A shared love of tools and carpentry had cemented their relationship and helped them become closer than many natural brothers. Certainly, Alan had been more like a brother to Will than bookish Simeon.

Even after Alan's marriage to Lucinda, he'd continued to stop by often and work on one project or another in the woodshop. But it was the project Alan had left unfinished that brought Will back to this place he himself had neglected for so long.

Will blew out a long breath, creating a misty cloud in the chilly evening air. The memory of the words he'd spoken to Alan so long ago returned to haunt him. Did that road run both ways? Had Will inherited what Alan had left undone?

The piece of cherry wood still fixed in the vise where Alan had left it said that he did. Alan had meant to finish the project for Lucinda's birthday last August.

Shame filled Will. He should have finished Alan's gift then and given it to her as Alan had wanted. But Christmas was coming.

He ran a piece of sandpaper along the rough edge of the plank, smoothing it. After checking for any missed splinters, he took the plank from the vise, set it aside, and replaced it with another rough-cut piece.

Alan had done much of the work. So if Will devoted an hour each day to this project, he should have it done long before Christmas.

"Will." Will turned toward Simeon's voice behind him. In the dim lantern light, Simeon's hard features looked as if they were chiseled from stone, a sight eerily reminiscent of Will and Simeon's dead father. "My wife's intent was not to anger thee. But she is right. It is unseemly for thee to spend so much time alone in the company of Lucinda Hughes. If thee cares naught about thy own reputation, at least think of thy sister's. I will speak with the other elders of the Meeting, and we shall see to it that Alan Hughes's widow is provided for." His voice took on a no-nonsense tone Will could imagine him using with an unruly student. "But as Naomi's husband and thy elder brother, I must insist that thee refrain from visiting Lucinda Hughes further."

Chapter 5

Lucinda waddled along the leaf-strewn brick walkway that led to Mercy's porch as quickly as her unwieldy figure allowed. How wonderful it would be when she could walk with ease again and carry her sweet child in her arms instead of in her belly. Thankfully, the weather had remained mild enough for her to continue making the daily trek. And because of that, her skill at the loom had markedly improved in the two weeks since she wove her first rug.

Thoughts of that day brought with it thoughts of Will. At the memory of their ride together on his wagon through the snowy twilight, warmth flooded her cheeks. She could still feel his hands, strong and secure, lifting her to the wagon's seat. How carefully he'd tucked a woolen blanket around her. Several times, he'd inquired of her comfort and had used his tall frame as a barrier to protect her from icy gusts of wind. And when they finally reached the cabin, he'd eased her down to the ground as if she weighed no more than a feather.

Remembering that moment, and how close she'd come to leaning her head against his chest and inviting his embrace, a blast of shame shot through her. What kind of woman entertained such feelings about a man—even a good man like Will—less than six months after she'd buried her husband? The husband whose child she would bear in little more than a month.

Knowing she couldn't allow another such moment to happen, she'd kept a more diligent eye on Mercy's mantel clock while working at the loom. Each day, she made sure she headed home a good hour before the grain mill's whistle blew, signaling the end of Will's work day.

She let herself in the front door as Mercy had instructed her to do. Inside, she was met by the welcoming scent of gingerbread. Not finding Mercy at the loom, she hung her shawl and bonnet beside the door and then followed her nose to the kitchen and the source of the delectable, spicy aromas.

"There thee is." Smiling, Mercy turned from rolling fragrant brown dough at the kitchen table. Her round cheeks glowed pink from the oven's heat, and her sleeves were rolled up at the elbows. Flour covered the tabletop as well as Mercy's hands, which gripped the worn rolling pin.

"Since thee has helped me get caught up on my rug orders, I thought this would be a good afternoon to do some Christmas baking." Mercy pressed the rolling pin against the shapeless piece of dough and angled a grin at Lucinda. "I was lookin' through my cookie recipes and ran across my mother's old gingerbread recipe. I thought maybe thee would like to help me make gingerbread men for the children at the orphanage."

Joy filled Lucinda's heart as she rolled up her own sleeves. "Oh yes. I'd love to." Though Christmases at home growing up were sparse, somehow Ma always managed to scrape together enough ingredients to make at least one batch of cookies with the help of Lucinda and her older sisters, Esther and Lydia. Those memories, among the few happy ones of Lucinda's childhood, brought unexpected tears to her eyes.

If Mercy noticed, she kept it to herself. She snatched an apron from a peg on the wall beside the stove and handed it to Lucinda along with a cookie cutter shaped like a little man. "Thee can begin cutting out the cookies while I start a new batch of dough."

Lucinda tied on the apron and then pressed the sharp edges of the tin form into the rolled-out dough, repeating the process until she had a dozen faceless, chubby, little men-like figures.

A sad smile graced Mercy's face as she poured a cup of sugar into a crockery bowl. "My, but this takes me back to when Jedidiah used to help me make these cookies. That is, before he got old enough to consider such things woman's work." She gave a little chuckle, but Lucinda thought she noticed tears glistening in the older woman's eyes. Mercy rarely mentioned her only son, who had worked as a brake-man on the Ohio & Indiana Railroad and died years ago in a train crash.

Struck by life's unfairness, something akin to anger flared in Lucinda's chest. Mercy didn't deserve to lose her son and later, her husband, any more than Lucinda deserved to lose Alan. Yet God had allowed their loved ones to die. Still here she and Mercy stood, making Christmas cookies to celebrate God's love in the person of the Christ Child. Did Lucinda even believe in God's love anymore? That was a question she wasn't prepared to explore. So she was glad when Mercy's bright voice intruded on her dark musings.

"Did I ever tell thee about my mother?" Mercy plopped the sticky blob of gingerbread dough onto the floured tabletop.

Lucinda shook her head. "No, I don't think so." She only remembered Mercy mentioning that she had been raised in Illinois and later came to Indiana with her husband, Ezra, whom she'd met at a Quaker yearly meeting.

"Well," Mercy said as she rolled out the dough, "Mama was quite a character. The black sheep of the family, thee might say. Papa always said she was as spicy as her gingerbread." She grinned. "Some say I take after her."

"Then she must have been a good cook, too." Using a spatula, Lucinda carefully lifted a dough man from the table and laid it on a waiting greased and floured jellyroll pan.

Mercy chuckled. "Oh no. Mama was a terrible cook. In fact, this cookie recipe was one of the few things she could cook really well. And what was worse, her family didn't even want her to make it. . .at least, not as any celebration of Christmas."

At Lucinda's puzzled look, Mercy explained that her mother had belonged to a sect of Quakers that did not observe religious festivals such as Christmas.

As she talked, Mercy reached into the flour sack for a handful of the white powdery stuff and gave the table, dough, and rolling pin all a generous dusting. "As a young woman, Mama craved anything exciting and interesting. And though her family refrained from sharing in the Christmas traditions of their non-Quaker neighbors, Mama was drawn to them. Like this recipe for gingerbread men, she collected anything associated with Christmas celebrations." She shook her head. "Well," she said with a huff as she began to roll out the dough, "as thee might imagine, that didn't set well at all with her folks. And then when Mama's appetite for excitement plopped her smack dab in the middle of Papa's family of river pirates—"

"River pirates?" At Mercy's stunning revelation about her family's history Lucinda's eyes popped, and she stopped in her work of decorating the cookies with pieces of raisins.

Mercy laughed out loud, and her blue eyes twinkled. "Don't gape, child! I will tell thee all about it later. But the upshot is that Mama learned that our lives don't always go as we think they will. No matter what happens, God still has a plan for each of us." She paused in rolling out the dough and cocked her head. Her forehead scrunched in a thoughtful expression. "I reckon thee could say He has a recipe for our lives."

Last year, Lucinda could clearly see God's plan for her life. But when Alan died, that plan, that recipe had become smudged and unreadable. She pressed raisin eyes into the round face of a gingerbread man. "But what if we can't read all of God's recipe for us?" She blinked back tears. "What if parts are missing?"

Mercy came around the table and took Lucinda's hands in her flour-covered ones. "Dear one, God is the only one who can see the full recipe." She sighed. "When I put this dough together I did it one step, one ingredient at a time. We must take each step in faith. Just be open to God's direction." She smiled. "Sometimes God surprises us, so don't reject His instructions just because they are not what thee expects."

"But how can I tell if it's God's direction, or just something I want?" Oddly, the image of Will's face flashed in Lucinda's mind.

"Thee should know by now that thee will only find discernment through prayer." An imploring look came into Mercy's eyes, and she gave Lucinda's hands a gentle squeeze. "Thee needs to come back to Meeting, Lucinda. The longer thee stays away, the dimmer the Light within thee becomes."

Lucinda slipped her hands from Mercy's grasp and turned back to her work at the table. She lacked the courage to tell the woman that she wasn't even sure if she'd uttered a single prayer since Alan's funeral. "Maybe after the baby comes," she murmured, forcing a weak smile. "Maybe I'll be ready then."

Mercy heaved a deep sigh and took the finished pan of cookies and put it in the oven. When she straightened up again, she fixed Lucinda with a somber gaze. "If thee wants to know if something is from God, just remember that God gives only good gifts. If something is good, it's from God."

Though Lucinda was tempted to say that God may give but He also takes, she bit back the retort. She would rather their cookie making not be marred by more sermons about her need to return to Meeting. So she nodded silently and went back to cutting out and decorating gingerbread men. As she and Mercy worked together, Mercy kept Lucinda enthralled with stories of her parents' daring exploits as young people in southern Illinois on the banks of the Ohio River.

Before Lucinda realized it, the afternoon had slipped away. She had just put the last pan of cookies in the oven when a knock sounded at the front door. Her heart jumped. Could it be Will coming to take her home? She hadn't heard the living room clock chime five o'clock, but she might have missed it.

Mercy turned from where she stood washing up the mixing bowls and utensils. "Would thee see who is at the door, Lucinda? I'm up to my elbows in soap suds."

"Yes." Hoping her voice didn't register her dismay, she headed to the living room. When she opened the door, a measure of relief washed over her. She couldn't think of a time when she was happier to see Naomi Davis.

"Good afternoon, Lucinda." Mild surprise edged Naomi's voice. "Is Mercy home?"

"Yes." She glanced toward the back of the house and the kitchen. "We were just making gingerbread cookies for the orphanage. Please, do come in." Remembering her manners, Lucinda backed away from the door, allowing Naomi to enter with a rather sizeable basket on her arm.

"That is very commendable of thee." Naomi's voice held little warmth. Her green-eyed gaze avoided Lucinda's and instead flitted about the room like an insect searching for a place to land. It finally rested on Mercy's loom.

At that moment, Mercy, with tea towel in hand, bustled into the living room. "Good afternoon, Naomi. How nice of thee to visit. Please come in and sit down." She motioned toward the bench against the north wall.

"Thank thee, but I can't stay." Naomi held out the basket. "I know it is late notice, but I've brought rag strips for a rug I'd like to have made before Christmas."

Smiling, Mercy took the basket full of balled cotton strips in hues of browns and greens and set it beside the loom. "We should get this done before the end of the week, shouldn't we, Lucinda?"

"Oh." The word came out of Naomi's mouth more like a gasp, and her wide-eyed gaze bounced between Mercy and Lucinda. She fidgeted, and her complexion reddened. "I—I didn't know that Lucinda wove rugs," she said as if Lucinda wasn't present.

"Yes." Beaming, Mercy glanced at Lucinda. "She just took it up a couple weeks ago, but she's already doin' an excellent job."

"I'm sure." Naomi's voice was weak. Her tortured smile looked more like a grimace. "As I plan to give the rug as a Christmas gift, I would really prefer that thee made it thyself, Mercy."

"Of course." Mercy's smile didn't waver, but Lucinda thought the lines around her mouth tightened. Suddenly, Mercy's eyes flew wide open, and she gasped. "Oh, I almost forgot that last pan of cookies in the oven! If thee will excuse me. . ." Without waiting for an answer, she bustled off toward the kitchen.

Naomi cast a worried look at her basket of rags as if having second thoughts about leaving them. Then, looking down her pinched nose, she ran a chilly gaze over Lucinda's form. "It's good to see thee looking so. . .well. Since I hadn't seen thee at Meeting for months, I supposed thee might have taken to thy bed. But I see that is not the case."

Lucinda managed a stiff smile. Though she would not question the woman's honesty, Lucinda found it hard to believe that Naomi wasn't aware of her general health. "I thank thee for thy concern, Naomi, but I am well."

Naomi's voice turned hard, dropping any pretense of friendliness. "Then I shall expect to see thee at Meeting this Sunday. For if thee is well enough to walk two miles every day to weave rugs, thee is well enough to attend Meeting." Her critical gaze sharpened to an outright glare. "I will tell thee plainly, Lucinda Hughes, Simeon and some of the other elders have begun to question if thee ever truly experienced sanctification and if thy name should remain on the membership rolls of Serenity Friends Meeting."

Chapter 6

We buried Pa last Tuesday.

Lucinda stared unbelievingly at the words on the page of her sister's letter. Despite the roaring fire in the belly of the coal stove a few inches away, she sat as if frozen to the bench along the wall of the mercantile that doubled as a post office.

She'd read Esther's announcement three times and still felt only numbness. Surely there must have been some scrap of tenderness between herself and Pa—something to evoke a smidgen of emotion. But nothing came. Not sadness. Not even relief. Nothing.

One image of Pa muscled out all others in Lucinda's mind. Her most vivid memory of him was the day she told him she'd be leaving their tenant farm and going to Indiana with the Quakers. She could still see him towering over her in a drunken rage. His slurred voice still echoed in her ears. "You leave this place with them black-hatted Bible thumpers, and you'll be dead to me, girl. You want to leave, then leave. But don't you ever come back, or I'll put you in the ground. I swear it!" After that he'd seared the air with obscenities, the memory of which still blistered her ears.

She shivered. If not for the half-dozen Quakers standing in the yard behind her, Lucinda had no doubt that Pa, in his fury, would have swung his raised fist and struck her down where she stood.

She blinked, willing the frightening image to disappear. When she focused again on her sister's letter, she found Esther's next revelation nearly as jarring as the news of Pa's death.

I'm fixing to have another young one next summer. Me and Lonny would like for you to come back down and live with us. You wouldn't know Lonny. He done found religion. He quit drinking and has started taking me and the children to church on Sundays.

Esther's words filled Lucinda with happiness for her sister as well as her little niece and nephew. But she found it hard to picture Lonny Ray Malloy as a teetotal churchgoer. In part, Lucinda's desire to escape the fate of her two older sisters had convinced her to leave home. Both Esther and Lydia had married men cut from the same whiskey-soaked cloth as their father—demanding when sober and cruel when drunk. Though she was glad for Esther, the notion of returning to the grim life of a tenant farmer held little appeal.

Still, as she read on, her sister's description of Esther, Lonny, and the kids searching the woods along Raccoon Creek for the perfect Christmas tree strummed a compelling melody across Lucinda's heartstrings. She liked imagining her child growing up alongside his cousins.

"I hope all is well with your family in Kentucky." The voice of Beulah Reeves, the storekeeper's wife, brought Lucinda's face upward.

"Yes." It was not a lie. Whether or not her siblings grieved Pa's passing, Lucinda knew his absence removed a constant danger. Feeling the need to digest all she'd learned before sharing it with anyone, she stuffed the letter back into its envelope and tucked it into her skirt pocket.

Beulah struck an expectant stance, her head cocked to one side and her arms akimbo as if waiting for Lucinda to divulge more of the correspondence. But when she failed to oblige, Beulah gave her a lukewarm smile. "Well, I have your groceries all boxed up. So unless you can think of something else you might need, I'll have my boy, Henry, carry the box to your buggy."

Lucinda rose from her perch on the bench. "Thank thee, Beulah. That will be all." She'd almost forgotten why she'd driven into Serenity in the first place.

Fifteen minutes later as she drove home, Esther's words still dominated her thoughts. *Me and Lonny would like for you to come back down and live with us.*

After Pa's hateful warning nearly two years ago, Lucinda had put all thoughts of ever returning to Kentucky out of her mind. But now, for the sake of her child, she must at least consider it.

Through a flurry of snowflakes, she guided Star along the dirt road toward home. *Home.* Was this place even her home anymore? Maybe Naomi was right and Lucinda had never experienced true sanctification, despite how real it had felt that night at the tent meeting.

Sniffing back a wad of hot tears, she flicked the reins against the horse's rump, urging the mare to a trot. If, as

Naomi Davis believed, Lucinda was not a true Quaker and didn't belong with the Serenity Friends Meeting, then what was there to hold her here?

The image of Will's face drifted unbidden before her mind's eye, setting her heart trotting faster than Star's feet. She sighed. So far, no amount of rug weaving or visiting Mercy had managed to diminish her uncomfortable reaction to Will. And he hadn't helped, insisting on coming by the cabin every few days to inquire about her health or comfort. Indeed, she'd made the trip to the store for groceries so he'd have one less reason to stop by her house.

Aside from her own disquieting feelings about Will, even more troublesome was her growing sense that he felt the same about her. And what *if* they should make a match? Her child would need a father. But Naomi and Simeon would doubtless stand squarely against Will marrying outside the faith. Will, too, would expect Lucinda to attend Meeting. And Lucinda would not sit in Meeting and falsely pretend a connection with God she no longer felt.

As she came to the spot where her lane converged with the road, Star turned unprompted onto the narrow path that led up to the cabin. "No." Lucinda surprised herself by speaking aloud. It would be better for both her and Will if she simply accepted Esther's offer and moved back to Kentucky.

The mare whinnied and bobbed her head as they rounded the curve in the lane that led to the front of the cabin. When the house came into view, Lucinda's heart turned a somersault. Will's mule, Bob, stood hitched to a flatbed wagon. But more remarkably, the cabin's front door stood wide open.

Lucinda reined Star to a stop behind the wagon. What could Will be up to that required the door to be open? And why would he go into her house without her there? Eager to learn the answers to the questions burning in her mind, she scrambled down from the buggy and headed to the front porch.

At the open door, she stopped, stunned. Will stood in her front room with a wrench in his hand, constructing something that looked suspiciously like a loom.

At a sound near the open doorway, Will looked up and his heart catapulted into his throat. Lucinda stood as if frozen in place, her eyes growing to the size of silver dollar pieces. This was not the way he had envisioned presenting her with her new loom.

"I hope thee doesn't mind me letting myself in." Could he have thought of anything more stupid to say? Of course she minded. Otherwise, she wouldn't still be standing there with her jaw practically scraping the floor. He wouldn't blame her if she turned tail and headed to Serenity to get Sheriff Brewster.

"What—what is that?" She finally stepped into the room, but her unblinking eyes never left the loom.

"It's a rug loom. See?" In what seemed even to him a ridiculous demonstration, he swung one of the moving parts of the contraption. After two hours of work, he prayed he had the thing put together correctly.

"For me? Thee got this for me?" Lucinda, who'd given the loom a wide berth as if afraid it might come to life and pounce on her, inched closer.

"Yes." Despite a chill breeze blowing through the open door, sweat broke out on his forehead. How could he explain why he had let himself into her house and built a loom in her front room without sounding overbearing, crazy, or both? "I thought thee might like to weave here instead of walking to Mercy's. I mean, in case it snows and thee can't. . ."

She reached out and touched a timber as if to assure herself that the thing was real. Then she turned and looked at him. Straight at him. Tears welled in her eyes, and panic grabbed Will's chest like an iron fist. She hated it.

"Please, do not be distressed. If thee does not want it, I promise I will have it gone within the hour." He moved to begin loosening the closest bolt. "It was wrong of me to—"

"Oh no!" She reached out her arms toward the loom in a protective motion. "I do want it. But I cannot accept such a gift. It is too dear. And I—I cannot pay thee for it." Her voice wilted, and Will's heart seized.

"Thee owes me nothing." He dropped the wrench into his toolbox with a clatter. "I am repaid by knowing that this loom will keep thee home safe and out of the weather."

At that her lips pressed into a straight line, and he knew he'd said too much. He groaned inwardly. He should have heeded Proverbs 13:3. "He that keepeth his mouth keepeth his life: but he that openeth wide his lips shall have destruction."

"So thee bought this to keep me home." There wasn't so much as a hint of question in her flat tone. Staring at the loom, she pressed her fingertips against her lips, hiding her expression.

"I'm sorry. It was wrong of me." Befuddled, he gathered up his remaining tools scattered around the floor. He needed to leave before he angered her any further.

A sputtering sound escaped from between her fingers then a full-blown giggle burst free. "Poor Will." Grinning, she gave him a piteous look. "Thee does not know me as well as thee thinks."

Will fought the urge to take her into his arms and declare that he would like to learn to know her better. But that could never be.

The mirth left her face, replaced by a smile so sad and sweet it made his chest ache. Then she stepped toward him, and his heart pounded like a bass drum. "Thank thee, Will." She placed her hand on his forearm, sending tingles dancing up to his shoulder. "The first rug I make on this shall be for thee."

Abandoning all caution, he took her hands into his and gazed into her cinnamon-colored eyes. "Lucinda."

"Will!"

At the harsh male voice, they both turned toward the open doorway to face a nearly purple-faced Simeon.

Chapter 7

Will touched his fingertip to the wood to check if the varnish had dried. When he felt no tackiness, he reached for the can of varnish on the shelf above the workbench and then drew his hand back with a sigh. Another coat of varnish would not improve it. Nor would varnish improve his mood.

Though pleased with the finished project, he almost hated seeing it come to an end. As long as he had something to keep him busy, to concentrate on, he managed to keep his anger in check. So he wasn't particularly pleased when Amos closed the mill at noon to make needed repairs, sending Will and the other workers home early.

At the memory of Simeon's actions last week, Will's simmering rage boiled again in his belly as if his insides were a cauldron. He'd been but an instant away from declaring his affection for Lucinda when Simeon had appeared at her door. Determined to protect her from any embarrassment, Will had insisted that he and Simeon take their conversation, which eventually escalated to a heated argument, outside away from the cabin and, he'd hoped, beyond earshot.

Though pride was sinful, Will couldn't help feeling more than a tinge of it. In the face of Simeon's demands that Will leave Lucinda's home immediately, he had stood his ground. Simeon then left in a huff, and Will stayed to carry in Lucinda's groceries and put her horse and buggy away in the barn.

But the worried look Will had seen on Lucinda's face after Simeon's departure told him she had indeed heard the argument, including Simeon's complaint about the money Will had spent on the loom.

Guilt lashed at his heart. The last thing he had wanted was for her to feel that she was to blame for the contention between his brother and him. He also hated that she might feel indebted to him or his family in any way.

The anger pulsating through him exploded, and he kicked the empty metal bucket near his feet clear to the other side of the barn. It smacked against the mule's stall with a clatter, causing the animal to jump and bray in protest.

A small measure of his frustration eased, Will blew out a long breath. "Sorry, Bob," he muttered and then looked up at the cobweb-covered rafters. "I know, Lord, I know. Proverbs, chapter nineteen, verse eleven. 'The discretion of a man deferreth his anger; and it is his glory to pass over a transgression.'"

With that thought, part of another scripture—Luke 6:37—came to mind. *Forgive, and ye shall be forgiven.*

Turning back to the piece of furniture he'd just finished, Will's heart throbbed painfully. In truth, no one, including Simeon, stood more in need of Lucinda's forgiveness than Will did. But she couldn't forgive him without knowing what he had done.

He picked up the ragged length of quilt he'd used to cover the object since beginning work on it and carefully swathed the varnished wood. Next week was Christmas. The moment he gave her this might be the perfect time to confess fully his transgression. At the thought, an icy chill slithered down his spine. Did he have the courage to face losing what small measure of affection Lucinda felt for him?

Leaving the barn, he stepped toward the house and groaned. He'd sooner stay out in the frigid December air than enter the chilly atmosphere that now held sway inside his home. Simeon and Naomi hardly spoke to him anymore. And when they did, their words held little warmth.

He looked back at the barn. The need to converse with a compassionate soul gripped him hard. His mind instantly flew to Mercy Cox. Aside from his own sainted mother, he could think of no one else who possessed more maternal wisdom and caring than Mercy. And at this time of day, she should be home and most probably alone since Lucinda was doubtless safely inside her cabin, weaving at her new loom.

With resolute steps, he walked to Bob's stall.

The mule lifted his nose from the manger and paused in chewing a mouthful of fragrant timothy hay.

Will rubbed the animal's velvety muzzle. "Don't get too comfortable with that hay, Bob. We have somewhere to go."

Lucinda walked to the jelly cupboard and pulled open one of the cabinet's twin drawers. Had it been a week since she found Will in her front room constructing the loom?

Remembering the moment he took her hands in his and gazed into her eyes, her heart throbbed with a sweet ache. For that one instant, the two of them had seemed to teeter on the brink of something special. . .until Simeon yanked them back to reality. What had Will been about to say before his brother interrupted? Part of her longed to know, while another part of her was glad she didn't.

But whatever affection she and Will might share, it didn't matter. Witnessing the argument between Will and Simeon had convinced her to accept Esther's offer and move back to Kentucky.

Glancing toward the living room, she smiled. Whether here in Serenity or down in Kentucky, Will's loom would continue to provide a living for her and her child. She was eager to try it out and make that first promised rug for Will. But until she could get thread for warp and material for weft, the loom would have to sit idle.

She rifled through the drawer in search of paper on which to pen a letter to Esther. "Where is that writing paper?" But all she found were her recipe books, some canning lids, and sundry kitchen gadgets.

She sighed. The sooner she could get a letter to Esther, the sooner her sister and brother-in-law could begin making plans to fetch her and the baby down to Kentucky in the spring.

Abandoning the first drawer, she tried the second but still found no paper. Suddenly she remembered the last time she'd written a letter to her sister. Mercy had provided her with the writing paper and envelope.

She glanced out the kitchen window where large snowflakes filled the air. The thought of leaving the warm cabin and going out into the snowy day made her shiver. Also, the winding lane with its steep downgrade in places could become slick and treacherous when snow-covered. On the other hand, the wind appeared light, and she'd walked the mile to Mercy's house through snow showers many times. And if Mercy could spare the warp thread, Lucinda could weave a rug for her in exchange for the paper and envelope.

After tying on her black wool bonnet and wrapping her warmest shawl around her shoulders, she picked up her market basket from beside the kitchen door and left. Outside, she pulled her shawl closer around her and grinned, thinking how Will would scold her if he knew she was out in the snow.

So far, the snow had hardly made a dusting on the frozen, packed dirt lane. Using extra care, she made it down the lane and to the road without any problem. She had gone only a few yards when she heard the rumbling sound of a horse and wagon in the distance behind her.

Moving to the edge of the road, she looked over her shoulder to see who was coming. Her heart jumped. Even at the distance of a quarter-mile, Will's mule, Bob, with his lop-ears and loping gait, was unmistakable.

Lucinda turned back and resumed walking. Hopefully, he would just give her a friendly wave and continue on down the road. But as the sound of the wagon and mule became louder, the clopping of the mule's hooves slowed.

"Lucinda." Will's voice held no censure, only mild surprise as the wagon and mule came to a stop. "If thee is going to Mercy's, I would be happy to take thee."

Lucinda's mind raced, trying to think of a credible reason to decline his offer. "I would not want to cause thee more trouble with thy brother." She wished her silly heart would cease its jubilant hopping. At least he would likely attribute any redness in her cheeks to the cold temperature.

His face turned as cloudy as the gray sky behind him. "Simeon is my brother, not my master." With that, he climbed to the ground and helped her up to the seat with the greatest of care.

"I was on my way to Mercy's myself," he said as he settled beside her and flicked the reins down on Bob's rump. He shot her a sideways grin from beneath the wide brim of his hat. "Thee was right. It was silly of me to think a loom would keep thee home. I hope I constructed it properly and it works well."

Lucinda turned her head away so her bonnet would hide her smile. "I don't know. I'm hopin' to get some warp thread and rags from Mercy so I can begin a rug."

"I'm sorry. I never thought. . .I reckon I should have brought thee some with the loom."

His penitent tone squeezed Lucinda's heart. How could he imagine he owed her anything more after gifting her with such an expensive item as a loom? She placed her hand on his forearm. "I didn't expect thee to bring me thread. Thee has done far too much already."

Will became quiet, and his pensive look filled her with regret. Was he thinking of Simeon's warning? They traveled the rest of the way in silence except for the clopping of Bob's feet on the frozen road.

Lucinda knew she should tell Will of her plans to move back to Kentucky in the spring. But they'd arrived at Mercy's house, and this was not the proper moment to blurt out her news. Will deserved a full explanation as to why she had made such a decision, and she needed time to give him one.

Will climbed down first and then helped her down. Would she ever again feel as safe as she did in Will's hands?

When they reached the front door, Will knocked twice. When several seconds passed and no answer came, he knocked twice again.

Still no answer.

"She's probably in the kitchen." Lucinda opened the door. "Mercy is always telling me that if she doesn't answer the door and it's unlocked, to just come in." She walked into the front room, but Mercy was nowhere in sight. "Mercy."

Only the crackling of the fire in the belly of the stove in the corner answered her call.

A sick feeling began to grow in the pit of Lucinda's stomach. She hurried to the kitchen with Will at her heels but found no sign of Mercy. Lucinda checked Mercy's bedroom on the first floor. It was empty as well. Will bounded up the stairs to check the two rooms there and then came down an instant later.

"She's not up there," he said, shrugging his shoulders.

The wad of worry balling in Lucinda's stomach grew. "I don't understand it. Where could she be?"

"She's probably just gone into town or to visit someone," Will said. Though his tone was light, Lucinda saw concern in his gray eyes.

Lucinda shook her head. "I've never known her to leave the front door unlocked when she leaves home."

Will smiled and put his hand on her shoulder. "Don't

worry. I'm sure she just forgot to lock the door. Stay here in the warmth. I'll go check the barn to see if her horse and buggy are gone."

Lucinda nodded, but unable to stay still, she headed for the kitchen the moment he closed the front door behind him. Something compelled her to open the back door and step out on the porch. "Mercy," she called.

This time a soft moan sounded just beyond the far end of the porch. Lucinda hurried to the spot, and terror leapt into her chest. Mercy lay in the snow, her bleeding head leaning against the house's stone foundation.

Chapter 8

The best I can tell, the bones are intact." Doctor Jennings finished tying the bandage he'd wrapped around Mercy's head. "But I fear thy head may be slightly concussed, and thee has badly sprained thy wrist and ankle."

At the doctor's diagnosis, Lucinda sniffed back tears and clutched Mercy's uninjured hand. She couldn't bear to think what might have happened if she and Will had not come by.

"Oh, don't fret thyself, Lucinda." Wincing, Mercy raised her head from the pillow and then sank back with a groan. "I'm just a little banged up. Nothin' Dr. Jennings can't fix."

"But thee could have died." Fresh tears rolled down Lucinda's cheeks, and Will slid a comforting arm around her shoulder. The doctor eyed the move with a critical glance, and Lucinda experienced a flash of concern that Dr. Jennings, an elder at Serenity Friends Meeting, might mention what he saw to Will's brother.

Mercy slipped her good hand from Lucinda's fingers and touched her bandaged head. "Reckon I deserved it for chasing that raccoon off my back porch with the broom, but the critter eats the scraps I put out for the barn cats." She gave another low moan. "I must have hit a patch of ice, because the next thing I knew I went flyin'."

"Well." The doctor snapped his black leather bag shut. "The raccoon is safe for a while. Thee won't be going out there again anytime soon. Actually," he said as he rose from the chair beside Mercy's bed, "I suggest thee have someone come here and stay with thee until that ankle heals, which will probably take two or three weeks."

"No." Mercy rolled her head on the pillow.

"Mercy." Will bent nearer to the woman's bedside. "I know thee is used to taking care of thyself, but now thee needs—"

"I know I will need help for a while, but I don't want to stay here." Mercy looked at Lucinda. "I might as well go to thy place now. I'd planned to stay with thee after the first of the year anyway." She grinned, and her gaze slid to Will. "And when my hand gets well enough, I want to try out that fine loom thee bought Lucinda." Now, she turned her attention to Dr. Jennings. "Can thee get me in thy buggy?"

The doctor scowled and grasped his chin between his thumb and forefinger. He bounced a narrow-eyed glance between Lucinda and Will. "Although I would normally recommend that thee stay put, in this case it might be best if thee did go to stay with Lucinda. I think with Will's help, and so long as thee doesn't put any weight on thy injured foot, we should be able to manage moving thee."

Lucinda bundled Mercy in a warm shawl and tied her black wool bonnet beneath her chin. At Mercy's instructions, Will gathered up spools of warp thread and bags of rug rags, so Lucinda could make promised rugs in Mercy's stead. Then with Will and Dr. Jennings supporting her, Mercy hopped out to the doctor's buggy. The four headed to Lucinda's cabin with the buggy in the lead and Will and

Lucinda following in the wagon.

A few minutes later, in Lucinda's front room, Will and Dr. Jennings ensconced Mercy in the big horsehair-upholstered chair that had once belonged to Alan's father. Under doctor's orders to keep her injured ankle elevated, Will brought a chair from the kitchen, and Lucinda placed a feather pillow on the seat.

Dr. Jennings eased Mercy's stocking-clad foot onto the pillow. Then taking a step back, he crossed his arms over his chest. After giving Lucinda a skeptical glance, he eyed Mercy. "Is thee sure thee wouldn't like for me to send another one of the ladies from Meeting to see to thee? I'm sure any number would be happy to—"

"Lucinda is quite capable, I'm sure." Giving her a confident smile, Mercy settled back in the chair.

Dr. Jennings dropped his double chin to his chest and gave a muted *harrumph*. "Of course." With that, he reiterated his instructions and took his leave.

Will lingered. "I will come by soon to check on thy firewood and see to thy outside chores." Though he spared Mercy a glance, his gaze rested gently on Lucinda's face.

The big chair creaked softly as Mercy sat forward. She looked first at Will and then at Lucinda. A hint of a smile touched her lips. And though it might have been but the reflection of the fireplace flames, Lucinda thought she caught sight of a knowing glint in the older woman's eyes. "I praise God that thee came by my house this afternoon, Will, but thee never said for what reason thee came."

Will's gaze dropped to the scuffed toes of his black boots

as if pondering his reply. Finally, he raised his face, and with a glance at Lucinda, he looked at Mercy and smiled. "I believe God sent me."

Two days later, Will's words still rang in Lucinda's ears as she sat weaving at the loom. Had God sent Will. . .not only to Mercy but to Lucinda as well? It didn't matter. In the spring, she and her child would be moving back to Kentucky. But so far, she hadn't found the words to tell Mercy of her decision.

She looked over at Mercy, who sat reading her Bible by the sunlight spilling through the front window over her shoulder. Lucinda couldn't remember the last time she'd even picked up the Bible, let alone read it. If she'd ever had any faith—any Light in the first place—it had obviously gone out. And it was high time she told Mercy.

After beating down a line of woven weft she paused, shuttle in her hand. "I'm moving back to Kentucky in the spring," she blurted.

Mercy looked up from the pages of her Bible, concern pinching her features. "But thy father warned thee not to come back. Thee must think of thy child. It may not be safe."

"Pa is dead." Lucinda turned back to the loom and her weaving. "I got a letter from my sister Esther. She told me that Pa had died and that she wanted me to come back and live with her and her man, Lonny. That's why I went to your house two days ago—to get some sheets of writing paper, so I could write and tell her to come and get me in the spring."

"Thee has stopped using the plain speech. Has thee turned from the faith, then?" Mercy's voice was tinged with sorrow.

Sighing, Lucinda faced Mercy. "I'm not even sure I ever had any faith. And no, I'm not a Quaker anymore." She swallowed down the wad of tears that had gathered in her throat. "Naomi Davis says I'm an impostor, that I was never sanctified. And she and Simeon don't like Will comin' here." She didn't even try to mask the bitterness in her voice as she recounted to Mercy what had transpired between Will and Simeon the day he brought her loom.

Anger flashed in Mercy's blue eyes. "Thy sanctification is not for Simeon and Naomi to judge, and I'd advise them to heed Christ's warnin' about doin' so." The anger lines left her brow, and she breathed a soft sigh. "Child." Her tone held patient kindness. "I saw thy convincement. I know it was real. But I fear thy faith was too new, too young and tender to withstand the gale of grief that assailed thee. Thee needs to nurture thy faith, not turn thy back on it."

New tears sprang in Lucinda's eyes, and she blinked them away. "And why should I have faith in a God who abandoned me?"

"Dear one." Mercy leaned forward in her chair. "God has not abandoned thee. He says in His Word that He will never abandon us." The pages of the Bible whispered as she thumbed through them. "'Be content with such things as ye have: for he hath said, I will never leave thee, nor forsake thee,'" she read.

She laced her fingers together and rested her hands on the open pages. "God's plan for our lives is like a road. For a stretch it may go in a straight line. But sometimes when we don't expect it, there is a fork in the road, and if we don't seek

God's direction, we can get lost."

Lucinda stepped on the treadle and slid the shuttle through the open threads. "But. . .but when we come to a fork, how do we know what direction to go?"

Mercy tapped the Bible. "It's all in here. Next week is Christmas, and Christmas is all about God sending His Son to find the lost and show them the way they should go." She grinned. "I think God has been giving thee signs all along as to what direction He wants thy life to go. Thee is just ignoring them." She paused. "Like Will, bringing thee this loom."

At Mercy's mention of Will, Lucinda froze and nearly dropped the shuttle. Recovering, she focused again on her work. "So what do you think God is trying to tell me?" She couldn't help the bitter tone that crept into her voice.

"I think," Mercy said, "that God is telling thee to continue thy weaving." Then cocking her head in a thoughtful pose, she gave Lucinda a knowing smile. "And maybe something more."

Chapter 9

Conflict swirled through Lucinda's heart like the gusting wind that swept showers of fine snow from the porch roof.

Would Will stop by on his way to the mill this morning? Did she even want him to?

In the days since Mercy's accident, many members of Serenity Friends Meeting had come by to offer their good wishes, prayers, and help. But Will had not been back. After Simeon's warning to Will and Dr. Jennings' critical looks, Lucinda couldn't blame Will for staying away. Still, it hurt to think that he had bowed to Simeon's wishes, especially since Mercy was here now to chaperone.

Hugging her wool shawl tighter around her shoulders, she took careful steps toward the diminishing woodpile next to the front door. Her hope gusted with the wind. Still, he *might* stop. He rarely allowed her supply of wood to dwindle lower than half a rick.

She lifted her face to the December wind that snatched at her hair. With a crooked finger, she caught an errant lock that had escaped its pinned moorings and tucked it behind her ear. Squinting, she peered beyond the snowy field across the road to the Davis family woods. The bare trees appeared sketched with charcoal onto the pristine whiteness of last night's snowfall.

Will always replenished her firewood from the cords

of cut wood he kept stacked near this entrance to his family's woods. If he had driven his wagon into the woods this morning, she should see some evidence in the new-fallen snow.

Yes, she could see tracks now, where the snow blushed beneath the kiss of the morning sun. Her heart quickened at the sight of the muddy gouges that disfigured the otherwise unblemished blanket of snow. The tracks made by a wagon's wheels disappeared into the shadows between the two large barren oaks that stood sentry on either side of the forest path. But her next thought reined in her galloping heart. The indentions might not have been made by Will's wagon at all, since he and Simeon allowed several of their neighbors to use the woods as well.

Lucinda breathed a deep, ragged sigh and rubbed her arms against the biting wind. Staring wouldn't cause Will's wagon and mule to materialize.

She emitted a small groan as she bent over her expanded waistline to lift three pieces of firewood into her arms.

Inside, she laid the largest—a chunk of maple—on the stone hearth that jutted out from the large fireplace.

From her perch on the horsehair chair, Mercy glanced up from sewing together strips of faded calico that Lucinda would soon weave into a new rug. "How much snow did we get last night?" Since their conversation three days ago, neither woman had spoken again of Lucinda's plans to return to Kentucky in the spring.

Lucinda cradled the two small pieces of willow wood meant for the cook stove in the crook of her arm. "Looks like about four inches."

"Thee should have waited to bring in the wood, Lucinda. If the pile of wood on the porch is as low as thee says, Will probably will stop by on his way to the mill to bring us more."

Fearing her face might reflect her hope that Mercy was right, Lucinda turned toward the kitchen. "Maybe. But that won't help me keep the fire going in the cook stove now."

"Thee should make biscuits, I think," Mercy called after her. "I would like some biscuits, and I'm sure Will would, too, if he should stop by."

Lucinda didn't reply but carried the two pieces of wood into the little kitchen.

Warmth radiated from the cook stove in which she'd earlier built a fire with corncobs soaked in kerosene.

Using a piece of quilted flannel, she pushed down the hot lever on the door covering the stove's firebox, swung the door open, and pitched in the two pieces of willow wood. The cold, wet wood sizzled and popped as she fed it into the hot stove, sending orange sparks flying.

Two pieces should be enough to bake biscuits. Mercy was right. If Will did stop by to bring them wood, he would appreciate hot biscuits.

As she reached for the flour sack on the shelf beside the cupboard, guilt nibbled at her conscience. If, as she suspected, Will did harbor a special affection for her, was it fair of her to encourage his affection when she planned to leave both Indiana and the Quaker faith?

Minutes later, her heart fluttered at the sound of a wagon

rattling to a stop in front of the cabin.

"I think thee has company, Lucinda." Mercy's voice held a noticeable smugness as she called from the front room.

Using a dish towel to protect her fingers, Lucinda reached into the oven and grasped the hot pan full of fragrant, golden-brown biscuits. She plunked the pan of freshly baked bread onto the stovetop and started for the front room.

Opening the door, she found Will peering around a pile of split maple wood in his arms.

"I see thee needs more wood. I have brought plenty for both the fireplace and the cook stove." He stamped on the porch boards, knocking snow from his boots.

"Thank thee, Will. I was hoping thee would come." The words leapt from Lucinda's mouth before she thought. Not only did they express her true feelings, but she realized that she had lapsed back into the plain Quaker speech. Just as well. Will didn't need to know that she had all but abandoned the Quaker faith. She moved aside, inviting him to come in, and admonished her racing heart, which refused to behave at his smile.

"Good morning, Mercy." Will stepped into the front room and turned his smiling attention to the older woman. "I pray thee is feeling better."

Dropping her work back to her lap, Mercy returned his smile. "I am. Thank thee, Will." She gingerly touched her fingers to the dark scab forming on her bruised forehead. "My cut is nearly healed." Then she lifted the forked stick she now kept beside her chair. "Lucinda found this outside beneath the big, old poplar tree in the yard." She grinned. "Just sitting in this chair gets powerful tiring, so with this I can manage to hobble around some." Half turning in her chair, she glanced over her shoulder toward the front window. "Does thee think it will snow again tonight?"

"Think so." He shifted the load of wood in his arms. "The wind has picked up, and it is coming from the north now." He shot a worried look at the lonely piece of wood lying on the hearth. "Are thee both staying warm enough?"

"Plenty warm," Lucinda chimed in. "In fact," she grinned at her houseguest, "Mercy more often complains about being too warm."

He left three more pieces of split wood on the hearth and then headed to the kitchen, Lucinda following behind him. "But we would freeze for sure if it wasn't for the wood thee brings," she said as he stacked six pieces of willow wood by the cook stove.

"I'll bring in as much as I can pile up by the hearth, then I'll finish the rick on the porch." A worried look etched a *V* between his pale brows. "But thee must be careful when thee goes out on the porch to fetch it. And do not carry too much at once." He glanced at her distended middle. Immediately, his face turned bright red, and his gaze skittered quickly away.

His sweet concern touched her deeply, bringing a knot of hot tears to her throat. She swallowed them down and forced a light tone to her voice. "Thee will stay for biscuits and coffee, won't thee?" She turned her back to him and began transferring the hot bread to a stoneware plate. If her eyes held hope, she'd rather he not see it.

His voice behind her smiled. "I was hoping thee would ask when I first walked in and smelled them. I would not want to miss *thy* biscuits, Lucinda."

When she turned back to place the plate of biscuits on the table, he leaned his face close to hers, sending her heart skipping. He lowered his voice to a whisper. "Thy biscuits are better even than Mercy's," he said with a glance toward the front room, "though thee must not tell her I said so."

At his nearness, Lucinda's breath left her lungs. Grasping the table's edge to support her suddenly weak knees, she caught only a glance of his grin as he turned and headed toward the front room.

Will's heart pounded as he stood at the back of his wagon and loaded his arms with wood. Guilt had smote him at finding such a small amount of firewood on Lucinda's porch. He should have come two days ago. But before seeing her again, he had needed to spend much time in prayer.

After the first of the year, Simeon and the other elders would likely meet with Lucinda and question the state of her faith. And if, as Simeon believed, she had turned away from the faith, Will might be forced to choose between her and his brother.

Last night as Will lay in bed, praying for God to give him the answer, one came. Not heralded by trumpet or an angelic choir but a still, small voice that spoke directly to his heart. The words he heard were simple. *"Love is to give."*

He needed to keep doing what he had been doing all

along—taking care of Lucinda. And as long as she allowed him to, that was what he would do.

He turned toward the cabin, and his gaze flitted over its weathered porch posts. The porch would need painting in the spring. Hefting the firewood in his arms, he prayed he'd be the one doing the work. But when he shared with her the burden he'd carried for six months, Simeon's opposition to Will seeing Lucinda would likely be rendered irrelevant

Sometime soon he would have to tell her. But not today. This morning he wanted only her smiles. Today he needed to go to the mill still believing that in the spring he would paint Lucinda's porch.

After building up the stack of wood on the porch and bringing in all that the hearth could hold, Will walked to the kitchen.

There Lucinda stood pouring steaming cups of coffee, while Mercy sat buttering biscuits.

"Sit down, Will." From the end of the table, Mercy motioned him toward the chair across from the one in which Lucinda had taken a seat.

He dragged off his hat and ran his hand over his hair in an attempt to smooth it down, aware that it must look like so much straw. After hanging his hat on the knob of the chair Mercy had indicated, Will sat down.

Mercy looked over at him. "Will, would thee say the blessing, please?" Although it was Lucinda's home, the older woman seemed to have assumed the role of host, as befit her age.

Will bowed his head over his plate of buttered biscuits

and cup of black coffee. "Lord, we thank Thee for this food and all Thy blessings and the opportunity to commune with Thee and dear ones of like precious faith. In Jesus' name, Amen."

When he raised his head, he looked across the table, directly into Lucinda's eyes. He hadn't seen her bow her head, but he might have missed it.

Her glance flickered from his face to the lone plate of biscuits. "I'm sorry I have no eggs to serve thee. The chickens have slowed down on their layin', but I haven't checked this mornin', so there might be some out there."

"Too cold." Mercy shook her head. "The cold weather always slows them down."

"Thee has no business traipsing out to the chicken house through this snow." Concern roughed his tone. Every time he thought he'd done all he could to keep Lucinda safe, another worry cropped up. "I'll feed and water the chickens and check for eggs before I leave."

A hint of a smile touched Lucinda's lips. "If thee finds some, maybe I could make a Christmas cake, if thee would care to share it with Mercy and me." Her cinnamon-colored eyes looked almost childlike in their hopefulness.

All morning, he'd tried to think of how best to invite her to the midweek Meeting on Christmas Eve, two days away. So her unexpected mention of the coming holiday seemed to present the perfect opportunity. *Thank Thee, Lord.*

Aloud, he said, "I would love to share thy Christmas cake. If thee would like, I'd be glad to take thee to Meeting on Christmas Eve." He fixed his gaze on his plate. In the past six months, she'd turned down every invitation to attend Meeting. But it was Christmas. He needed to try.

She paused and then exhaled a long sigh that frayed at the edges. "Yes, I think I'd like that. Thank thee."

It took him a couple of seconds to accept what he'd heard. "I'd best come by about six thirty then. Meeting is at seven." He tried hard to keep the surprise from his voice as his ridiculous heart sang.

His joy immediately withered.

I'll tell her then. I'll have to tell her then.

He couldn't allow it to go on. She had to know. And if telling Lucinda the truth killed all hope of winning her love, then so be it. Maybe he deserved that. Maybe that would be fit penance. The burden had grown too heavy. On Christmas Eve he would lay it down.

Chapter 10

Six o'clock Christmas Eve, Lucinda frowned at her reflection in the oval dresser mirror. Tugging at her best black bombazine dress, she wished it fit better. She'd been able to let out enough pleats to accommodate her swollen belly, but it seemed to hang all wrong. Hopefully, her black wool shawl would hide a lot.

Had she made a mistake in agreeing to this? How would the congregation she had so long shunned receive her? Worst of all, would God view her as a hypocrite? Well, it was too late to change her mind now. She'd promised Will and couldn't bear the thought of disappointing him.

Chiding herself for her case of nerves, she slipped another pin into the coil of hair she'd twisted into a bun at the back of her head.

Outside, the jangling sound of a wagon sent her to the front room, her heart racing with her feet.

"Will is here," Mercy called unnecessarily from her chair in the front room.

When Lucinda answered the knock at the door, her focus shifted from Will's face to the long, narrow parcel wrapped in brown butcher paper that he held in his hand.

"Good evening, Lucinda, Mercy." He knocked the snow off his boots and stepped into the front room.

"What has thee brought?" Curious, Lucinda followed him as he stepped to where Mercy sat.

"Merry Christmas, Mercy." He held the package out to her.

Mercy accepted it with a puzzled grin. "What could thee have brought me?"

"Open it up and find out," he said, his smile stretching his face wide.

"Yes, Mercy, open it up!" Leaning forward, Lucinda clasped her hands together, trying to guess what Will's gift to Mercy might be.

Mercy tore away the paper to reveal a wooden stick. But the gift was more than a stick. It was a lovely, varnished cane of dark wood. Lucinda guessed black walnut. The end was crooked like a shepherd's staff and padded with black cotton material.

"I thought this might work better for thee than the forked poplar branch."

"Oh, thank thee, Will! It is perfect. Exactly what I need." Mercy's eyes filled with wonder and tears. She immediately used her new gift to stand and gave Will a hug.

Lucinda's heart swelled at his sweet gesture. Was there ever a kinder, more thoughtful man? She didn't want to contemplate how empty and sad her life would be without him.

Oddly, without saying a word, he went out the door again. A few seconds later, he returned holding a large object wrapped in a crazy quilt. "This is for thee," he said to Lucinda.

Her mind whirling, Lucinda stepped back to allow Will and his mysterious burden into the front room. Her curious gaze followed the quilt-wrapped gift as he set it down in front of her. "But thee already got me the loom. Thee didn't need to—"

"I'm really just delivering this," he broke in, his tone almost apologetic. "Alan started it," he said, stealing away her breath. "I only finished it."

❉

Will held his breath as he lifted the quilt from the cherry wood cradle. How would she react?

Still no words.

Mercy emitted a soft gasp.

Lucinda's trembling fingers ran tenderly, almost reverently over the varnished red-gold wood, her large eyes questioning, unbelieving, helpless. At last she turned them to him—huge brown eyes glistening with tears.

The silence lengthened until he could no longer bear it. He had to fill it.

"He'd started working on it right after he learned about the baby. He'd planned it to be a birthday gift for thee last August." Will squirmed, his nervous hands crushing his good black hat.

Her tears escaped their beautiful confines and slipped silently down her cheeks.

"I hope it does not offend thee that I finished it. I thought he would want. . ." Will felt lost now. Floundering. Unsure.

"Yes. Yes, that's exactly what he would have wanted." Her voice quivered, but he marveled at her courage and how her words had hastened to his rescue. "Thank thee for finishing it and bringing it to me." Her words lent the impression that she'd sensed his discomfort and wanted to console *him*!

His heart writhed. If only he could put his arms around her. But that wouldn't do, especially with Mercy looking on.

But Mercy's glistening eyes were fixed on the cradle. "It is a beautiful cradle, Will. I can see the love shining from it."

"Thank thee," Will mumbled and then cleared his dry throat.

An hour later, in the midst of the midweek Meeting, a peace Lucinda had not felt for many months settled over her heart. The Prince of Peace. Moments ago, she'd sung those words in a carol along with the rest of the congregation.

Entering the meetinghouse, she'd expected snubs and even outright hostility. Instead, she'd been met with smiles and welcoming hugs. Even Naomi and Simeon Davis had greeted her with smiles, albeit a tinge stiff.

In the congregation's loving embrace, Lucinda realized the truth in Mercy's words. God had not abandoned her nor had the congregation of Serenity Friends Meeting. Lucinda was the one who had left them. She had let her anger at God separate her from His comfort, His peace, and His Light.

When they left the meetinghouse, Will tucked Lucinda's arm securely around his and helped her across the snowy ground to the wagon. As they walked, she glanced up at the quiet figure of the man beside her. God had not left her alone. Whenever she needed something, Will had been there. He never gave up on her. As he was doing now, he'd quietly provided caring support. Patiently and lovingly, he'd nudged her back to God's guiding Light. And with that Light shining brightly within her once more, she could now see clearly God's direction for her life. And that direction was not back to Kentucky but right here in Serenity with the man to whose arm she clung.

As Will ensconced her on the wagon seat, wrapping her in a quilt, Lucinda returned his smile. She no longer needed nor wanted to deny what her heart felt for him. At last she could unflinchingly call it by name—love. Yes, love.

Her heart twirled with joy at the admission. Oh, love hadn't come with the sudden loud clatter of a summer thunderstorm as it had with Alan. This time, love had crept slowly, quietly, like a winter snowfall, covering her heart like a soft, warm, comforting blanket.

Will's fingers tensed around the reins as the mule pulled the wagon away from the meetinghouse. When would he tell her? How would he begin?

The wagon had come up even with the cemetery's wrought iron fence when she pressed her hand against his arm. "Will, stop for a little."

"Is thee warm enough?" Concerned, he reached to snug the lap quilt around her.

"Yes, I am warm." Her sweet smile relaxd his worried frown.

The time to tell her had come.

"Lucinda. . ." Praying for courage, he hesitated.

She waited quietly for him to continue. Their gazes drifted to the cemetery, which looked serenely beautiful in the moonlight. The new snow covered all the reality, white fluffy caps softening the headstones.

Will cleared his throat and began again. "There is something I need to tell thee. Something I should have told thee before." He took a deep breath and then allowed the words he'd harbored so long to escape in a rush. "It should have been me, not Alan." There, he'd said it.

"No, Will. Thee mustn't say that."

She didn't understand. He would have to finish it. His courage nearly deserted him. He kept his gaze directed toward the vicinity of his friend's grave. If he looked into her beautiful brown eyes, he'd be lost.

"Amos had asked Alan to make the trip to the railroad depot with the wagon that day, but he wasn't in the notion, so I went instead. If I had just refused to make that trip, Alan would not have been at the mill when the explosion happened. I will understand if thee never wants to see my face again."

Lucinda watched Will's Adam's apple bob with a hard swallow, his gaze firmly fastened on the cemetery. Her heart ached for him. How quietly he had carried the burden all these months. How needlessly he had suffered.

She gently covered his large hand with hers, praying for words that might lift the undeserved burden from this sweet man's heart. "I know. Amos told me at the funeral. Will, I lost one man I loved. I don't think I could bear to lose another."

His face swung toward hers, his gray eyes growing wide

with wonder. When their gazes locked, a sweet understanding swept away all uncertainty. For a moment, his eyes glistened in the moonlight before closing, and he lowered his lips to hers.

Lucinda's heart sang as she welcomed his kiss. She'd found where she wanted to be—where she needed to be. After a long moment, she dropped her gaze to her lap, feeling oddly shy. "I'm sorry I don't have a Christmas gift for thee after thee gave me the loom and then the cradle. Just a Christmas cake. Maybe the cake. . ."

"Sweetheart." Will gently took her face into his hands and tipped it up to his. "Thee has given me better gifts than I could have ever hoped for. They are the same gifts the Christ Child brought to the world that first Christmas—the gifts of love and forgiveness." His calloused thumb prickled against her skin as he brushed a tear from her cheek before tenderly kissing her lips again.

"Take me home, Will." She barely breathed the words, allowing her gaze to melt into his.

His smile nearly split his face as he snapped the reins against the mule's back. "Come on, Bob!"

Along the road, they passed a group of young people caroling outside a farmhouse. The words wafted through the frigid night air and wrapped tenderly around Lucinda's heart.

"'How silently, how silently, the wondrous gift is given; so God imparts to human hearts the blessings of His heaven.'"

Snuggled in the warm circle of Will's arm, Lucinda

knew that God had indeed blessed her.

Resting her hands on the mound beneath her heart, she felt a tiny kick and thought of the cradle. Quietly, but clearly, God's voice spoke to her heart. The life that she and Alan had begun, she and Will would finish.

She'd learned something else this extraordinary Christmas Eve. The best gifts were the ones wrapped in pure love, exchanged silently from one heart to another. She and Will had exchanged such gifts. Gifts they would share for the rest of their lives.

Ramona K. Cecil is a wife, mother, grandmother, freelance poet, and award-winning inspirational romance writer. Now empty nesters, she and her husband make their home in Indiana. A member of American Christian Fiction Writers and American Christian Fiction Writers Indiana Chapter, her work has won awards in a number of inspirational writing contests. Over eighty of her inspirational verses have been published on a wide array of items for the Christian gift market. She enjoys a speaking ministry, sharing her journey to publication while encouraging aspiring writers. When not writing, her hobbies include reading, gardening, and visiting places of historical interest.

PIRATE OF
MY HEART

Rachael Phillips

Dedication

My applause and gratitude to Wendy Lawton, Janet Grant, and the rest of the Books & Such Literary Agency bunch. Working with you is a joy.

Special thanks to the friendly, helpful citizens of Cave-In-Rock, Illinois (formerly Rock and Cave), Cave-In-Rock State Park, and the Harrisburg District Library, Harrisburg, Illinois.

Blessings on my novella partners Lauralee Bliss, Ramona Cecil, and Claire Sanders. Also many thanks to Kim Peterson and Jaclyn Miller, dear friends who edited my manuscript with caring, critical eyes.

Most of all, glory be to God the Father, who "has rescued us from the dominion of darkness and brought us into the kingdom of the Son he loves, in whom we have redemption, the forgiveness of sins" (Colossians 1:13–14 NIV).

Chapter 1

Mama said the red shawl was of the devil, but Keturah begged to differ. Its luxurious warmth around her shoulders made this blustery September morn even more special.

"Where did you get it? How did you leave the house with it?" her friend Delilah whispered after Papa's wagon rumbled down the dusty road to the village stable.

Keturah chuckled softly as they walked away from Scott's General Store, owned by Delilah's father. Caleb, Keturah's older brother, trailed after them with his usual gangling, un-hurried gait.

"The shawl came from my aunt Rachel in Pennsylvania. She sent barrels of castoffs in answer to Mama's appeal for the poor here in Illinois."

"Surely she knew your mother would not allow this shawl in her house." Delilah's shoebutton eyes twinkled.

"Surely she did." Keturah kept her expression demure, though she longed to laugh aloud. "Aunt Rachel is her sister. She also knew Mama would no more give this shawl to the poor than she would stolen alms."

"Quite convenient for Keturah that our rich aunt should be read out of Meeting for marrying a Methodist," Caleb drawled. "Perhaps in the next barrel, thee will find geegaws fit for the Christmas thy soul craves." He grinned. "Or thee could marry a Methodist, too."

Caleb often teased Delilah, who was a Methodist. Keturah tolerated his frequent reminders that she, at twenty, was past the usual age of marriage. But his poking fun at Christmas ruffled her. Why did Mama consider it wrong? Even Papa and other Friends discounted it. *Should we not celebrate the birth of the Son of God, the Light of the World?*

Keturah decided not to waste her breath on Caleb. With a winsome smile, she said, "How fortunate for our parents their son's affections dwell safely within the Friends' fold."

His face turned pink. "Thee art mistaken."

"Perhaps." Keturah glanced down Rock and Cave's main road. "Still, Priscilla Norris doubtless would welcome a greeting." She steered him toward the gray-caped blond girl carrying a large basket. Keturah hoped to keep her giggles inside until she and Delilah managed to lose their chaperone. "Good day, Priscilla."

"Good day. And to thee, too, Delilah and Caleb." Priscilla's childlike voice feigned innocence, but her knowing blue eyes searched Keturah's.

Delilah echoed the greeting, but Caleb turned red as Keturah's shawl, as if Priscilla had said something bold.

"Would thee join us for a walk?" Keturah edged Caleb toward Priscilla.

"I would, but I feel ill." Priscilla sighed. "My basket is heavy—"

"I will take it." Caleb moved faster than Keturah thought

possible. He clasped the handle. "Perhaps thee should rest under that oak."

"Carry it to her house," Keturah urged him.

Caleb hesitated. "But Pa—"

"Papa would want thee to help a lady in need." The firmness in her voice sounded so much like Mama's, it startled her. "We shall not wander far."

Caleb opened his mouth for a token protest, but Priscilla captured him. "I am thankful for thy help, Caleb. God Himself must have sent thee my way."

"God smiled on us all," Delilah whispered as Caleb trailed after Priscilla, unblinking as if under a spell.

Laughter bubbled in Keturah, but she and Delilah held their peace until the couple disappeared around the corner. They laughed at poor, lovesick Caleb as they headed toward the Ohio River shore.

"I'm so glad your father does business in Rock and Cave rather than taking Ford's Ferry across to Kentucky." Delilah almost skipped along.

"So am I." Keturah squeezed her arm. Otherwise how would they, years out of school, see each other? "Papa questions Mr. Ford's honesty."

"Nor should he trust many who run Rock and Cave." Delilah never hesitated to voice her opinions. "They say river pirate days are gone, but I don't believe it."

The gleeful wind pulled at Keturah's shawl, and Delilah, fingering its silky fringe, forgot about pirates and corruption. "You did not tell me how you escaped wearing this."

"I slipped it out of the rubbish bin and washed it while

Mama rested. Then I hid it in the washhouse." Keturah hugged herself. "When I brought it today, dear Papa tried to object. But he said, 'That is the color of the cardinals outside our window,' and I knew he would not forbid me to wear it."

"It is red as holly berries at Christmas." Delilah's dark eyes widened with longing. "I would save it to wear to the Christmas dance."

"Thee knows I cannot join in such revelry." Keturah sighed and then straightened. "But I intend to celebrate Christmas this year any way I can."

"Perhaps I can teach you carols and customs we keep," Delilah offered.

Keturah squeezed her arm gratefully. "I'll be asking thee as Christmas nears."

The girls sorted through bits of ripe news and gossip like persimmons in a basket. Half Keturah's mind grasped every sight, sound, and smell of the village—even the stench of animal skins drying behind the tanner's—framing them like portraits to be viewed later without limit. Although Papa's farm was only three miles from the village of Rock and Cave and the Ohio River, she rarely joined him on a trip to town. Only Papa's gentle maneuvering—and Mama's dislike of poetry—had freed Keturah from the usual drudgery of housekeeping.

"Did you recite Shakespeare aloud to your mama?" Unlike her biblical namesake, Delilah had a heart of gold—but her wicked smile suggested at least a small kinship.

Keturah nodded. "Shakespeare, Burns, and Blake!"

"'Tis small wonder she relented. You should read her poetry every day."

Keturah giggled, but a voice in her head waged an indignant protest. *Why must I scheme like a naughty child to spend a few hours away from the farm? And from Caleb?*

The vast green and gray Ohio River absorbed the road, reminding her that Mama feared it like a monster serpent coiling among forests and farms.

Keturah shook herself. The day was too precious to waste. Thin crimson threads embroidering the green maples along the shore reminded her of the skeins she'd bought earlier with her birthday money, thread she would work into a special Christmas sampler.

The wind's gusts died. The sun ceased its coy hide-and-seek among the clouds and shone warm on her back. She loosened the shawl and let it hang from her shoulders. She and Delilah gloried in the giant river's beauty, watching muscled boatmen keel and steer boats, some eighty feet long, around snags and other perils. The friends exclaimed as a majestic steamboat appeared, trailing a train of black smoke as if to say *the queen has come to Illinois*. Men wearing top hats and elegant ladies strolled down its tiered decks.

Yearning caught in Keturah's throat like a fishbone. During the past decade, steamboats had become a common sight. But she never had stepped foot on even a keelboat. *If only I could go, too.*

"Would you ladies be needin' a ride to McFarlan's Ferry?" A leathery-faced man offered them a near-toothless grin from the village's wooden dock. He held out a clawlike hand. Other boatmen stared at them with hungry eyes.

"No, thank you." Keturah grabbed Delilah's arm and hurried away. She longed to escape to McFarlan's Ferry

Golconda, even down the Mississippi to New Orleans! But not on that boat.

Her shawl suddenly left her shoulders as if the man had grabbed it. Fingers of terror stole down her back. But when she turned, only the impish wind dangled it, swirling it—and her life, it seemed—toward the water.

"No!" She chased the shawl, skirts clogging her steps. Delilah darted beside her, but they could not outpace the wind. Guffaws from the keelboat met Keturah's ears, but she ignored them and dashed down the pier.

If only she could grab—

Splash.

She dropped into a cold, green underworld, ramming against the rock-strewn river bottom. She lay stunned and bruised, undulating skirts binding her like bandages. Gold strands of light writhed in the water, water that filled her eyes, her mouth, her throat. She retched, only to swallow more. Mama had never allowed her to swim.

Something gripped her shoulder. A mental picture of Jonah and the big fish in Papa's Bible filled her with fresh terror. She kicked and tore at the thing with her nails. Iron-like bands pinned her arms to her sides. She felt as if her eyes would burst.

Dear Lord Jesus. I am going to die.

Suddenly she broke the surface. Coughing and shivering, she shook her sodden hair from her eyes and realized a stranger held her in his arms.

❄

From the boat he saw her fall and go under, her friend screaming from the dock. He leaped into the river.

182

Now, standing in the water and holding her as she coughed and spit on him, he shared her stupidity. Catcalls from other boatmen greeted them—the silly girl who ran off a pier, nearly drowning in only five feet of water, and the soaking-wet fool who jumped in to rescue her. He would never hear the end of this. Still, her eyes, greener than the water, locked him in a vise. He trembled—but not because of cold.

"Keturah! Are you all right?" The girl's friend stretched out a hand.

"You that hard up, Henry?" Old Sol cackled from the deck. "I know where you can find a woman that will hug ya up good without drownin' ya dead!"

"Not as pretty as that 'un though."

The boatman's tone wrenched Henry's eyes away from the girl's. He hated the look the man gave her. Turning away, he waded ashore, still carrying the girl who lay limp in his arms, her eyes like green stars. "Sol. You got a blanket?"

The old codger pulled one from his poke, jumped from boat to pier, and brought it to him. The girl's friend scurried close behind.

Keturah. What a pretty name.

Sol shook the tattered brown blanket out. "Wrap her up good, boy."

The girl wriggled to free herself. His arms did not want to release her, but he set her on the grassy shore and covered her. Her friend hugged her.

"I—I thank thee." The girl avoided his eyes now and looked to the older man. "And I thank thee for the blanket,

Friend Sol, is it?"

"Yes, ma'am. Hope you're feelin' better." The man turned back to Henry. "We got to go. You comin' with us to McFarlan?"

He needed the work. He did not need to waste an afternoon with a girl who didn't have the sense to swim when she fell in. And she, hearing Sol's words, said nothing. She did not need him.

But he could not bring himself to leave.

Sol chuckled. "I see. You're gonna stick with this here damsel in distress. Just be sure you bring my blanket back."

Sol returned to the keelboat. With a final round of catcalls, the boatmen guided it out of the dock.

The girl searched behind Henry as if for something lost. But she addressed him in a polite voice. "I am sorry for the way I behaved. I thought—"

"People who think they are drowning do strange things." He stared at the ground.

"I—I cannot swim."

"You should learn. Then a few feet of water will not scare you." He stole a glance, hoping to regain the communion of those wonderful eyes. But they still darted behind him, scanning the river. "You lose something?"

"My red shawl." She struggled to rise, her soggy clothing weighing her down. "The wind blew it into the river. I chased it and fell in."

"Shawl?" He felt like tossing her back.

"I must find it." She struggled free of the blanket, rose, and stepped toward the shore.

Her friend grabbed her arm. "Keturah, you'll catch your death of a cold."

When Keturah's steps grew more determined, her friend picked up a long, gnarly stick from nearby underbrush. "If you insist, perhaps we can fish it out."

Henry retrieved Sol's blanket. "Wait. This is bound to be dryer than a shawl fresh from the river. Better wrap up. Please, or you'll get sick." Why did he feel compelled to accompany her?

"I thank thee." Though dripping hair clung to her cheeks like river weeds to white stone, her smile outshone her eyes. "I am Keturah Wilkes. My father owns a farm outside Rock and Cave. This is Delilah Scott."

Why had he not seen her before? He bobbed his head as steamboat gentlemen did. "I am Henry Mangun. I work on the boats." He did more than that, but she need not know.

"We had better hurry." She turned toward the river, brandishing her stick like a child. "My brother, Caleb, will return shortly."

At his name, Delilah rolled her eyes. "How will you explain—"

"Let's not think about it." Keturah swished the stick in the now dark-gray water.

As they searched the shallows, clouds bullied the sun into hiding. No one had given Henry a blanket to ward off the sharp breeze rising from the west. Not a pinch of fat to keep him warm as Ma said. And his cold, wet leggings and coarse blue linsey woolsey shirt rubbed him raw.

"This is useless." Keturah threw the stick into the river.

Delilah gave a sigh of relief. He almost followed suit—except he feared Keturah would disappear, leaving him empty as an upset bucket. Still he must end this futile search. "A red shawl would stand out in the water. It must have been swept into the drop-off."

Keturah tossed the blanket aside, kneeled, and removed her still-soppy moccasins.

"Keturah Wilkes, whatever are you doing?" Delilah squealed.

"I'm going to find my shawl." Her chin rose.

"You want to jump into the river again?" He *had* rescued a crazy woman.

"No. But I must." Her trembling cheek looked lily-petal soft. His hand ached to touch it.

He heard himself say, "I will look for the shawl."

All his life he had doubted the sanity of the people around him. Now he wondered if she had driven him to madness. He plunged into the chilly water.

Like a catfish, he slid along the river bottom. When he found nothing, Henry gulped fresh mouthfuls of air and swam well past the pier's mossy posts. Nothing. Popping through the river surface, he opened his mouth to tell her he was done. Finished.

She was yelling for him to try that spot. He already had searched near the drop-off twice. He might have told her to find another madman for her task, except with the wind sloshing waves up his nose it was simply easier to drop back down into the water and look. Perhaps. His open eyes, braving the silt, burned.

There, caught among the weeds. He grasped the shawl, wadded it into a shapeless mass, and held it close to his body with one hand as he made for shore. Planting his feet in the muck, he held up his trophy.

At the joy on her face, his irritation evaporated. She splashed in, and he handed her the muddy, slimy shawl. Clasping the blanket around her with one hand, she hugged the shawl. He wished he could take its place. But she did hold out a hand, and though he did not feel worthy of its whiteness, he clasped it as if he were the one drowning.

"Keturah Wilkes."

The bass voice sounded more powerful because the man did not raise it. Keturah, clinging to her filthy bundle, dropped Henry's hand as if it contained hot coals. She turned slowly around. The birdlike friend on shore gave a funny little chirp.

Henry did not want to look up. But he lifted his chin and looked squarely into the rock-like gaze of a big man with Keturah's eyes.

Chapter 2

Perhaps thee would like to explain?" Papa's tone, though controlled, spoke more words than his dictionary.

"My shawl blew into the river." Keturah knew only the truth would set her free. "I fell in, trying to retrieve it. This person witnessed my misfortune and helped me to shore."

She dared not look into Henry's odd, yet wondrous, golden-hazel eyes again, eyes that had imprisoned her when he pulled her out.

"That does indeed relieve my mind." Her father's probing gaze did not soften. "I thought perchance thee had grown too warm in thy lovely shawl and decided to take a cooling bath in the mud." He gestured toward the village. "Perhaps thee knows Caleb's whereabouts?"

"He carried Mistress Norris's heavy basket to her house," Delilah chimed in. "She was ill."

"Of course." Papa nodded sagely. "The air fairly reeks with charity today. Would thee be so kind, Delilah, to go ask Caleb to meet us at the edge of town?"

With a wave, Delilah skittered away. Keturah, wading ashore, looked after her in despair. After this escapade, who knew when she would come to town again?

Papa turned to Henry, still standing in water. "I would be far remiss if I did not thank thee for helping my daughter. What is thy name?"

"Henry Mangun."

"God bless thee, Friend Mangun." Papa pointed to the blanket wrapped around her. "This belongs to—"

"Sol. I work with him."

Keturah tried not to shiver as she handed it to Henry. "I will use Papa's horse blanket on our ride home." She wrinkled her nose at the thought of the smell.

"That will no doubt complete thy elegant toilette." A tiny smile escaped Papa's mouth.

Perhaps there was hope, after all. And thanks to Henry, she still had her shawl. "I cannot thank thee enough."

He smiled for the first time, a slow light that filled his tanned face like a sunrise. Almost before she realized it, he had disappeared into the nearby forest.

Caleb, his mouth hanging open like a sheep's, joined them in the near-silent ride home. Wrapped in the scratchy horse blanket, Keturah held her nose. She checked the wet red-and-green crewel in her pocket. Hopefully her unexpected bath had not affected the bright colors. She anticipated no further remarks from Papa. He would say little to Caleb— usually the dutiful son—about leaving his sister unescorted in town. Papa would assume both had learned from their misadventures and would adjust their ways accordingly.

But Mama? She, Caleb, and Papa had left the mighty Ohio behind, but Keturah knew they all were preparing for the flood of reproaches that surely would sweep them away.

❄

Henry stuck his fingers in his ears and tried to invite sleep back into his dark, musty loft. He liked fiddle music and sang a good ditty. Though he tended to watch more than participate, he liked parties. But not this kind, especially after several hard days of loading and keeling boats.

Ma's hee-haw laugh scared away any lingering dreams. He flipped off his cornhusk tick, crawled to the ladder opening, and stuck his head into the room below.

"Ma, you trying to wake the dead?"

She laughed uproariously. "Boy, when things is good, I gotta dance."

Several people clapped as his red-haired mother, hands on ample hips, never missed a step in her jig to someone's wild fiddling. Her feet blurred, she danced so fast. He couldn't help grinning. Nobody could outdance Ma.

"Henry, you missed the best loot ever." Charlie, his brother, raised a gourd filled with wine. "Rich farmer on his way home from New Orleans. But we were kind. Left him his underdrawers."

The room rocked with huzzahs and toasts. Charlie's eyes glittered with a look Henry had come to dread.

He pulled back and flopped on his tick. As children he and Charlie had been the best pickpockets at the docks. Now Henry only stole when he or his family were hungry. But Charlie wanted to get rich. Someday he would trespass on James Ford's territory one time too many. Or worse, join Ford in his schemes to lure travelers to Potts' Inn and rob and kill them.

I'll never touch Ford or Potts, no matter how poor we get.

He lay sleepless until they grew too drunk to notice his leaving. He grabbed his poke and climbed down the ladder, navigating dancers and snoring bodies on the dirt floor. He unlatched the door, welcoming the forest's fresh, chilly air as he escaped to the limestone bluffs along the river, honeycombed with caves he'd explored since a child. Not that he would go to the big pirate cave. He would never go there again. Ever.

Henry, using the silent walk his Shawnee-Indian father had taught him, meandered through the forest to his secret cave. Even Charlie didn't know this favorite spot, big enough for him to build a fire and lie down for a rocky but peaceable night.

❄

Tea-kettle-tea-kettle-chee-chee-chee! One Carolina wren woke Henry. Soon several chattered outside. He dragged his aching body to a sitting position. Sly sunbeams peeked through a small opening in the cave's roof, teasing him to come outside. Henry, swathed in the blanket he kept in the cave, munched a piece of hardtack from his poke. He did not work on Sunday—a welcome rest from his usual backbreaking labor. Beyond that, Sundays had always seemed special. For the life of him, he could not imagine why. After Saturday nights, his home looked like a pigsty. He would not return there today. The peaceful village streets drew him, but churchgoers wearing their Sunday best eyed him. Their faces told him ragged half-breeds did not belong.

Henry pulled a small worn book from his poke and opened it under the sunbeams. Ma hadn't given a fig whether he went to school as a child. But he went because he liked the teacher and wanted to read.

As a teen, he stole a Bible because he'd always wanted one. He read it off and on, trying to sound out the hard words. Now he scratched his head, deciphering a New Testament verse: "Therefore if any man be in Christ, he is a new creature: old things are passed away; behold, all things are become new."

What did it mean? At twenty-five he felt old and hard as the cave. "Any man," it said. How could any man—especially him—become new, like a baby?

The memory of Keturah, her softness and sparkling eyes, invaded his thoughts as they had many times the past week. Despite the cave's chill, his face heated like an iron skillet. He should not think of scripture and Keturah in the same moment. Yet he felt they were linked. She and her father were obviously Quakers, saying *thee* and *thou*. Keturah and her pa sounded as if they had stepped out of the Bible.

But other things about them intrigued him. Keturah told her pa the truth about her "swim." She could have made up a story, even blamed him for dumping her into the water. But she didn't.

Her pa's patience surprised him, too. Men swore and struck their families when they annoyed them. Henry had never seen an angry man show such calmness. He had called Henry, a river rat, *friend* and blessed him.

Keturah and her pa must know God. Something inside him leaped. But was it the girl or her God that excited him more?

He would have to think on it. Clutching the Bible, Henry shouldered his poke and headed for the river. He hunkered down on top of a cliff overlooking the water sparkling in the sunshine as if God had just made it. Humming a scrap of a hymn he'd learned at school, he opened the Bible again.

❋

Keturah tied on her First Day bonnet. Mama gave the kettle of beans baking in the fireplace's coals a final stir. They joined Caleb and Papa, who had driven the wagon to the door of their cabin.

"Thee is ready for Meeting?"

Papa's words meant more than finishing chores and donning their best clothes. Keturah nodded. Although sitting in silence strained her ready tongue, she genuinely loved First Day, when a few area Quaker families gathered in the tiny cabin that served as a meetinghouse. Sharing God's Light and listening for His wisdom, rather than scrubbing and cooking, seemed an excellent use of time to Keturah. Did Mama like sitting still? She hid a grin.

Keturah enjoyed the meetinghouse more during summer, when the wide-open wooden shutters let in the forest's fresh scents. But the candles Mama brought for the table at the front glowed like the Light within. Sitting beside her on the women's side of the room, Keturah pondered the scriptures Papa had read at breakfast, all about becoming a new creature in Christ. At times her thoughts and actions had nothing to do with Christ's Light. As one Friend spoke of God's refining fire, and another rose to praise God, Keturah asked Him to make her the woman He wanted her to be.

Yet she could not believe God had designed her like Mama or most Quaker women, who married at sixteen or seventeen, kept house, raised children. Her heart longed for adventure, for learning, for newness of life she had not yet tasted.

Keturah felt an odd sense of someone watching. To be sure, she had felt boys' covert stares at Meeting throughout the years. Now, the group's marriageable young men had all found wives. She rejoiced in their happiness—and her own respite. Why this uneasiness?

She turned her head, coughed into her handkerchief, and cast a glance behind. Large golden eyes met hers. A tall, thin figure sat on a bench at the back. Henry Mangun. Why had he joined them? How had he slipped in without anyone hearing?

Henry blinked and then stared at the floor. She shifted back to the front, surprised to find herself blushing as Meeting ended.

"Friend Mangun?" Papa strode to the door.

Papa remembered his name, too. Henry looked as if he wanted to escape. But as Papa talked, he asked hesitant questions, then more. With the buzz of the women's after-Meeting conversation, Keturah heard little. But they appeared to discuss the scriptures read. Henry said nothing to her before disappearing into the forest as he had done after rescuing her.

She knew all—including Mama—were bursting with curiosity, but they would keep their post-Meeting discussions to spiritual and family matters. As she expected, Henry's attendance came up at dinner.

"Who was that boy?" Mama ladled beans onto their

plates. "Is he from Rock and Cave?"

She frequently sent food and clothing for the village poor with Papa, but she had not set foot there in years.

"Henry Mangun. Lives downriver." Papa drank his cider, taking care not to look at Keturah.

"Why would he come? How could he know where we meet?" Mama sputtered.

"Perhaps—" Papa put his cup down. "Perhaps he is looking for God."

Chapter 3

Two weeks later, Mama's small hands pounded bread dough on the big oak table in their cabin's main room. "Thee *shall* see the man."

"Mayhap thee might tell me before inviting a gentleman to keep company." Keturah pounded hers harder. "I am not a child."

Mama stoked the big stone fireplace. "Perhaps thee knows another grown woman who swims in the river wearing her best dress?"

Keturah gritted her teeth. Mama would display this unfortunate incident like a prize ribbon until Keturah turned eighty. At least she did not know about the shawl.

The set of Mama's mouth told Keturah further argument would be a waste. In silence they formed the loaves of white bread they ate only on First Day or when visitors came. Keturah's kneading almost matched her mother's. But that did not guarantee baking success. Often Mama hid Keturah's bread from company—especially male company.

"Bring in a ham." Mama chopped apples for pies as if wielding a battle-ax.

Keturah welcomed an escape to the smokehouse. The brisk October air cooled her hot cheeks as she detoured into the drafty washhouse. Keturah pulled the red shawl from its hiding place behind pokes of rags Mama kept to make rugs. She threw it around her shoulders, parading past big wooden tubs, imagining she wore it openly today. Especially on Christmas Day. Every day if she chose.

If she chose. The words rattled in her mind, useless and noisy as stones in a bucket. She wished she dared shout from the rooftops that she harbored no interest whatsoever in Thaddeus Squibb, son of wealthy Friends from northern Illinois.

Keturah could not recall Thaddeus, though Mama said they met at the last yearly Meeting. Keturah enjoyed those rare gatherings of Friends from across the state. But this was not the first time a man only Mama remembered had appeared afterward at their door, eager, suitable, and impossibly dull. She considered appearing at dinner wearing the shawl. Friend Squibb, seeing her in all her scarlet glory, would disappear like a bad dream.

She giggled but then felt a little ashamed. People prone to rash judgments annoyed her. Should she not keep an open mind, too? She had not told her parents a deep part of her longed for a strong man's love. He had not yet appeared. If God chose to bring him with Mama's help, who was she to reject him without so much as laying eyes on him?

Remembering the river episode, Keturah realized her mother was right about her occasional lack of common sense. Reluctantly, she restored the shawl to its hiding place. She dashed to the smokehouse and cut down a large ham. Carrying her greasy bundle, Keturah hurried into the cabin and managed to slice it for frying without wounding herself. She raised cloths covering the rising bread to check its progress and sighed. Mama's loaves looked perfect. Hers were lopsided.

As a final peace offering to Mama and Friend Squibb, she made gingerbread cookies using Grandmama's recipe, the only dish she never ruined. As she rolled and cut the rich brown dough into circles, she recalled that, long ago, her Methodist aunt Rachel had told Keturah her Quaker grandmamma secretly called them Christmas cookies. Keturah had followed that example. Now the cake-like treats added their aroma to the cabin's mouthwatering aura.

Keturah tidied up and set the table with Mama's white tablecloth and dark-blue and white crockery, brought precariously downriver from Pennsylvania. The room with its scrubbed wooden floor, cozy rag rugs, and polished pewter would smile a welcome to Friend Squibb.

Keturah washed up then clambered up narrow stairs to her bedroom. She brushed her hair until it glowed like summer wheat and donned her best dress—without the red shawl.

❄

Friend Squibb did not appear nervous, if one judged by appetite. He ate as much as Keturah's father and brother combined. Had he devoured a whole pie? But he also was making Keturah's Christmas cookies disappear. Between bites, he declared he had not eaten such a feast since his dear Sally departed this life.

Keturah choked on her pie. One glance told her Mama had known. *No wonder I did not remember him. He has to be at least fifteen years older than I.*

Still, he was handsome, an enormous tanned, blond-haired man. She brushed away a biblical reference to the giant Anakites of Canaan from her mind and tried to smile. She did not have to make conversation, for Friend Squibb devoted his whole attention to eating. Due to a full mouth, he rarely answered. At least not so she could understand. Keturah tried not to panic when Papa and Caleb left to do chores after dinner without inviting their visitor to join them. Her mother accepted Keturah's fervent offer to help with dishes but went to fetch heated water from the washhouse.

She hoped Friend Squibb's heavy meal would make him drift off. Instead his alert blue eyes surveyed her with a pleased air. Keturah gulped.

"Thee has been well?" Friend Squibb gave her a huge, toothy smile.

"Very well, indeed." She could not tell him his manners nauseated her.

"Thou art tall and strong, not frail and fussy, like so many young women." He cocked his head to one side. "Thee likes children?"

"Yes." She began to regale him with tales of their neighbor girls, when the words died on her lips. "Dost thou have children?"

"Seven sons." He chomped more cookies. "But my quiver is not yet full. I would have seven more to work my farm and a lovely girl or two—like thee—to care for and civilize the household."

"Civilize," Keturah said faintly. A vision rose before her of a gargantuan table surrounded by wide-mouthed blond Anakites with her and two skinny, pitiful girls shoveling food like hay. She broke out in a cold sweat.

Friend Squibb gave her a gooey smile, and her gorge rose. With a stammered apology, she ran out the door toward the barn.

Papa's hands held her head as she retched. After she washed her face, he seated Keturah in the empty but still-warm washhouse. "I will inform Friend Squibb of thy illness."

But Mama, returning from the house, already had done so. "When I said thee was feeling delicate, he expressed thanks for the meal, but said perhaps he should leave thee in the tender care of thy mother and father."

Keturah twisted her apron.

Her mother's fine eyebrows drew together in a straight black line. "What did he say to thee? What did he do?"

"Nothing dishonorable," Keturah assured her. "He complimented my good health. He wishes to marry and have seven more sons—"

"Seven!" Caleb appeared out of nowhere, as usual. "Seven who eat like him?"

"Seven *more* to help run his farm." Keturah shuddered.

She knew Papa was searching for something positive to say. "Friend Squibb appeared a very. . .hearty man."

Keturah bowed her head. "I—I did try to like him, Mama."

"I am glad thee did not. He would work thee like a slave." Mama sniffed. "I had not seen him at table. His god is his stomach."

She laid a rough hand on Keturah's cheek. It felt good. Her mother hastened inside to scrub Friend Squibb's presence from her table.

Papa's glance followed his wife fondly, and then wrapped Keturah in a gentle embrace that quieted her heart, mind, and insides.

Perhaps Mama would think twice before finding her more suitors.

Chapter 4

Henry dropped his lunch poke. Beautiful Keturah looked straight at him. Standing near Scott's store beside her brother, Keturah did not blink. Henry avoided her at Meeting each week, but now he could not escape that jeweled green gaze. His legs teetered, but his feet refused to move.

"Henry."

Keturah's smile devoured his breath. He looked away, trying to inhale.

"Henry?"

Was there a note of hurt in her voice? He rose from his seat on the ground, flattening his voice into politeness. "Miss Keturah, how are you? And you, Mr. Wilkes?"

Caleb nodded.

She giggled. "By now thee should know we Friends do not give each other titles."

Last month she had played the fool, falling into the river. Today he was doing everything wrong.

"Do not worry thyself." Keturah read his uneasiness. "Call me *miss* if thee wishes."

"I—I don't want to be too familiar."

"Thee rescued me, and now thee knows my name. I know thine, as does Caleb. We worship together. Are we not friends?"

He let himself smile. "We are."

"Would thee like Christmas cookies?" She eyed the leathery dried fish in his hand.

He puzzled at this, since it was only October. But his stomach growled at the sight of plump brown gingerbread cookies. "I would not eat your vittles."

"We have eaten plenty." She held them under his nose. "Even Caleb has had enough."

Caleb nodded, his gaze wandering.

Henry took two. *Mmm.* Sweet and spicy. Like Keturah. She must be a wonderful cook.

Caleb's stare fastened on a blond girl down the way. "Keturah, may I assume thee will not swim?"

She shot him an annoyed look. "I promise."

"Remember what Mama said. Stay within my sight."

Watching Caleb amble off, Henry laughed. "If you do fall in, I will teach you to swim. At least I will not have to seek your shawl."

Her smile faded. "I do not trouble Mama further by wearing it in public today. She does not think bright colors proper." Keturah set her jaw. "But I wear it often alone, especially when I stitch my Christmas sampler."

"Why does she dislike color?" He was being too bold but could not restrain his curiosity. "At Meeting, all wear gray or dark clothes."

"Friends prefer to keep their lives simple and free from pride. I see their wisdom." She raised her chin. "But surely the God who created cardinals, dandelions, and pumpkins, who paints the sunrise each day, does not forbid the joy of color to His people."

He nodded. Looking into her emerald eyes, he knew their Creator must take even more pleasure in them than he.

"I want to open my life to beauty." Keturah cupped her hand over her eyes to scan the Ohio. "I was born here yet know the river so little because of my mother's fears."

"Why is she afraid of the river?"

"Her sister drowned one spring."

No wonder. He'd seen the river flood, changing overnight into a roaring monster that swept dead people and animals downstream before his very eyes.

"That was years ago." Impatience tinged her voice. "Tell me what thee has seen."

He didn't want to frighten her. "I see it sparkle in the sun's light and hear its voice in the dark. I've keeled many boats, even past where the Ohio meets the Mississippi."

"Thee has ridden a steamboat?"

He basked in her smile of admiration. "Occasionally." Twice, actually.

"Thee has met travelers. How exciting." She gestured to the east. "And has thee explored the big cave?"

Henry nodded, but uneasiness chilled him. Pa knew the big cave too well.

"Thee must have many stories to tell." Like a little girl, Keturah hugged herself. "I would see the cave, but Papa forbade it. I heard pirates once lived there, preying on passing boats. Some say they still stop boats—even steamships—and demand money. Did thee ever meet up with pirates?"

His soul dropped like an anchor. Finally, he wet his lips and said, "Yes. A time or two."

❄

How glad Keturah was that Mama, regretting Friend Squibb, allowed her to go to town now. She wanted to know Henry better. Once past his first shyness, he seemed almost light-hearted with a boyish smile that warmed his feline eyes. As they talked, she felt more comfortable with him than with her own brother. But now his face stiffened. He said little as she chattered. Still she was disappointed when Caleb and Priscilla walked toward them.

"I must go." She sighed. Back to the farm where adventure consisted of runaway livestock. "I will see thee at Meeting?"

"I would not go elsewhere."

The hunger in his voice startled her. She had gone to Meeting every week since a babe and never encountered such fervor.

"Come then, and feast," she said impetuously.

His face lit up.

"Till then. Good-bye."

Henry nodded and faded into the forest. She blinked and turned to her brother. "How does he vanish like that?"

"Because he looks like a walking sapling." Caleb waved farewell to Priscilla. "Except for the black hair."

"The sapling calls the sapling thin." Keturah crossed her arms.

"He is much thinner than I."

She was about to say, *He does not eat as many cookies.* Instead she said softly, "He does not eat as often as we."

Caleb nodded, his eyes suddenly serious. He said no more

as they walked back to Papa's wagon.

"What, thou art not late? Nor soaked?" Papa gave them a quizzical look. "To what do we owe this strange state of affairs?"

Keturah impulsively held his hand against her cheek. "Sometimes Caleb and I forget to be thankful for all we have."

Papa looked pleased but more puzzled than ever when Caleb did not add a retort. As he urged Sam on home, Keturah thought perhaps the farm with its snug four-room cabin, full table, cellar, and smokehouse was not a bad prospect, after all.

❄

"Where you goin' so early?"

Hand on the door latch, Henry felt Ma's words hit him between the shoulder blades like birdshot. "I can't sleep."

"You're goin' to see that Quaker girl."

Ma knew. How? He dropped his head.

"I saw you talking to her in town. Pretty. You have an eye for the ladies. Like your Pa."

Pa was dead, shot in Kentucky when vigilantes hunted down his pirate gang. Why couldn't Ma let him die? He wanted to run but faced her. "I'm going to Meeting."

Ma's face and hair had absorbed the gray morning light. Her weary mouth twisted in a chuckle. "Henry, I'm your ma. You may present a fine front to others, but don't try it on me. Meeting? You, a Quaker?"

"Don't know if I'll be a Quaker. But I find peace there." He took a deep breath. "I find God."

"And that girl has nothin' to do with your gettin' religion?"

He knew his face was turning red. He threw the door open. *Today I'll do it. I'll run and run and never come back.*

"Henry!" Her tone dropped to almost a whisper, a thin chain that pulled him. "This foolish dream can't come true. She and her thee-and-thou family will never think of you as anything but dirt. She doesn't know you—"

"You don't know me, Ma!" The cry ripped from his chest as if she had opened it with a knife. "You never have!"

He ran for the meetinghouse as if his life depended on it.

❆

"Therefore if any man be in Christ, he is a new creature: old things are passed away; behold, all things are become new."

Papa had read this scripture weeks ago. The words sprouted in her daily thoughts, and now, sitting before the crackling fire on a gloomy October afternoon, she stitched them onto the sampler she had marked herself.

"I am glad to see thee so industrious." Mama, trimming candles they had made, smiled approval, but her voice held a note of amazement.

Keturah did not wonder; she had cared little for samplers—until now. "This scripture comes to me during Meeting. I think on it almost every day."

The verse was not among other familiar passages women sewed. Keturah feared Mama would remark on the bright-red crewel, which had not faded during her unplanned bath in the river. She soon saw, however, that Mama was not about to discourage this combined spiritual and needlework miracle.

Nor did Papa as he brought in more wood. "An excellent verse." He beamed. "Friend Henry questioned me about it. I loaned him my pamphlet on the Corinthian epistles. That boy asks good questions."

"*Humph.*" Mama sniffed.

Keturah feared her mellow mood had departed with Papa. Mama eyed the decoration Keturah had marked on the sampler. "Roses? Such large roses."

"Yes, Mama. One above the scripture, one below." Green pine needles and holly would give it a Christmas air, but she wouldn't point that out.

"Lilies would match the verse's meaning better."

"The rose does symbolize love." Keturah knew what Mama feared: romantic overtones would feed local gossip. "But Christ's love makes us new. What better flower for my sampler?"

Mama nodded. Though she lived her faith and her love, her mother did not speak easily of either. Mama bustled upstairs to battle imaginary dust.

Keturah chuckled then hummed "While Shepherds Watched," a carol her friend Delilah had taught her. Her awkward fingers gained speed, stitching the wondrous words and Christmas roses in bright red.

❄

"Henry!" She waved from the bench outside Scott's store and readied her Christmas cookies. Sharing them had become almost a ceremony, though she now added thick bread-and-butter sandwiches and apples to her food packets.

He joined her, his face rosy with the brisk October

day. While he munched, she read poetry, including a Robert Burns poem, sung in Scotland on Christmas and New Year's Day.

"*Should auld acquaintance be forgot, and never brought to mind? Should auld acquaintance be forgot, and days o' auld lang syne.*"

He grinned. "I doubt that would be read at a Friends' Meeting."

"Mama likes Christmas songs no more than she likes red." Keturah rolled her eyes. "But I have decided this year to celebrate Christ's birth with poems and carols."

"My grandmother sang carols in French every Christmas." His eyes glistened a little. "Sometimes Ma sings them."

"Is thy papa French, too?"

"He was a Shawnee." Henry's eyes hardened to sandstone.

"Thee has not yet eaten thy cookies." Although itching with curiosity, Keturah changed the subject. "I shall finish mine. When Caleb returns, he may try to steal them as he only ate a dozen before we left home."

The strained lines around Henry's mouth relaxd.

Until a teasing voice broke in. "You could share one with your hungry little brother."

Turning, Keturah nearly dropped her treasured book of poetry into the mud.

Wide, dark eyes fastened on hers. Rich black waves of hair curled on his bronzed forehead and neck. The most handsome man she ever imagined gave a slight bow. He took her limp hand in his and kissed it.

Chapter 5

Y ou going to introduce me, Henry?"

"Guess you've done that yourself." Heat and ice fought in Henry's stomach. He tried to steady his tone. "Keturah, this is my brother, Charlie. Miss Keturah Wilkes."

Charlie did not drop her hand. "So glad to make your acquaintance."

Of that Henry was sure. "Thought you were headed downriver today."

"Ma asked me to change my plans." Charlie sounded like an obedient choirboy.

"Of course she did." If Ma couldn't shipwreck his friendship with the "Quaker girl," she would do it through Charlie the Lady-killer.

Keturah gave Charlie the same smile Henry remembered when she spoke of her red shawl. "If thee is hungry, I gladly share my cookies." She handed all three to Charlie.

"I would not think of it." He returned them, looking hopefully at Henry.

He clutched his Christmas cookies like a greedy five-year-old. But he offered his brother two.

Charlie ate them slowly, telling Keturah how delicious they were. She forgot to eat while he told stories of fascinating ladies and gentlemen who traveled on the river—neglecting to mention he often picked their pockets.

You do it, too, Henry's conscience prodded him. Faces of their thievery peered around the corners of his mind, shrinking away in terror. As Charlie continued the I'm-so-wonderful script Henry knew well, he sat mute.

When Caleb returned from his rendezvous with Priscilla, he raised his eyebrows at Keturah, who did not notice. Henry wanted to escape, but he would not leave Keturah and Caleb alone with Charlie. Finally Friend Wilkes drove up. Henry watched Charlie assess Keturah's father. A Quaker, but a big one with a shrewd eye, not to mention an adult son and a hunting rifle beside him. For now the Wilkeses were safe.

As they drove away, Keturah turned and waved. "See you at Meeting!"

He marveled that the frost on the ground did not melt from her smile's warmth.

But did she smile at him? Or at Charlie?

❅

Henry and his brother had left town, yet Charlie still wore his choir-boy face. "You could have given me more than two cookies."

"Or I could have knocked you down." Henry held his fist under Charlie's nose. "Thinking of robbing them? Don't try it."

Charlie threw him a scornful look. But at Henry's intensity, he stepped back. "What's gotten into you? We were the best together, even as boys."

"You mean the worst."

Charlie laughed. "And proud of it. Until you started reading too much." He rolled his eyes heavenward. "Why did you have to steal that Bible?"

Henry felt the familiar flood of shame but glared at Charlie. "It wasn't my idea to rob a circuit preacher."

"I figured on Monday he'd be carryin' a fat offering." Charlie snorted. "His wallet was skinnier than he was."

"What made us think we knew anything about preachers?" Henry shook his head.

"You're gettin' along good with them now."

"Quakers don't have preachers. They believe God has put His Light in all His followers."

"That would be you, right, Henry? And Keturah." Charlie cast sly eyes at him. "She makes you feel downright holy, don't she?"

Henry ached to beat his brother into the mud. He could do it, despite Charlie's muscles.

Charlie knew it, too. He took off like a deer, and Henry darted after him. They wound through the forest, panting, sweating, running all four miles. How many times had he chased Charlie home? He had lost count.

Henry ran most of his fury off. Drawing near their cabin, he wondered if he had overreacted. Still Ma might try anything to keep him away from the Quakers. And he wouldn't put anything past Charlie, especially when it came to a pretty girl.

He was breathing down his brother's neck as Charlie burst through the cabin door. "Hoping Ma will protect you?"

Charlie turned with his infuriating smile. "She always does."

A snore fairly shook the cabin walls. Ma, her mouth as

open as the big cave's, lay on her cornhusk tick. They knew better than to awaken her.

Charlie rummaged an old wooden box they called the cupboard. "No hardtack."

"Any cornmeal?" Henry rummaged another. Nothing like food concerns to unite enemies.

Charlie shook his head then headed for the loft ladder. "Oh well. Got to catch a few winks."

"Business tonight?" Henry glared. "Make sure it's not with Keturah's family."

"I got better things to do." Charlie climbed the ladder, yawning.

Likely thieving and drinking. One minute he wanted to kill Charlie. The next, he worried his brother was getting in over his head.

Henry's near-empty stomach growled. If he wanted to eat, he'd better get moving. Henry picked up his gun and headed into the forest again.

❄

"*Mmmm.*" Keturah, stitching a rose in her sampler, inhaled the fragrance of the sweet buns Delilah took from her dutch oven. "Those smell almost as good as Christmas gingerbread."

"Like all excellent cooks, we must make sure our food tastes good." Delilah laughed as she poured hot cider. They "tasted" two buns apiece.

"It is almost time to walk to the river." Keturah loved fun times at Delilah's house, but she had waited all day for this moment. She donned her red shawl. "At Meeting last week, Henry told me he had a surprise for me."

Delilah put her hands on her nonexistent hips. "You've been meeting Henry for weeks. Do you think this friendship is wise?"

"Henry is a good friend, but a friend only," Keturah stammered. She did not dare mention Charlie. Her cheeks felt as if she faced the fireplace.

"Do tell." Delilah gave Keturah a schoolmarm look.

"You will come with me, Delilah, will you not?" Papa would never accept her going alone!

"Of course. I must ensure my best friend's well-being." She grinned. "And I must see this surprise."

As they walked Rock and Cave's main road, Keturah thought of Mama fussing because Caleb, gone on business for Papa, could not accompany them. Mama need not worry. Delilah would keep her sharp eyes on Keturah.

Would Charlie come today, too? Her pace and heartbeat increased.

Sure enough, in the usual meeting place, Charlie's broad-shouldered figure stood beside Henry's tall, thin one.

Henry greeted them, a rare ear-to-ear smile on his face. Surely his shining eyes were the color a crown must hold. Charlie stooped to kiss her hand. When he also kissed Delilah's, her friend's mouth froze into a large *O*.

"Would you like a keelboat ride?" Henry pointed toward the river. Sol, who had lent Keturah the blanket after her "bath," waved cheerfully from a small boat beside the dock.

Delight filled her. "Have you always owned a keelboat?"

Charlie laughed. "Did he tell you that?"

"I told her no such tale," Henry said stiffly. "We do not

own a boat. Sol found a small one we could use for an hour."

"I—I would like nothing more. I have long dreamed of this moment." The Ohio, borrowing blue satin finery from the calm sky, beckoned. She longed to ride through its quiet ripples. Even on this chilly day, she wanted to leave the shore, the solidness that had bound all her life. But desire was a futile dream.

"I am sorry, Henry. I cannot without telling Papa, and he will not return until later."

To her amazement, his grin widened. "I spoke to him after Meeting last week. He agreed, if we take only a short ride."

She did not know which startled her more, Henry's audacity or Papa's permission. Obviously, he had not discussed this with Mama.

"Let's take the boat down to McFarlan's Ferry." Charlie struck a dramatic pose. "I will show the lady sights she has never imagined—"

"Too far." Henry sounded almost like Caleb.

She felt annoyed then remembered Henry planned this lovely surprise. She restored his smile with her own. "Of course it is too far. We will go only a short distance. May Delilah join us?"

Henry nodded. His mouth still curved upward, but his face had lost its glow.

This boat ride has become complicated. She turned to Delilah. "Do you think your father will agree?"

"Yes, since yours does. Keturah, will you come with me to ask him?" Delilah's words came a little slowly, like cold molasses poured from a pitcher.

Reluctantly, Keturah left the brothers to eye each other like roosters in a barnyard.

As they strolled to the store, Delilah whispered, "Do you really believe he asked your father and he said yes?" Her keen eyes searched Keturah's face.

She gaped. "Of course."

"How do you know?"

Keturah paused. She said quietly, "I believe Henry."

Delilah gave a rueful smile. "I do, too. Why, I'm not sure."

"He is a good man." Keturah didn't know what else to say.

After a pause, Delilah opened the store's door. "All right. Let's ask. Though I do believe those two would rather I stayed on shore."

"*Pshaw*," Keturah said, though she feared Delilah spoke the truth.

Mr. Scott, who also knew Sol as trustworthy, agreed, and they ran back to the dock.

The boat was small, tapered at front and back, with a patched canvas awning at the stern. But Keturah pretended she had stepped into Papa's history book. She became the ancient queen Cleopatra, about to board her barge on the Nile.

"Afternoon, ladies." Sol gave them his friendly, toothless grin. "Little warmer than usual in November. Good day for a ride."

"I promise not to fall in." Keturah returned the grin.

"Henry here will keep a good hold on ya."

The remark made her blush. She couldn't look at Henry, so she looked at Charlie. Was he born with that smile, glittering like the water's surface in the sun? She pictured him in a dashing gentleman's garb, silk hat in hand.

"I'll assist the ladies." Charlie lifted her onto the boat as if she weighed no more than a milkweed seed, taking his time about releasing her.

Friends helped her down from wagons all the time. But Charlie's touch made her want to fly!

Henry, his face turning dull red, extended his hand to Delilah. He loosened the boat from the dock.

"Ladies, hold on to the tent, please." Sol took charge. "Get them settin' poles, boys, and give us a push out into the river."

Henry accepted a pole from the other oarsman, a big, silent man whose cheek bulged with a large tobacco chaw. Charlie manned his pole at the opposite side.

Keturah hoped the atmosphere would lighten as they sailed. The brothers dug their poles into the river bottom, and the boat nosed off the dock as if eager to be free.

Suddenly, Keturah floated down the Ohio, vast and blue. She felt as if they skimmed on sky. Wonderful. Frightening. She gripped the awning's splintery wooden frame, her knuckles whitening.

"Are you well?" Delilah gave her a quizzical look. "'Tis but water."

"Mama never even let me have a swimming hole—"

"You should have had more brothers." Delilah clicked her tongue. "But look yonder at our oarsmen. Perhaps their skill will ease your mind."

"Give the ladies a song, boys!" Sol called without a break in his rowing. "*En roulant ma boule,*" he sang in a booming voice.

Henry and Charlie, pulling on big oars, answered him in harmony.

"En roulant ma boule roulant, en roulant ma boule."

The spritely song tweaked frowns into smiles, fears into fun. Keturah would not allow her wayward feet to dance to the happy rhythm, but her fingers tapped against the awning's frame.

Henry grinned as he rowed, his rich, strong baritone weaving through Sol's solos and Charlie's higher tones. She'd heard Henry mouth a few notes, but now he sang full voice. What a gift God had given. If only he could sing at Meeting. Perhaps he would sing some French Christmas carols for her. Keturah hummed along, though singing was not her strong point.

"What does it mean?" Delilah asked when the singing boatmen paused for breath. "How did you learn it?"

"Henry and Charlie's grandpa taught it to me before you was born," Sol answered. "Good song to keep us rowin'."

"*Grand-pére* sang it to us when we were little." Henry's face softened as he pulled. "The chorus is about rolling a ball, and while he sang it, Grand-pére rolled a rag ball to Charlie and me."

Keturah smiled at the picture of an old man playing with two dark-haired little boys—until Charlie spoke.

"You were his favorite." His smile did not fade, but his lips tightened away from his white teeth like an animal's.

Keturah started. Delilah gave Charlie a sharp look. Henry pulled steadily at his oars, eyes straight ahead.

"*Alouette, gentille alouette, alouette, je te plumerai,*" Charlie sang, giving Keturah a wink.

She couldn't help laughing, but judging from the look in his eye, she did not ask what this song meant. Instead she swept her gaze over the river, an everlasting poem of liquid and light. Occasional grayish-white limestone cliffs jutted ancient chins above black leafless trees along the shore, raising their branches in salute to their Creator.

"O Lord, our Lord, how excellent is Thy name in all the earth." Keturah could no more keep the psalm from her lips than she could stop breathing. Her gaze caught Henry's. Though he said nothing, she knew his silent song matched hers word for word.

Charlie shook his head, chuckling.

"Slow that rowin', boys," Sol drawled. "Have to turn around soon and pole, so take a break."

Henry released his oars and unfolded his long frame, his gaze still intertwined with hers. "So, you like the water, after all?"

"I like this view of it," she said softly. "I thank thee. No one could have told me how grand it is."

The glow on his face warmed her. "I think it even more beautiful in winter than summer."

"But never lovely as you." Charlie's glinting smile melted into a look of little-boy adoration.

Delilah yanked her arm. "Come, there is something on your face." She pulled Keturah into the awning and brushed at her cheek.

"Did I not wash the crumbs from my face before we left?" How annoying, in the midst of such poetry, such romance, to present a face like a dirty urchin.

"No crumbs," Delilah hissed in her ear. "But do not let him cast his spell on you."

"Whatever does thee mean?" Keturah pulled away.

"Charlie would turn any woman's head. He no doubt has turned many." Her friend's eyes bored into hers. "Would you encourage such boldness?"

Keturah wiped her cheek to continue the facade and tried to speak lightly. "Thee acts as if I have pledged marriage. A few pretty words mean little."

She brushed past Delilah to the deck, back to the sweet freedom of the river flowing on forever, the wind in her face, and Charlie's velvet gaze.

"Pole us home, boys." Sol swung the sweep to steer the boat back. Guiding it close to the shore where the current was not as strong, he sang new verses to "En roulant ma boule." Charlie almost danced along the gunwales of the boat as he sang and pushed his pole into the river bottom.

Though the water seemed gentle, all four men joined in poling the boat back to the Rock and Cave dock. Delilah stood at her elbow—silent, thank heaven—and Keturah savored the last stretch of her first boat ride. The afternoon sun, a rotund King Midas, turned everything in its path to gold. Charlie, bronzed like an Egyptian god, guided their river chariot away from danger. Keturah clapped her hands to the men's rollicking song, letting its magic pump through her veins.

Only later, after Papa's pleased grin at her ecstasy and their wagon ride home, did she realize Henry, while poling back, had not sung a note.

Chapter 6

Henry knew the look all too well: The shining blankness in women's eyes when they looked at Charlie, as if they had turned into empty-headed china dolls in a store window. Why had he thought Keturah different?

He dove into his cornhusk tick without undressing and pulled the ragged quilts over his head. Out of habit, his fingers sought the leather pouch hidden under his shirt and felt the coins he'd hoarded for her Christmas gift. A shudder of anger passed through him. Just let Charlie try sleeping in the loft tonight. He felt like flinging the little bag into the river. Instead, he tossed and rolled, his muscles reminding him of extra hours he had loaded and rowed to make the money. Would he let Charlie push him into throwing away something so valuable?

Try as he might, he could not forget Keturah's wonder at the river's beauty, the way she spoke of its Creator as he did. He pictured those soft red lips pressed against his. His hands cupped her face as he and the sun's rays played with stray wisps of her golden hair.

He sat up. *Stupid!* How could he, lanky, silent Henry, who long had played second fiddle to Charlie's charms, hope to kiss Keturah? She had forgotten his existence—almost didn't say good-bye when they landed at the dock. Not that he had lingered.

He buried his face in his hands. *Oh God, why did You ever let me see her, hear her voice?*

No angels answered. He did not expect any. Neither did he expect this odd Quiet to invade him. Its current felt strong as the Ohio's after a storm, yet it gently floated his wounded heart along like a leaf.

A door opened downstairs. Footsteps shuffled like milling cattle. Probably his uncle. A faint catlike tread of moccasins. Charlie. Henry felt as if someone had dumped hot coals into his clothes. His body tensed, his fists clenched, readying for the fight of his life. But the Quiet swirled through his rage like a river of peace, leaving him limp. He flopped onto his mattress and listened.

No more steps. No ladder creaks. Henry gave a silent, mirthless chuckle. Above all, Charlie protected himself. If he were smart, he would not come to the loft tonight, nor tomorrow, nor next week.

The Quiet continued flowing over Henry's seething insides. He wanted to tell it to go away. Yet he wanted to say, *Stay forever.* Finally, he gave a weak shrug. *All right, God. I won't kill him. But if I don't, he'll hurt Keturah.*

Tears, like hot springs, welled in him. Keturah again in his mind's eye, the river behind her, the psalm on her lips. Keturah, her eyes locked with his in something bigger than an embrace.

Did God mean Charlie would not win her, after all? Joy and caution collided like boulders, sapping the last of his strength. Finally, he folded his hands in prayer. *Please take care of her.*

He dropped into a coma-like sleep.

❄

Henry no longer sat in the back at Meeting. When he moved behind one large Quaker family, they blocked his view of Keturah.

With his eyes off her shining hair, he regained his mind. Henry saw the plain truth: if he had indeed held Keturah, he had lost her. Of that he was certain. If, during their weekly get-togethers, Henry spoke to Keturah of village news or dared offer a fragment of his deeper thoughts, Charlie pickpocketed them as smoothly as he did his victims' money. Within seconds his gilded, counterfeit charm dazzled Keturah so that she saw no one but him. Henry wondered if he should stay away. Would Keturah notice?

The elderly man sitting in front of Henry turned and cast him a curious glance. Had he said her name aloud? He stared at his hands, chiding himself for thinking about her. Henry focused anew on the speaker's ministry about the Light of Christ who dwelt in His every follower, giving guidance and hope throughout one's life.

Henry had heard such claims since he first came to Meeting, but today, he listened well to God and the Friends He inspired. The man's words filled Henry's empty heart until he thought he would burst, yet he longed for more. Keturah or no Keturah, he believed what he heard. Why nibble scraps of truth when a feast awaited? He wanted nothing more to do with the sin and pain of his pirate past. He would not face life any longer without the Light of Christ inside.

After Meeting he spoke to Friend Wilkes as he often

did. Instead of discussing the latest pamphlet he'd borrowed, Henry expressed his desire.

"Thee has experienced convincement?" The man's kind eyes searched Henry's face and, he felt, his soul.

He answered steadily, "I have."

"Now is a hard time for thee." A statement, not a question.

So Keturah's father had sensed the growing gap between Keturah and him. The man's gentleness eroded Henry's resolve to appear strong. "It is."

His voice squeaked. He wanted to hide, but he lifted his chin. "In the midst of hardness, we learn true wisdom. Isn't that what the scriptures teach?"

"Indeed." Friend Wilkes laid a hand on his shoulder. "But I would that thee be sure. Will thee lay over several weeks before declaring thy intentions?"

"*Lay over?*"

"Ponder, pray, consider, so thee can make a solid decision."

He wanted to belong now. And never look back. Disappointment sucked the air from him. Why did Friend Wilkes suggest delay? Did Quakers try to discourage others from joining? Or only him?

"I will continue to hold thee in the Light and advise thee." Friend Wilkes clasped Henry's hand. His fatherly smile eased Henry's anxiety. "And I will rejoice when thee becomes a part of us."

He meant it. Henry had no idea why the man advised postponement, but he would do as Friend Wilkes said.

❄

"Delilah, I thank thee for rescuing us from the cold." Keturah threw her arms around her friend. The group sat on hide-seated chairs and stumpy logs around the crackling fireplace, warming blue hands in the Scotts' hospitable cabin.

"Pa said we can get together to talk in his store's back room from now on. But today, we have a party." Delilah's dark eyes sparkled. "After all, it soon will be Christmas."

"You saved our lives." Charlie made a gentlemanly bow. Zechariah, Delilah's new, very large beau, hovered nearby. Keturah noticed Charlie did not kiss Delilah's hand.

Henry nodded his thanks and drew closer to the fire. Thin as a lathe, he froze outdoors. Sometimes he coughed, worrying Keturah.

Delilah and her mother handed out hot cider and sweet buns. They all sang to Zechariah's fiddle and played Blindman's Buff and Who's Got the Thimble?

"No fair!" Keturah laughed when Charlie cornered her the fourth time. "Thee always finds me."

"'Tis true." Delilah stared at Charlie's blindfold, but with her mother's warning glance, she began gathering mugs.

Henry, who had been laughing like a boy, grew quiet.

Keturah sighed. Henry said less and less. Although Charlie's face and gallantry thrilled her, she missed talking with Henry about God, about poetry, about everything. Perhaps when she gave him her Christmas gift, he would entrust her with his smile again and feel freer to share his mind.

Too soon it was time to go. As usual Caleb and Priscilla wandered off while they waited outside the store for Papa.

Keturah handed each brother two small brown packages she had decorated with yew sprigs and their red berries. "Merry Christmas."

Henry's face lit up as he unwrapped the stockings she'd knitted. Although her sampler was progressing, the red shawl had performed no miracle to improve her poor attempts at other housewifely arts. At least the baggy stockings would keep his toes warm.

"Thank you, Keturah."

That measured, golden look. Henry could not begin to equal Charlie's charm, but his gaze, unchanged since the day he rescued her from the river, washed over her, warm as July.

"I will treasure them forever." Charlie kissed her hand, but he looked and sounded impatient.

She cringed as they opened their second packages. What had possessed her to experiment? "I tried a new honey cookie recipe—"

Henry munched a gluey "treat" with a determined smile. "Very, er, sweet." His words sounded muffled.

"I will cherish them." Charlie carefully re-wrapped the cookies. "But now, dear Keturah, I have a gift for you."

He opened a blue velvet box. In the white satiny folds lay a gleaming silver locket, the likes of which she had never seen. Charlie pressed the locket open. Inside lay a curl of his shining black hair. His finger outlined her face with a feather-light touch that left a burning trail in its wake.

When she came to herself, Caleb was waving good-bye to Priscilla, and Papa was driving up. Her heart thumped loud as a churn, but she put the locket into her pocket and kept her face calm while Charlie helped her into the wagon.

Henry was nowhere to be seen.

Chapter 7

"Keturah, I would speak with thee."

She almost dropped her needle. Since childhood, Caleb had teased her. But today his serious tone matched his face as he stood in their cabin's doorway. She stuck the needle into her Christmas sampler and drew the red shawl around her. "Close the door before we catch our deaths."

He thumped it shut then faced her. "Does Charlie have thy heart?"

Heat rose in her cheeks. She fingered the sampler's corner. What business was it of his? If only Mama and Papa had not gone visiting.

His blue eyes probed hers.

She tried to laugh. "Surely thee knows I would make no promise to him. He has not yet spoken to Papa about courting me—"

"Nor is he likely to." Caleb sat opposite her in Papa's big chair and scanned her face with a keen, very un-Caleb look. "I fear an unworthy man has stolen thy heart."

She glared. "Does thee judge a man by his cabin and livestock and money? Papa never taught us so."

"I do not." Caleb paused. "I did not when Henry pursued thee."

She looked down at her hands. "Thee art mistaken. Henry desired only my friendship." Apparently no longer.

How she missed his odd but refreshing wisdom and slow, rich smile. He even missed Meeting two weeks straight—though Charlie now attended on First Day! She smiled, hopeful he would come to love God as she did.

Still, Caleb's stare disturbed her. "Thee is an intelligent woman, Keturah, with much learning. But thee knows little of men."

She did not know which bewildered her more, the compliment or the insult. But she would not swallow this outrage. "Certainly thee is an authority on women—"

"I am not. Or I would have persuaded Priscilla's mother to let me marry her." His head dropped.

Despite herself, sympathy softened her armor. "Perhaps thee would have been wise to avoid falling in love with an only child."

His eyes shot blue sparks. "Thee talks of wisdom! Surely thee knows Charlie's attendance at Meeting is only to win thee. He cares nothing for God or His ways."

"Like God, thee can read his heart?" She crossed her arms.

"I do not need to. Charlie is often mentioned as a thief. Some even link him to the vile happenings at Ford's Ferry and Potts' Inn."

Fury spurted through her veins. "Dare thee speak of whisperings with no evidence—"

"Thy locket is evidence enough." His face hardened. "How would a poor boatman come upon an expensive trinket?"

Tears boiled from her eyes. "It belonged to his mother. She wanted him to give it to the one he loves most."

"Mayhap, Charlie took it from her. Or she herself stole it." Caleb tried to capture her gaze. "Keturah, open thy eyes. Some say Charlie's father and grandfather were pirates who preyed on innocent folk."

She sprang from her rocker. She crossed the room and turned away. Silence, like an enormous ax, fell between her and Caleb, broken only by the fire's mutterings.

Finally she spoke. "Charlie's family has long lived in darkness. So the Light of Christ cannot dwell in him. Thee believes this?"

"Thee knows I do not. Henry lived with the same evils, yet spoke to Papa of convincement until—"

"Until Charlie came to Meeting, too." She whirled around and glared at him.

"Until thee made a fool of thyself over Charlie. Can thee not see?" Caleb's words exploded like live coals in a barrel of gunpowder.

"So I have neglected to use my influence on Henry, yet should not do so with Charlie." She lifted the latch and slammed the door behind her, clutching her red shawl like a best friend as she ran for the washhouse.

Henry held his breath, motionless in the thicket. Early evening darkness cloaked Ford's Ferry Road, the only road to Potts' Inn. The few remaining leaves hanging from overhead branches gave their death rattle. He'd heard nothing more. So far.

For a moment Henry wished he'd brought whiskey. But a jugful did him no good after he lost Keturah. It would do him no good tonight. Charlie's life might depend on his keeping a clear head.

Charlie deserves what he gets.

True, but ever since Ma told him she'd overheard Charlie's plans to ride Ford's Ferry Road, he'd stuffed his mind's whisper into a bag and tried to drown it.

Ma taught her sons to be thieves. But she didn't want them to be murderers. If Charlie "guided" travelers from Ford's Ferry to their deaths at Potts' Inn, he might as well wear a noose around his neck. Ma had heard that the brash new constable planned to raid the inn.

Charlie had stayed away from home—wisely—after giving Keturah that locket. Yet now Henry was trying to save his neck. Charlie, who stole people, just as he stole valuables. Charlie, who stole Keturah.

He deserves what he gets.

Let Charlie destroy himself. It would be so easy to go home to his warm loft. No more of Charlie's lies. No more taunts.

You'd have Keturah to yourself.

A vision of her gleaming hair glowed in the shadows like a thousand candles; her warm, laughing face and lips so close, she lit his. A rush of heat ran down him. Keturah might be his—if he let Charlie reap what he had sown, as he had read in the Bible.

A tiny star gleamed through the clouds above the road, capturing Henry's eye and sending it heavenward. Then the star fell, its showy path snuffed out in a moment. His inner flames died with it, leaving him dark and empty as the night. But another faint star escaped the murky clouds, refusing to be devoured. To his surprise, the yearning for God bubbled up inside him. The Quiet answered it, filling him till he thought he would explode from joy and anguish. Why would God want anything to do with him? Didn't He know about his drinking and returning to the old ways—about the hatred inside him, the rage at Charlie that could make him a murderer, too?

What do I do? He almost cried aloud. *Do I warn Charlie? Do I go home?*

A baby's soft cry nearly made him jump out of his moccasins. Down the road, Henry spied two horse-sized shadows and recognized his brother's stealthy gait. Horror clogged Henry's throat. Children as well as adults disappeared upon entering the inn's welcoming, deadly door. And Charlie was leading a family there.

Potts would never let a constable take him alive. Would these innocent people survive a gun battle? He heard another child's voice.

Henry whistled the redbird's call he and his brother had, since childhood, used to indicate danger.

He saw Charlie lift his head then raise his rifle. Henry stuck a leg out of the thicket and shuffled his moccasin through dead leaves. If Charlie was drunk and trigger-happy, he'd rather take it in the leg than the chest.

"What's this, Henry?"

He sounded annoyed but stone sober. Maybe Potts or Ford had threatened him to stay away from drink. A tall figure rode the horse behind Charlie, even taller because he wore a stovepipe hat. Henry addressed the man. "Sorry to bring you bad news, sir, but Mr. Potts sent me to tell you the inn is full."

A young woman's voice wailed from the other horse. "But Mr. Ford said the inn would accommodate us!"

"Are you sure?" The man spoke loudly because the baby now screamed at the top of its lungs. "The children are in need of shelter."

Sending up frantic silent prayers, Henry kept his voice calm. "It would be unwise to travel eight more miles, only to be turned away."

Finally Charlie spoke. "Perhaps a family in Rock and Cave will take you in."

Charlie understood! Giving thanks, Henry held his breath. Would the man believe him?

"If that is our only choice." The woman almost moaned.

The man swore at his horse as he turned him. "Take us there."

"We will do our best to find lodgings," Henry promised.

"You mean *you* will," Charlie hissed in his ear.

Henry nodded and pressed his thumb hard into Charlie's arm. Another signal he should lie low. Charlie slipped to the side of the road.

"Are you not going with us?" Anger filled the man's voice. "What about the money I paid? And why should we trust him?"

"He is my brother. You can trust him," Charlie said.

If things weren't so desperate, Henry might have laughed. Instead he said, "I will guide you to the village free of charge."

The man gave a grudging assent, and Charlie disappeared into the underbrush.

Henry clasped the woman's bridle and began the slow, dark journey through the forest to Rock and Cave. Where would he ask? He dare not take them to those he knew, to be stripped of their belongings like a Christmas goose of its feathers.

If only the Wilkeses lived in this direction. Memories of Delilah's large cabin prodded his mind. If the Scotts could not help, he would check with Priscilla's family. He did not know them except for Meeting, but he could not imagine Quakers leaving a mother and children out in the winter darkness.

He wiggled stiff fingers. His weary legs felt like logs. As he led the horses back to Rock and Cave, the faint star brightened, reminding him of the Christmas story. How had Joseph felt, guiding a woman about to give birth along a dark, dangerous road? Keturah also showed him the terrible story of King Herod's attempts to kill Baby Jesus. Tonight, as Henry guided the angry man and sniffling family to Rock and Cave, he prayed God would send angels to protect them all—and his scheming, conscienceless brother.

❄

"Mama?" Keturah, amazed as if the skeletal trees had budded green, stared at the stout figure walking toward Papa's wagon. "Is she going with us to town?"

Papa flicked the reins. He did not look at Keturah. "She has not seen her friends for many months."

A small circle of dismay spun in Keturah's middle. "But

she hates the river—"

"Thy mama has been known to change her mind." Papa turned to meet his wife.

Mama knew the only way to make beds. To braid Keturah's hair. To stir soup. When had she changed her mind about anything?

Mama's black Meeting dress rustled as Papa helped her up beside Keturah. She cast a glance back at Caleb. He looked away.

What had transpired? Whatever it was, she liked it less and less.

Her mood did not lighten when they pulled up to Scott's store. Henry had absented himself from the group again. But Charlie's smile sent a thrill through her as if she had touched lightning.

Until Mama followed them into the store. Thankfully, she remained out front while Keturah, Charlie, and the others found seats in the back room. Oblivious to naught but each other, her friends murmured and giggled.

Charlie kissed her hand. "My love, I have waited all week—"

"Thank you, Friend Scott," Mama's words boomed like cannon shots. "I would like two bags of flour."

Keturah tried to ignore the conversation. "I wear thy locket close to my heart—"

"Thy hog butchering went well?" Mama continued. "I declare, we didn't get half enough liver or sweetbreads—"

Keturah almost gagged. Mama knew full well she despised both. Mama chattered on with the storekeeper, then with his wife, until tears of fury blinded Keturah. Were not she and Charlie adults? Had they not remained with the group as was proper? If only they could spend time alone— or at least without an accompanying hog-killing dialogue. She might even talk with him about God, as she did with Henry. A flash of brilliance lit her despair. She addressed Priscilla.

"We do not know when we will see the sun again. Why not walk by the river?"

Caleb's taut mouth told Keturah he knew exactly what she was doing. But Priscilla, delighted, pulled him to his feet. Delilah told her father where they were going. Once they left the store, the group would slowly, quietly separate into couples.

Mama, tying her bonnet, met them at the store's door. "Wonderful idea."

No. No. She wouldn't—

"We do not know when we shall see the sun again, do we?" Mama almost marched them toward the river, her steps firm and unswerving.

"Exactly what Keturah said," Zechariah said innocently.

Caleb grinned.

Even the brisk breeze could not cool Keturah's burning cheeks. Charlie wore a pained smile. Mama stuck to them until they returned to the store. While the group drank sassafras tea, she babbled on and on to anyone who would listen.

"Can I meet you alone?" Charlie whispered.

"I do not know!" Keturah gritted her teeth. She felt like a chastened, naughty child.

"At your house?" His warm breath caressed her cheek.

"Tomorrow, when my parents visit friends. But Caleb will be home." She thought quickly. "No one will be working in the washhouse on First Day."

"I will meet you there." He lowered his voice to a husky plea. "Do not disappoint me, my love."

Chapter 8

Henry glanced at Charlie, sitting next to him during Meeting, feigning attentiveness to the speakers. Did his brother hear even one word about the goodness of Christ? Henry, back at Meeting for the first time in weeks, listened. Despite his pain at seeing Keturah and the insanity of Charlie's presence there, he practically wallowed in the warmth of the Light of Christ. Never again would he allow anyone or anything to separate him from God.

Afterward the Friends did not quiz him on his absence or ask what brought him back. Instead they welcomed him with smiles that made him feel as if they really were his friends. Friend Wilkes rested his big hand on his shoulder, eyes filled with gladness. "Would thee read a pamphlet on God's charity toward us?"

"I would." Henry could hardly wait to explore its depths.

Friend Wilkes's delight faded as he greeted Charlie. Other Friends spoke kindly to his brother, who was on his best behavior. But for the first time Henry could remember, Charlie did not overwhelm a group with his charm. Although the Friends did not know Charlie, they knew him.

"Thee has returned."

He had not noticed Keturah's approach. *God, do not let me falter.*

Her dazzling smile was genuine, but her brilliant eyes, ever forthright, did not meet his. They drifted with only glances at Charlie instead of the usual adoring gaze. Henry's breath quickened. Did she know the truth about his brother?

But the glances shared between them were still potent. The faint flutter of hope Henry harbored dissolved. Only a fool would not sense their attraction. But Keturah seemed uneasy. And her cold hand, extended in fellowship, clung to his shocked fingers an extra moment. "I am thankful to see thee."

Charlie edged her away. Henry felt almost grateful. He could hardly bear her troubled glance. Then a torrent of fear swept him away.

He had protected travelers on Ford's Ferry Road from Ford, from Potts, and from Charlie. What had he done to protect Keturah?

❅

She shivered despite the red shawl. Mama and Papa had left an hour ago. Caleb snored in the cabin by the fire. Surely Charlie would come soon.

The washhouse's rickety door opened. Charlie, sporting a dashing black cloak, clasped her cold hand to his warm lips. Could any girl wish for a more handsome beau?

"Ah, a smile." He tapped her lips with his finger. "Now you look like my Keturah, the most beautiful girl in Illinois. No, the most beautiful girl in the world!"

"Flatterer." But her pulse soared at his words, his touch.

"I only speak the truth." He drew her to him.

How she yearned to melt into his arms. But she could not dissolve the unease she felt at deceiving Mama and Papa. Even Caleb with his self-righteous sermonizing.

Not that she had lied about Charlie's visit. She simply had not mentioned it—

"The smile disappears again?" Charlie gently turned her chin up.

His luminous black eyes nearly undid her. But she needed to talk. "I—I do not like to mislead my parents." There. She finally said the words that pestered her like cawing crows.

"Nor do I." Charlie drew back. "But your ma would smother our love. And though I come to Meeting, I fear your pa does not accept me."

Indignation spurted through her. Why did they not believe a man could change? Surely the Light of Christ could accomplish all things.

"I understand their doubts, my love." Charlie looked at her gravely. "I have done many things I am not proud of."

"As have we all."

He patted her cheek. "But as time passes, God will help them understand."

She hugged him fiercely. He drew her eager lips to his in a long, tender kiss. Her heart stopped. Would the wonder of his kiss steal her very life? If it did, oh, dying was worth it.

Minutes passed by with Keturah in a happy daze. How amazing to laugh, talk, and hold Charlie, as a woman—without a parent's critical eye, Caleb's sermons, and the Friends' scrutiny. At the thought, her celebration dimmed a little.

"You need my help to smile again."

Charlie knew her feelings. She loved that about him.

"Next week we will talk about your special Christmas

gift." He touched her hair.

"But thee already gave me my locket." She gently pulled it from beneath her dress's high neckline.

"But this is something you have wanted a long time." Charlie's eyes shone. "A steamboat ride!"

She felt her jaw drop. "How? When?"

He laughed until she cautioned him to take care. "I will tell you next First Day when we meet here again. But say nothing. It will be our secret."

Still stunned, she pressed her cheek against his broad chest. "Charlie, my first Christmas with thee will be the best ever."

Henry watched from the underbrush at the village's edge. Was Keturah's mother trying to avoid Charlie? She and her daughter entered Scott's store alone, well ahead of their usual time.

He breathed a prayer of thanksgiving. He had had no idea how he would talk privately with Keturah. Now there was a chance—if God indeed was guiding his steps. *Lord, give me the right words.*

He pushed through the store's door before he talked himself out of it. Keturah looked like a storm cloud. But he dared not risk losing this opportunity. "Friend Wilkes, may I speak with Keturah? Alone? It will not be long."

Keturah's eyebrows shot up. Her mother's eyes scoured him. But she gave a slow nod. Henry hustled Keturah back by the shovels and hoes.

"Henry, what would thee say to me?" Keturah's eyes

shifted behind her as though she were listening for her mother. Or Charlie?

Keturah's sweet, puzzled question nearly destroyed his resolve. Had she truly no idea of the warning he must give? "I would not upset you, Keturah. But I have prayed much about this. I can no longer keep quiet."

She paused. "Say on."

He stumbled on his words. "Charlie may have made you promises, but he's made them to many women."

Silence. Then, "He himself has told me of his past."

"But I do not speak of his past. I speak of now." Henry fought to keep his voice under control. "Charlie comes to Meeting. But he lives a true devil of a life. He knows nothing of the Light of Christ."

He thought his words would shrivel her. Instead she gave him a piercing, sorrowful look that bled his heart. "Thee, Charlie's own brother, would join in the attack on him? I thought better of thee, Henry." Her snow-white front teeth bit down on her red lip.

"Do not think better of me." There. He finally said what he dreaded to tell her. "Although I hurt no one, I was his partner in theft. The Bible I now read I stole from a circuit rider." He hung his head. "But God's Light has changed me."

"Blessed be God's Light." Her voice softened.

To his amazement, she clasped his hand. "I would that we be good friends, Henry. I miss thee."

Paralyzed, he did not know what to say. What to do.

"I can only hope thee will see how God is changing Charlie as well."

With that she swept back to her mother, her head high—like a graceful, lovely doe with no inkling of the hunter who waited in the shadows, sharp arrows in hand.

❄

Why had Charlie wanted to ride the steamship at night?

Keturah knew the answer. Her parents, who now dogged her every move, would never consent, even if in broad daylight. An invitation to accompany her and Charlie would be rejected. Their stubborn refusal to open their hearts to him angered her. Still, creeping out of bed with the mantel clock's eleventh chime—two hours after the family retired—awakened niggling doubts. Waiting in the washhouse without a lit candle gave her the shivers. She snuggled into the red shawl, glad the night felt more like fall than almost Christmas.

The door gave a welcome creak. "Are you ready, my love?"

Relief swathed her like the shawl. She'd known Charlie would come. Her family—and Henry—would one day understand. She took his hand and stepped into the silvery world. The moon's friendly face smiled down on them as they slipped through the trees to Charlie's horse, tied a few hundred yards away.

His hands lifted her high to the saddle. Breathless, she felt as if she had grown wings. He vaulted to a place behind her, his brawny arms surrounding her. What would it be like with Charlie in her life every day, every moment?

Riding through the silent fairy-tale woods with him was better than any Christmas gift she could imagine. As they neared Rock and Cave, she realized they were not mounted on the old brown nag she'd seen Charlie ride, but on a spirited black stallion. "When did thee buy a new horse? Or did thee borrow one?"

He gave an odd chuckle. "I borrowed it. But I will own a new one before long. Maybe two. Or three."

As if to celebrate, he pulled her to him and kissed her, hard and quick.

Her heartbeat sped up, but his kiss, which often left a spicy fragrance of horehound or sassafras, tasted as if he had consumed turpentine. "What on earth did thee drink?"

He gripped her shoulder. "How will I surprise you if you ask all these questions?"

What more could he do to make this night complete? "Thee already told me the Christmas surprise—the steamboat ride."

His white teeth flashed in the moonlight. "You misjudge me, my love." He pulled her face to his again. "You have no idea what wonderful plans I've made."

Chapter 9

Charlie had not mentioned walking to the big cave. Remembering Papa's refusal to take her as a child, she savored an additional moment of triumph. Along with riding the steamboat, she would visit the cave. Still its giant stony mouth, facing the river's broad silver black water, gaped as if she were a choice victual.

Behind her Charlie gave a chittery birdcall. Startled, Keturah halted. Charlie nearly fell over her and swore. She turned to him, grieved he would use such language on their special night.

"You're not afraid, are you?" In his gentle tone, she heard a note of derision. "It's not that dark inside the cave. They've built a fire to keep you warm."

"They?" She frowned.

He took her arm. "Friends I invited to share the steamboat ride."

She found herself swallowed by gloom, her feet swishing and stumbling through stinking dead leaves in a surprisingly large passageway. A team of horses could drive through here.

A glower of firelight pocked aged limestone walls scabbed by fungi. In the semidarkness, her ankle scraped against sharp rocks protruding from the cave floor. She stopped again. "Do I know thy friends?"

He almost pushed her forward. "More questions." He clicked his tongue, almost like Mama. "How disappointing. I thought you liked adventures."

Stung, she raised her chin. "If thee likens adventures to filthy caves, then no, I do not."

He laughed. "Now that's my Keturah. Full of fire."

Without warning, he swung her into his arms and whirled her into a large circular cavern as if they had entered a ballroom. She tingled at his embrace, but the echo of savage laughter, blended with Charlie's, pierced her.

Dusky light of the tiny campfire's coals carved three men into ogres. Shining eyes, reflecting its glow, burned her cheeks. The turpentine odor she smelled on Charlie's lips reeked from every nook. Whiskey. It had to be. She did not know what wretched trick Charlie was playing, but this had gone far enough. She turned to him and said in a low voice, "Please take me home."

"I would not think of it." His beautifully shaped lips met in a little-boy pout. "I promised you a steamboat ride. And I always keep my promises."

The men laughed again. So did Charlie. He poured whiskey from a jug into a gourd and turned to her. "Never too early for a Christmas toast. Drink to our health and happiness."

When she said nothing, he downed it in one gulp. She fought panic that soured her throat like bile. He swilled another.

"We better git movin'." One man slid a knife into a sheath hanging from his belt.

She thought she could not feel more frightened—until Charlie pulled an even larger blade from a poke lying on the cave floor. She could not breathe.

"True." He held the weapon up, smiling as red light glinted on the metal. "We will meet our steamship soon. You and Ned go ahead."

As the men left, Charlie turned and gestured carelessly at the shortest man. "Stay with him till I return."

Sudden fury poured from her. "If I choose not to?"

"You disappoint me again, my love." He sheathed his knife and reached for her cheek, his dark eyes molten.

When she shrank away, he yanked her to him, stripping her shawl from her shoulders, forcing his lips on hers.

Fight him. Scream. Someone must hear—

The other man chuckled. "Got a lively one, Charlie."

She bowed in pain, Charlie's iron hands jamming her wrists together behind her back. The short man bound them with rough rope and then tied her feet together and stuffed a greasy bandanna into her mouth. She choked, trying not to vomit.

"Why must you be so difficult?" Charlie chucked her on the chin. "I was hoping you would see the light."

She shuddered with outrage. How dare he use a sacred phrase?

Charlie laughed, threw her over his shoulder and then dumped her into the darkness of a small side chamber. He kissed his fingers to her. "Farewell, love. I will see *thee* soon."

She lay bruised on the muddy floor, her stomach roiling.

"If you touch her, I'll cut your hands off." Charlie's deadly voice floated from the "ballroom" to her prison.

"Ye know I wouldn't," the man protested.

"Good." Charlie must have slapped his back. "Plenty of women when we land in New Orleans." He laughed again. "Plenty for all of us."

Chapter 10

Had she dozed a few minutes? A few hours? Did it matter?

She saw weeping shadows on the cave's ceiling and walls. Pointed rocks wounded her ribs, her shoulder. Gravel was embedded in her right cheek. She commanded her muscles to move so her pain would lessen. Helpless, they could not obey.

Would Charlie kill her before they left Rock and Cave?

His face was a cat's. She was his prey. How long would he toy with her? Would she live to celebrate Christmas Day? If so, what a merry time it would be. Keturah wept with the shadows. What a blind fool she had been.

God, I thought I knew Thy Light. Yet I did not listen to those Thee sent.

Mama. Papa. Even Caleb. The horrible gag muffled her yearning to a tiny moan. Was it only hours ago she'd sat by their fire, plotting wrong as Papa read the Bible?

Henry. His honest eyes as he tried to warn her. Her hot tears added to the dampness of the evil-smelling floor. Henry was a man of true faith and love. She chose what was false.

The chittering call again. Footsteps. Charlie.

God, forgive me, though I do not deserve it. Save me—if not in this life, in the next.

"Henry!" Her captor's voice sounded pleased. "You goin' with us to New Orleans?"

Henry? Gladness shot through her. Henry would help. He would rescue—

"Sure am. Told Charlie he can't have all the fun."

Henry's voice. But—but he talked like Charlie. *Oh, God.*

"Good. I was afraid you got religion. Though Charlie said you saved his hide when that new constable caught wind of Ford's plans." The man chuckled knowingly. "Mebbe your brother'll thank you by sharing that pretty Quaker back there that's goin' with us."

"Maybe." Henry sounded as if they were speaking of hand-me-down horses. "She's a looker, but..."

She almost felt his shrug.

"In New Orleans, there'll be plenty of women to go round," the pirate finished.

Had it all been a ruse? Henry's supposed faith to impress her parents? His "warning" an effort to steal her from Charlie? She writhed, the rope's roughness skinning her limbs.

Henry, a pirate, too? *God, I cannot bear it.*

She heard the gurgle of whiskey pouring again. Her imagination already had painted ugly portraits of what she would suffer with Charlie. But Henry...

Numb, her mind and body turned to stone. Words, laughter. She heard but understood nothing. Deep inside, she pleaded with God to die, to sink into the cave's floor and become part of it forever.

A thump opened her eyes. Henry's tall silhouette held a knife. But instead of cold steel at her throat, ropes loosened. He set her, as if she were a doll, on her feet and wrapped her shawl around her. "I know you feel faint," he whispered. "But we must run. Now."

She moved her foot an inch. Two. Joy cascaded over her like a waterfall as he half-guided, half-carried her past the sprawled-out man.

"Smacked him with the whiskey jug," Henry answered her look.

Out, out, they hurried, into the blessed, clean December air. The glimmering wide ribbon of the river wrapped the night like a gift.

Henry lifted her off her feet and plunged into the thickest woods. She clung to him, ducking branches, feeling his long limbs eat up ground. Suddenly, he skidded to a stop. "Keturah, I mean no disrespect. But I can run faster if I carry you over my shoulder."

The polite request almost broke her. She nodded, and he hoisted her carefully over his shoulder and ran like the wind through the night. A bumpy ride. She would be sore tomorrow as if she had ridden a pony in the Christmas race. But thanks to him, she dared hope she would see another day.

Henry wound his way among bare-branched thickets, behind scraggly junipers, to a limestone cliff's wall. He slid Keturah from his shoulder. "Thank God, it's like an October night, rather than December. We'll hide here. In my prayer cave."

That she hung back did not surprise him. "I'll go in first."

He knelt and slipped through the narrow opening. A few bats flapped past him. He listened. Knife raised and shoulders hunched, he wound a path into the empty narrow room with moonlight leaking through the small opening in the top. It had never looked more beautiful. He returned to Keturah and coaxd her inside. He took his blanket from its oilskin packet and wrapped it around her. "Sorry. No food here. It would draw critters."

She stared past him, fascinated by the silvery lamp lit for them.

"Why, it shines like the Christmas star." Childlike, she stepped into its glory.

The star he'd seen the night he rescued Charlie had sent his mind heavenward as well. He longed to share a thousand treasures he'd crammed into his heart, but he gently pulled her back into the gray shadows. "We must keep quiet. We'll talk tomorrow. Tonight, I promise I will protect you. And I keep my promises."

Her eyes widened with new terror, and she shuddered uncontrollably.

What had he said? How could he take away her fear? He ached to hold her. But after her ordeal, she might scream, revealing their hiding place, or run away, an easy target for Charlie and his gang. In desperation Henry dropped the mask he'd worn all his life, putting every feeling he harbored for her on display. He prayed aloud. "God, please protect us. Help Keturah not to be afraid."

Slowly, she took his hand. "God keeps His promises, Henry." Her face mirrored the light. "I know thee will, too."

❄

She felt as if she had been beaten with a log. When one big hand shook her shoulder, she choked.

"Keturah. It's me."

Henry?

Her eyes opened to dim gray light. She leaned against hard, damp stone walls. A cave. She was in a cave. Spasms of panic shook her.

"There, there. You're safe." His long arm encircled her shoulders, and she remembered how they had agreed to share the blanket. The last thing she recalled was Henry sitting erect, his eyes like a hawk's, watching.

She clung to him. He touched her cheek. "Sorry I had to wake you so early. Surely Charlie wanted to hunt us down. But after stealing a steamship, the constable, not to mention James Ford, will chase after them. Ford doesn't like small potatoes like Charlie homing in on his territory."

She tried not to enjoy the picture of Charlie afraid, running for his life. Charlie captured and given what he deserved. Her head bowed. Not that she had been given what she deserved.

Henry went on, "If we go to the constable's now, perhaps we can take you home before your parents worry to find you gone."

Papa. Mama. She tried to scramble to her feet. She so hungered to see them. But how would she face them?

"I'll help you explain, if you want." Rising, Henry steadied her.

He risked his life to save her from her own folly. Now he offered to help her. "Henry, I do not know how thee came to rescue me—"

"When Charlie joined in James Ford's evil doings, I feared for you and for him. I followed him on his night

253

prowlings and saw him take you into the cave."

How she wished she could disappear. Instead she took his hands and forced herself to look him in the eye. "I have a world of apologies to make to thee, but we must go. I will begin, however, by offering my thanks."

He said nothing. But his tired face shone with such kindness. Last night she thought she would never kiss a man again. Today, how he drew her, but would he ever think of her in the same way? Tears dribbled down her cheeks. Weak and wounded, how could she make it through this day? Yet she must. Gently dropping his hands, she tried to brush dirt from her shawl and First Day dress, now in rags.

"Come, there will be time later to primp." For the first time, his voice held a note of amusement.

She stopped. "Thou art right. We must leave."

He hesitated. "Shall I carry you again?"

The thought brought a blush to her cheeks. "If I cannot keep up. But I will try."

"Perhaps we should pray?"

"Certainly. God has been so good to me." She took Henry's hand again. "If I needed God's help last night, I surely need Him today as I go home."

He squeezed her fingers. They bowed their heads in silence. *Lord Jesus, Giver of undeserved mercy, I thank Thee for Thy protection of Henry and me. Please guide our hearts and words today.*

❄

"Mama! Papa!" God's timing, certainly. She dashed toward her parents, who had just pulled up to the constable's small cabin, their faces old and shriveled in the early morning grayness.

"Keturah!" Papa vaulted from the wagon and ran toward her, her stout mother not far behind. They devoured her in their arms, her mother weeping as if she could not stop. "We thought thee would never come home. We thought thee was dead."

Mama cupped her dirty, wounded face with trembling fingers. "Child, what happened to thee? What happened to my Keturah?"

"I am so, so sorry." She cried tears and tears. How freeing to sorrow for the ignorance, the willfulness, the sheer stupidity of her actions.

"What goes on here?" The stocky constable, still wearing his nightcap, stuck his head out the cabin door. He glared at Henry, looking awkward and filthy, who said nothing. "What is the meaning of this?"

Sudden silence. Keturah felt the muscles in Papa's arms tighten like wire. He spoke very slowly as if digging the words out of hard places. "Henry, what is this about?"

She broke loose from him and ran to Henry, then turned to her parents and the constable. "I tell thee truly, if Henry had not risked his life, I would not stand before thee alive." Her voice broke. She hugged Henry fiercely and then faced them. "Will thee hear our story?"

The constable's wife poked her head out. "Come in and get warm. He'll dress directly and then speak with you." She pulled her husband inside as if he were six.

Still distraught, Keturah hid a tiny grin. So like Papa

and Mama. Her eyes returned to her parents. How she loved them. How she wished she had spared them such hurt. Would they forgive her?

They rushed to embrace her again. "Thee art our daughter, now and always," Papa said. He turned to Henry, his face working. "And if thee, young man, has indeed protected my child, I shall forever be in thy debt."

"We are Friends." For a moment Henry's calm faltered, and his eyes glistened.

What a world of meaning he put into few words. Keturah felt so proud of him and so ashamed of herself, she could not speak. But when he offered her his arm, she clung to him and followed Mama and Papa into the constable's home.

Chapter 11

Mama's First Day table outshone any Keturah could remember. Surely heroes did not die from gratitude, but if Mama had her way, urging seconds and thirds, Henry might be the first. She marveled he had room for both berry and apple pie.

Mama probably had not noticed today was Christmas. But Keturah, for the hundredth time since waking, gave silent thanks for life and for Immanuel, God with her always. Even in the cave.

Papa vigorously stirred honey into his hot cider in an attempt to hide his emotion. "Thee is such a blessing, Henry."

"And you have blessed me."

Keturah had not seen Henry's face glow like this in many days. Perhaps because Papa had told him at Meeting he would support his convincement. Perhaps because, though the ugly details of Keturah's ordeal were known only to weighty Friends, all quietly showed their appreciation for Henry's character and actions.

She found it harder to glow. True, everyday blessings, such as waking in her feather bed and hearing the *plop-plop* of Mama kneading bread, filled her with joy. Still, shame clouded her days. She had confessed her sins to God and to Friends, yet her past foolishness weighed her down. Going to Meeting took more courage than she possessed. Papa's gentle urging and Mama's inviting Henry to First Day dinner helped. But now dinner was done, and she almost hoped Henry would leave.

Instead he lingered, talking with Papa and Caleb by the fire while she and Mama cleared up. Reluctantly she sat in the rocker. Knitting, though it continued to try her patience, busied her hands and eyes.

"Friend Wilkes, may I speak with Keturah?"

Startled, she rocked on her foot.

"You may." Papa rose.

Mama stuck her needles into the ball of yarn as if this were normal. She followed Papa toward their room. "We would rest a little and read."

Caleb jauntily adjourned to saddle his horse. Priscilla's mother finally had consented to a weekly visit.

How Keturah would have treasured this moment, if only—

"Merry Christmas." Henry handed her two brown-papered packages from his poke and sat in Mama's chair beside her.

She did not know what to say. She did not know where to look. So she opened the first.

A Bible. A beautiful Bible that had cost him many, many hours of labor. Perhaps even many meals.

"Oh, Henry." She ran her finger along its fine leather cover.

"I did not even steal this one."

She had never seen him look mischievous. Laughing and crying, she tried to thank him.

"It is I who thank thee." Henry's use of the word seemed

natural. "I was drowning in darkness, trying to escape the thievery that came so naturally. If I had not met thee, would I have learned of the Light of Christ?"

She had not thought of it that way. "But I was such a terrible example—"

"Perhaps. And I would have preferred thee had not near-drowned me in the river."

She giggled, but her mirth faded quickly. "I failed thee. I—I failed Charlie." She covered her face with her hands.

"Thee believed his lying heart." She felt Henry's long fingers gently pulling her hands away, his face only inches from hers. "I failed Charlie as well. If I had shared the Light instead of hating him for taking you away from me, he might not be running for his life. Sooner or later, I must try to find him." His sad face brightened. "But does not Christ light our darkness and take away our sin—all of it?"

She felt as if a summer sun bloomed inside. "I have another Christmas gift for thee."

She pulled it from her knitting basket and held it in front of his startled eyes. Carefully, he undid the blue hair ribbon binding the brown package. He held the Christmas sampler she had stitched and framed, reading aloud: "Therefore if any man be in Christ, he is a new creature: old things are passed away; behold, all things are become new."

He said nothing.

She winced. Her blind side had shown itself once more. While Henry might appreciate the Bible verse, what man wanted frippery with red roses?

Wait. Did his eyes look moist?

"How could thee have known? I—I read this verse the first time just before I began to attend Meeting, and I've read it many times since. In a way, I understood as I learned more about the Inner Light. But not as I do now."

She nodded. "Sewing it, I believe, was Christ's gift to me as well."

"No better Christmas gift on earth." Henry clasped her hand.

Sitting beside him near the fire's cozy warmth, speaking of God's goodness—Keturah wanted to savor the moment forever.

Henry picked up his other gift. "This is nothing profound. But I thought thee might like it."

"I'm sure I will." Was it a picture? No, a poem printed on heavy paper with a scrolled border, called "A Visit from St. Nicholas."

"It's a children's Christmas poem." Henry looked a little shy. "I bought it from a peddler from the East."

She had never read anything like it—St. Nicholas, Christmas stockings, gifts, and reindeer. If the scripture made her feel brand-new, the story gave her the joy of a child! "Henry, it is a wonderful gift."

The look he gave her made her heart flutter. After all she'd put him through, could he still think of her as—as—

"I've heard flowers on ladies' samplers are symbolic." He ran his fingers over her imperfect embroidery. "What do roses stand for?"

"Love, usually." Quickly she added, "I wanted roses to remind those who view it of Christ's love."

"How wonderful." He touched her chin and gently turned her face to look at him. His golden-hazel eyes held hers as they had the moment he brought her up from the river. "Could they also stand for the love of Christ between a man and a woman?"

Her lips fumbled her breath. She finally squeaked out, "They could."

His lips rested oh so lightly on hers only a moment. "Perhaps, over time, they will."

Epilogue

December 24, 1826

Keturah donned her First Day bonnet and smoothed the silvery-gray silk dress Papa had insisted on providing. Mama justified the extravagance by pointing out that every married woman needed a nice dress for occasions of note throughout her life.

As they waited for Papa's wagon, however, her mother did not speak of practicalities nor guard against vanity. "My Keturah, thou art lovely, inside and out. God bless thee."

Keturah hugged her, feeling Mama's tears.

"Goodness, I'll stain thy dress." Mama dabbed at Keturah's neckline with a handkerchief then at her eyes. She pulled a package from a cupboard. "I wanted to give this before thee leaves."

Keturah chuckled. "Mama, our cabin is almost next door." She opened the gift, and her knees nearly gave way.

"I knew this meant much to thee," Mama said.

Keturah's hands held the red shawl. She thought Mama had burned it. Instead she'd washed and mended it. Now Keturah's tears threatened the new silk dress.

"If thee wears the shawl today, I will say nothing." Mama set her lips with heroic determination.

Keturah giggled, then cried, then giggled again. "'Twould be a memorable wedding."

She hugged her mother tight. "I thank thee, Mama. I will wear it as Henry loves the color on me. But not to Meeting."

Mama breathed a visible sigh of relief and then climbed into the wagon. They sat close together as they rode to the meetinghouse.

Keturah felt a little shy as she entered. But how handsome Henry looked in his black suit, his thick black hair shining in the candlelight. Mama had fattened him up, but he remained long and lean. Keturah knew the strength of those arms.

He saw her. His face lit up the world.

How fitting that on the Eve of Christ's birth they would celebrate their new life as one.

She and Mama sat by Henry's mother. After Henry's fruitless search for Charlie in New Orleans, she began to seek God, though she rarely came to Meeting. Keturah patted her hand.

One Friend delivered a short sermon, but the Spirit moved few. No doubt He understood they had waited long for this day, praying, studying, and counseling with her parents and other Friends. Now at Papa's nod, she joined Henry before the platform.

"Friends, I take Keturah Wilkes to be my wife, promising through divine assistance to be unto her a loving and faithful husband until it shall please the Lord, by death, to separate us." Henry's voice rose, warm and sure.

Hers wobbled as she repeated her vows, but with everything in her, she meant them. A Friends' wedding did not include a kiss. But seeing a lifetime of embraces in Henry's

263

eyes, she figured she could wait.

❄

"I'm sure Henry here will keep a good hold on ya," Sol said.

Keturah smiled, remembering her first keelboat ride. Now Sol worked on this small steamboat. Not only had he arranged for their free ride together to McFarlan, but he had also helped Henry get a job on the vessel.

Meeting over, she reveled in the red shawl's warmth. She and Henry snuggled close as the boat chugged away from the dock, their families waving. Her first steamboat ride! How many dreams come true could one day hold?

Henry chuckled. "Thy Mama does not like this."

"But she likes thee." Keturah gave him a coy look. "I like thee, too. But no stealing kisses until we are out of sight."

He shook his head at her. "Thee knows I'm a pirate."

How healing that such pain could be altered into laughter. "Thee did pirate me away from the pirates."

They chuckled again, but Henry's mirth quieted into thoughtfulness. For a while they stood in silence, watching the glistening river flow before them like the future.

"What are thy thoughts?" She learned each time she asked.

His grin surprised her. "I was thinking how God stole me from under the devil's very nose—through the birth of a Baby."

"As He did me. And through thy love." She gave the awaited kiss, long and sweet. Henry did not have to steal it.

Light of the World, Thee spirited us away from darkness. Every Christmas we will celebrate Thy birth together, giving thanks to Thee, blessed Pirate of our hearts.

 Rachael Phillips is a freelance writer in Indiana. Married with three children, she has written four previous Heroes of the Faith books. Visit Rachael's website (www.rachaelwrites.com) and learn more about her and her upcoming projects!

EQUALLY YOKED

Claire Sanders

Dedication

To my daughter, Grace, who lives up to her name every day

*Be strong and of a good courage, fear not, nor be afraid of them:
for the LORD thy God, he it is that doth go with thee;
he will not fail thee, nor forsake thee.*

DEUTERONOMY 31:6

Chapter 1

Southern Ohio, 1838

Susanna Griffith closed her eyes and burrowed deeper into the quilts. For a few moments, she'd been a girl again, picking blackberries from the brambles in her father's southern pasture and eating one sweet berry for every handful she dropped into the bucket. The summer sun had warmed her back as she searched for the ripest berries, while the blossoms' fragrance enveloped her. Perhaps she'd lie down in the soft grass and watch the pristine clouds float against the azure sky. It was so pleasant to be a girl again, free from responsibilities—and loneliness. Then the jarring crow of the rooster had woken her.

Weak rays of sunlight crept through the cabin's single window, reminding Susanna that it wasn't July, but November. She reached across the bed for her husband.

Nathan wasn't there.

His pillow was as cold as a January frost, and their wedding quilt lay straight and unruffled on his side of the bed. The rooster bellowed another raucous greeting to the morning, and Susanna groaned as reality replaced her dream.

Why even get up? There was no husband who needed breakfast, no work to do that couldn't wait. Why not stay in bed? Perhaps she could recapture the pleasant dream the rooster had interrupted.

As if scolding her laziness, the rooster crowed a third time. The bird knew that morning meant breakfast, and Susanna's idleness was no excuse for neglecting her duties. It wasn't like her to be petulant. If she looked into the small mirror that hung over the washstand, she'd probably see her lower lip sticking out. But she was no longer a child afraid of being alone. She was a wife now. A wife whose husband had important work to do.

She pushed back the covers and dashed to the fireplace to stoke the fire. Then she crossed to the window. Above the trees she could see smoke curling from the chimney of her in-laws' farmhouse. Her sister-in-law was already up and preparing breakfast, though her newborn son had undoubtedly kept her awake most of the night. Miriam was truly a virtuous wife. Didn't she rise while it was yet night and provide food for her household?

And there she was, feeling sorry for herself because she was alone. The least she could do was take care of the livestock while her husband was away. It was bad enough she'd argued with Nathan before he left, had whined like a child instead of being a supportive helpmate. She had a lot of apologizing to do when he returned.

Nathan had built their cabin so well it warmed quickly. Susanna dressed, remembering her father's pronouncement when he'd inspected it a few days before her wedding. "Snug," he'd said. "It'll protect you from the coldest Ohio wind."

Nathan had chafed at what he'd considered to be faint praise, but Susanna had known better. Her father's words had been his way of agreeing to the marriage. "A man who cares for your physical welfare will surely care for the rest of you," he'd explained to her later. "I can go home and not worry about how well you're being looked after."

Had it really been only five months since Susanna became Mrs. Nathan Griffith? Making Nathan's cabin into a home had been her delight. The embroidered table scarves and bed linens she'd brought in her wedding chest had softened the cabin's rough edges, and the pewter candlesticks her parents had given her were still new enough to gleam on the mantel.

After tying a woolen cape over her shoulders to protect from the autumn chill, Susanna stepped outside and tended to her morning chores. When she finished, she changed her apron and reached for her bonnet. She fingered the stiff brim, a sigh escaping her lips. Before she married, she'd spent many an afternoon decorating her bonnets with ribbons and ruffles. When her mother-in-law had given her the plain white cap and black bonnet, Susanna had no doubt she was expected to wear it.

"Now thee looks like a proper Quaker wife," Nathan had said with an approving smile.

Susanna had grinned up at her husband. He'd taken a chance at marrying her, an outsider, but he'd reassured her that none of the Friends would doubt his choice of wives. "Thee is good and kind," he'd said, "and thy light shines for all to see."

Susanna said a quick prayer for her husband's safe return, then tied the bonnet over her linen cap. She gathered her basket of sewing and started down the wooded trail that led to her in-laws' farmhouse. Geese honked overhead, their arrow-shaped formation pointing due south.

"It's about time you were on your way," she said to the birds. "You're going to be late for the family reunion." Until that week, the autumn of 1838 had been mild. Couldn't blame the geese for tarrying while food was plentiful. But yesterday the north wind had brought a chill to the Ohio River Valley, signaling the birds that the scarcity of winter was near.

The Griffiths' dog, Jasper, bounded out of a thicket and bowed at Susanna's feet. "Well good morning to you, too," she said, chuckling. Jasper barked and rolled onto his back, his tongue lolling out of his teeth. "I still think you're more wolf than dog." Susanna rubbed his belly with the sole of her walking boot. "But I'm not scared of you anymore."

Jasper scrambled to his feet and bounded down the trail, announcing her arrival. Susanna stepped into the clearing and caught sight of Miriam crouching near the door of the springhouse.

"Let me get that for you," Susanna called, and hurried to Miriam's side.

Miriam straightened slowly, both hands on the small of her back. "I thank thee. Didn't think it would be so hard to bring in a crock of butter."

"It's too soon for you to be doing so much work. Your son is only two weeks old." Susanna handed her basket to Miriam and nestled the heavy crock of butter in the crook of her arm.

"How's Mother Griffith this morning?" Susanna followed

Miriam along the stone path to the farmhouse door.

"Much better. Still coughing but no fever, thank the Lord."

"I'm sure the poultice you made helped. Have you heard from Father Griffith?"

"Not since his last letter. Although I did hear Reverend Mahan's trial has been set for the thirteenth. We'll know something soon enough."

"That poor man's been in jail for more than a month."

"And from what I hear, the mob's growing stronger each day. I know Father and Nathan want to be close enough to help Brother Mahan if the mob attacks. Still their absence is hard on Mother."

And on me, Susanna thought. Her husband of five months had abandoned her and willingly put himself in harm's way, just so he could offer protection to another man.

A ripple of shame passed through Susanna. Nathan hadn't actually abandoned her. His family was close enough to help if she needed it. She should be proud of Nathan's commitment to the abolitionists' cause instead of complaining about her minor hardships.

Miriam placed a hand over her brow and scanned the bluff that formed the eastern boundary of the Griffith farm. "I see our watchman is still on duty."

Susanna followed Miriam's gaze. An icy hand squeezed her heart at the sight of the lone rider atop the bluff, his figure clearly silhouetted in the morning sun. "Where's your husband?"

"Eli's helping Brother Jackson bale hay this morning.

277

Don't worry. Ever since Brother Mahan's arrest, we haven't had any special guests. That bounty hunter can sit up there until judgment day. He won't see anything worthwhile." Miriam opened the door and stepped aside, allowing Susanna to enter the kitchen. Then she hurried to the cradle near the fireplace.

"How's Samuel this morning?" Susanna removed her cape and bonnet.

"Fine as goose down and growing faster than a weed." Miriam patted the sleeping infant.

"Has Mother Griffith eaten?"

"Not yet. The biscuits are in the oven."

Susanna used the lifter to carefully remove the lid from the dutch oven. Although she was twenty years old, she could still hear her mother's stern voice, scolding her for spilling ashes in the food when she'd been a child. Six golden-brown biscuits smiled up at her. "Shall I bring some tea and biscuits upstairs?"

"That would be so helpful, Susanna. And ask Mother if she's up to eating more this morning."

A short time later, Susanna climbed the stairs to her mother-in-law's bedroom. Martha Griffith, propped up by pillows, smiled when her daughter-in-law entered.

"Thank thee, Daughter," Martha said as Susanna set the tray on the bed. "I hope thee brought two cups, so we can visit for a while."

"Of course I did. Do you feel like eating more than biscuits this morning? How about some eggs?"

"Not yet, dear, but I am determined to get out of this

bed and downstairs tomorrow. Now pull the chair closer and talk to me. Has thee heard anything from Mason County?"

"Not a word." Susanna moved the small rocking chair away from the fireplace and placed it beside the bed. "But Miriam says the trial date has been set. Surely Nathan and Father Griffith will be home shortly after that."

"I pray it may be so."

Susanna poured the tea then ran her finger around the rim of her cup. "I know the Bible tells us not to worry, yet it's hard to keep my mind from imagining the most horrible things."

Martha stretched out her hand, and Susanna clasped it with her own. "I know, Daughter. I find much solace in the psalm, 'cast thy burden upon the Lord, and He will sustain thee.'"

If only Susanna could, but stopping her worries was like trying to stop the rain from falling. They came of their own accord. "I try, Mother Griffith. Honest, I do. And yet I find worry creeping into my thoughts like weevils into grain."

"Then go to the Lord again and again. Every time thee finds thyself fretting over Nathan, picture our Lord walking beside him, guiding and protecting him."

Would she ever be as faithful as Mother Griffith? When it came to trusting in the Lord, Susanna was a caterpillar, and her mother-in-law, a beautiful butterfly.

"Did thee bring thy sewing?" Martha asked, withdrawing her hand and sipping from her cup. "I cannot wait to see the little coat you are making for Samuel."

"I've only begun Samuel's coat. I wanted to finish the

vest for Nathan before working on it. Do you think he'll be home by Christmas?"

"I pray they will be home long before the twenty-fifth. Susanna, has thee spoken to Nathan about celebrating Christmas?"

Susanna noted the concerned frown on her mother-in-law's brow. "Nathan told me the Friends don't observe Christmas, but I thought it would be all right to give him a small present. Do you object?"

"I do not object, but I fear our Quaker ways have been difficult for thee to accept. For us Friends, every day is a gift from God, none more special than the rest. How does thy family celebrate Christmas?"

"We go to church where we sing Christmas songs. Sometimes the children reenact the story of our Savior's birth. Then we share a meal with our friends and family and exchange gifts."

Martha's eyebrows drew together as she gave Susanna an assessing look. "As thee knows, we Friends do not believe in music at our Meetings. Our testimony of silence allows us to listen for the Lord's still, small voice. The expectant waiting is a powerful time."

"I've come to enjoy the weekly respite that quiet time with the Holy Spirit gives me."

Martha's knitted brow told Susanna that her mother-in-law was not appeased by her answer. "And where does thee stand on the issue of becoming one of the Friends?"

That was the question everyone wanted her to answer. Martha had made no secret of her disapproval of Nathan's choice of a non-Quaker to be his bride. Susanna had tried to win her approval, and Martha had been kind and loving in so many ways, yet intractable on this one issue. "I–I'm still praying about it, Mother Griffith."

Martha sighed, a sound of long-suffering and strained patience.

Time to change the subject, Susanna thought. She removed a bundle of gray cloth from her basket and spread the vest on her mother-in-law's lap. "All that's left to do are the button holes. Friends don't have anything against buttons, do they?"

Martha inspected the garment. "The Lord has given thee a wonderful talent, Daughter. My own mother despaired of ever teaching me to make stitches as small and straight as thine. And while it is true that we Friends believe in plain dress as a way to honor the beautiful spirits our Lord gave us, I have yet to hear anyone speak ill of an unassuming button."

As night fell, Susanna sat in her chair in front of the cabin's fireplace. Shadows danced on Nathan's empty chair, and a new pang of longing passed through her heart. How much longer until she reunited with her husband? It wasn't fair to be a newlywed and yet be alone. If only the Griffiths hadn't thrown in their lots with the Mahans, Nathan and his father would be home where they belonged.

Brother John Mahan had preached at her home church a few years ago, urging her neighbors to stand together against slavery. Susanna's father had declined to join the abolitionists. "I have a family to provide for and children to protect," he'd said, "but I'll pledge a yearly sum to support you."

Why couldn't Nathan have done the same? He should be sitting in their cabin instead of a strange boardinghouse on the other side of the river, where pro-slavery mobs threatened to tear down the jail and lynch a godly man accused of helping runaways.

The logs shifted in the fireplace, and Susanna added another piece of wood. She really should bank the fire and go to bed, but emptiness awaited her there. Spending the day with Mother Griffith and Miriam had helped the daylight hours pass quickly, though the night stretched before her like a shadowy cave. Perhaps she should have accepted their invitation to spend the night at the farmhouse, but she had wanted to return to her cabin. At least here, she could see Nathan's handiwork and feel his love for her in every carefully crafted mortise and tenon. She pulled her shawl around her shoulders, blew out the candle, and rested her head against the back of the chair, waiting for sleep to claim her.

A few hours later, a knock on the cabin's door startled her awake. She leaned forward, her fingers grasping the arms of her rocker, her pulse thundering in her ears. Who would dare to call so late at night? Should she pretend no one was home? The fire had burned down, sending the barest light into the cabin. Whoever was outside couldn't know for sure she was there.

"Griffith?" a man's voice called. "Nathan Griffith?"

Tension coiled in Susanna's shoulders. She didn't recognize the voice, but surely a thief would not call her husband's name.

The man knocked again. "My name is Simmons. I've

come with a special guest."

A special guest. That meant only one thing. A fugitive slave sought Nathan's help. What should she do? If she didn't answer, would the man go to the next safe house? Where was the closest safe house?

Eli would know. She could send the man to the Griffiths' farmhouse. Perhaps the runaway could stay with her until Eli came. If the bounty hunters spotted Mr. Simmons, he could be introduced as a relative, traveling to visit family.

Struggling to settle her heartbeat, Susanna touched a piece of straw to the embers, relit the candle, and made her way to the door. Perhaps she should take down the flint-lock from its place over the mantel—but Nathan had never answered the door with a gun in his hands. With one last look at the musket, she slid the bolt and opened the door.

The man, short and squat as a rain barrel, had a whiskered face and a patched coat. "Nathan Griffith?" he asked.

Susanna shook her head. "You'll have to go someplace else. My husband can't help."

The man frowned. "Got no place else to go. This guest has got to get to the Quaker settlement in Bear Valley right away."

It was wrong to invite a man into her house when her husband was gone, but the longer the man stood in the doorway, the more likely it was that someone would spot him.

"Come in," she said.

"My name's Andrew Simmons." The man removed his hat and stepped through the doorway. "This cabin was mighty hard to find. Whoever built it didn't want just any-body stumbling upon it. Where's your husband?"

Surely she shouldn't admit she was alone. "A trail leads through the woods to the farmhouse. Go there and ask for Eli Wilson. He'll know what to do."

He frowned. "Wilson, you say? I don't know anyone by that name. I was told to find Nathan Griffith, no one else."

"Eli is married to Nathan's sister. He'll know the best place for you to take your guest. Make sure you're not seen because bounty hunters have been watching the road and our homes."

Mr. Simmons shook his head and made a sound like an angry dog. "I knew it was wrong to come to someone I didn't know. But with the hornet's nest that's brewing in Mason County, my usual contacts have disappeared."

An idea popped into Susanna's mind. "Perhaps you could take your guest back to your house. Come back in a few weeks."

"Not possible. This is a young woman searching for her husband. She got word he's with the Quakers, and she's got to get there. Tomorrow wouldn't be too soon."

Susanna didn't know how Nathan and the others man-aged their clandestine journeys, but surely the runaway could wait until a safer time. "Where is your guest?"

"I put her in your barn," he said with a jerk of his head.

"I'll go for Eli," Suzanna said. "You can wait here."

Mr. Simmons slapped his hat against his leg and mut-tered under his breath. "No, I'll go. No need to send a woman out in the middle of the night. Where's this trail?"

"I'll show you."

Susanna lit candles inside two punched tin lanterns and closed the apertures before stepping outside. A bounty hunter would have a hard time seeing the faint light, though the lantern would be enough to help Mr. Simmons find his way. She gave one lantern to the man and led him to the trail. "It's a well-worn path," she said. "No roots or branches to slow you down. The Griffiths have a dog, but they let him sleep in the kitchen on cold nights. He won't bother you. What's your guest's name?"

"Phoebe," he said and started down the trail.

She hurried to the barn. The mare nickered a greeting as she closed the door and exposed the candle's light. "Phoebe?" she called softly. The mare stamped her front hooves. No other sound met Susanna's ears. "Phoebe, my name is Susanna Griffith. Mr. Simmons told me you were here. I've come to help."

A timid voice, soft as the spring breeze, answered. "Yes, ma'am."

Susanna turned toward the voice. The lantern light illuminated a figure huddled in the corner of the barn. "I want you to come inside, Phoebe, and get warm. Mr. Simmons will be back soon, and you'll be on your way. Are you hungry?"

"Yes, ma'am. Thank you kindly."

Susanna walked slowly toward the woman. She hadn't seen many slaves in her life, but Phoebe was a surprise in many ways. She was tiny, barely reaching five feet, and her thin clothing was little more than rags. As Susanna's gaze traveled down Phoebe's slight figure, she gasped.

Phoebe smiled. "Yes, ma'am. I'm going to have a baby. Granny said it's almost my time. That's why I had to leave."

Susanna couldn't begin to understand why the imminent birth of her baby had forced Phoebe to escape, but that didn't change the fact that the runaway was in her barn, asking for help. "Let's get you into the cabin," she said. "I'm sure I have an extra cloak you can use to keep you warm for the rest of your journey." After concealing the lantern's light, Susanna opened the barn door. "Stay close to me. I don't dare use more light."

Phoebe touched Susanna's skirt. "I'll just hold on to your dress, if it's all right. I won't lose hold of you."

Susanna smiled at the younger woman. There was something about the tiny dark woman that Susanna liked. Obviously courage didn't come in proportion to size.

Once inside the cabin, Susanna rebuilt the fire and filled the kettle with water. After hanging it from a crane, she swung the kettle over the fire. "We'll have some tea in a few minutes. Now sit here by the fireplace so you can warm up."

Phoebe eased herself into Nathan's chair, and Susanna passed a woolen blanket to her. In the firelight, Susanna could see Phoebe clearly. Had the poor girl actually walked this far with bare feet? Her frayed cloth dress barely reached her ankles, and she wore a faded blue covering over her hair. "I don't have much to offer you in the way of food," Susanna said. "But I'll get started on some griddlecakes."

"Thank you, ma'am."

Susanna set the long-handled skillet on the gridiron and turned to the task of mixing the batter. "Where are you from?"

Phoebe didn't answer. Susanna glanced over her shoulder to find Phoebe sleeping quietly. How exhausted she must be to fall asleep so quickly. She looked at the wet batter in the bowl and wondered if she should complete the simple meal. Then realizing she could send the griddlecakes with Eli, she finished the job.

Susanna had just removed the last cake from the griddle when she heard Eli's voice.

"Susanna? May I come in?"

She crossed to the door and let Eli and Mr. Simmons into her cabin.

Eli's gaze fell on Phoebe, who continued to sleep soundly in Nathan's chair. "Is everything all right, Susanna? I hope thee is not scared."

"Not now," she said. "I confess Mr. Simmons gave me a start, but I'm all right."

"Are those griddlecakes?" asked Mr. Simmons.

"Yes, would you like some?"

"Don't mind if I do." He seated himself at the table.

Susanna set the wooden bowl of griddlecakes on the table and added a small crock of honey. She turned to get him a knife and fork, but when she turned back, Mr. Simmons was already devouring the cakes with his fingers. Her gaze connected with Eli's.

Eli smiled and shrugged, then pointed to the door. "Let's talk outside."

Susanna took her shawl from the peg and followed Eli. "What have you decided?"

"It takes about four hours to get to the Quaker settlement

287

at Bear Valley, and dawn's only an hour away. Phoebe will have to wait until tomorrow evening. I'll take her back to the farmhouse. She can rest up and eat before starting on the last part of her trip. How old does thee think she is?"

"Younger than I," Susanna answered. "My guess is sixteen or seventeen. Did Mr. Simmons tell you she's in the family way?"

"Yes, but that can't be helped now. She's here, and we'll do the best we can for her. Mother Griffith says for thee to come to the house as usual, because the bounty hunters have been watching us for so long, they know our routines. If they don't see thee making thy daily visit, they're likely to pay a call to find out why."

"I'll be there."

Eli touched Susanna's arm in a supportive gesture. "I'll see thee at breakfast then?"

Susanna nodded. "I'd offer to bring griddlecakes, but I don't think there will be any left."

❄

Eli, Miriam, and Martha were gathered at the kitchen table when Susanna arrived. "Good morning," she said. But anxious silence met her greeting. "What is it? Has something else happened?" Susanna's hand went to her throat. "Did you receive word from Nathan or Father Griffith?"

"No, Daughter," Martha said. "I am sure Nathan and Thomas are fine. Sit down, and we will tell thee what we have decided."

"Thee is not going, Mother," Miriam said. "Thee has barely recovered from a bad case of the grippe. The journey would put thee either back in bed or in thy grave."

Susanna looked at Eli. "I thought you were going to take Phoebe to Bear Valley."

Eli opened his mouth to respond, but his wife answered. "Eli can't go either," Miriam said. "Those shameful bounty hunters have left the bluff and set up camp on our property. There are two of them now, watching Eli's every move. Brother Jackson came over at daybreak to tell us."

"Those scoundrels showed up at our back door shortly after Eli returned from thy cabin," Martha added. "They did not recognize Mr. Simmons and suspected he had information about a runaway. I have to give Brother Simmons credit. He was as calm as a pond at sunset. He did not give away a thing."

"They asked to search our house and barn," Miriam said. "Eli let them in, but they didn't come close to finding our secret room. Still it's obvious they suspected something."

"Phoebe's still here?" Susanna asked.

"Of course she's still here," Miriam said. "I brought her breakfast and told her she'd be leaving today."

It was all happening too fast for Susanna. "If the house is being watched so closely, maybe she should stay until the bounty hunters move on."

"Too dangerous to let her stay," Eli said. "That's why I'm taking her tonight."

Miriam groaned. "Please don't risk it, Eli. There are others who can take Phoebe. Men who don't have newborn babies to watch over. If thee leaves, who will protect us the next time those rogues knock on our door?"

"It is not right to put our problems on our neighbors' shoulders," Martha said. "God sent Phoebe to us, and it is up to us to do what we have pledged. I will take the hay wagon to the Quaker settlement with Phoebe hidden in the secret compartment. I am able to drive a wagon."

"For four hours in the cold November weather?" Miriam asked. "Not to mention the clouds building in the north. They look like snow to me. Thee would be risking thy life just as much as Eli if thee did that."

Susanna's in-laws fell silent. There seemed to be no solution acceptable to all of them, but Susanna knew what needed to be done.

"I'll take her," she said.

All eyes turned to her. "What did thee say?" Martha asked.

Susanna could barely believe the words had come out of her mouth, but there was no better solution. "I'll take her. I know where the Quaker settlement is. My family's farm is east of there. I'll go tonight."

"No," Eli said. "I won't allow it. It's my place to take Phoebe. Thee never pledged thyself to this cause."

"It's too much to ask, Susanna," Miriam said. "Thee has never done anything like this."

"If you didn't have Samuel to care for, would you do it?" Susanna asked.

"Of course, but I'm older. And I've made the journey with my father."

"I've made the same journey with my father," Susanna reminded her. "I admit we didn't travel in the dark, but I'm sure I can find it."

The three were silent as the possibility of Susanna escorting Phoebe seemed to solidify in their minds.

"I don't think the bounty hunters have been watching Nathan's cabin," Eli said. "With him gone, there's no reason to watch it."

"Susanna *can't* go," Miriam repeated. "She's too young."

"Which is why she is beyond the bounty hunters' suspicion," Martha said. "Both Susanna and I will go."

"No," Susanna said. "You're not well yet, Mother Griffith. I agree with Miriam. You must get better."

"I won't let thee go by thyself," Miriam said.

Susanna almost smiled at her sister-in-law's forceful tone. Surely Miriam could see Susanna was the only choice. "If Eli accompanies me, he'll bring attention to us. And like Mother Griffith says, Phoebe is our responsibility."

Silent seconds passed. When each person met her gaze and smiled, Susanna knew they'd reached the same conclusion.

Martha reached across the table and took Susanna's hand. "Yet who knows whether thee has come to the kingdom for such a time as this?"

Yes, Susanna thought. Like Queen Esther, she was in a unique position to help her new family.

Eli ran his hands through his hair and shook his head. "Nathan will have my hide for this."

Susanna smiled in return. She was going.

Chapter 2

On the fourteenth of November, Nathan Griffith and his father, Thomas, stepped out of the boardinghouse and walked along the muddy main road in Washington, Kentucky. Everywhere he looked, Nathan saw evidence of fear. Windows were shuttered and barred, water barrels filled in case of fire, and men buying extra ammunition. Rumors of a slave revolt or of abolitionists riding into town to free their comrade floated through the town like cinders from a brush fire.

"It is a good thing we came," Thomas said. "Brother Mahan should not have to face this alone."

John Mahan had been in jail for nearly two months, shackled like a murderer and forced to endure hardships he didn't deserve. "The trial is set to begin at eleven o'clock," Nathan said. "As soon as it's over, we should return home."

"I agree, but we will have to see how things turn out. After that false start yesterday, who knows what today's proceedings will bring."

"I hardly know which will fare better for him. If he's found guilty, the mob will surely hang him. But if the jury declares his innocence, the mob may still attack out of anger."

"I believe he will be cleared of the trumped-up charges. My hope is that we can help him get across the river and on his way home before the mob has time to form."

Nathan prayed for their success. As Quakers, he and his

father believed that violence was a sin, but Nathan knew peaceful reconciliation would not be an option for a hate-crazed mob. They could do little else for Reverend Mahan except visit him in jail and offer their help.

At the small jailhouse, Nathan and Thomas checked in with the jailer, walked down the narrow stairs to the dirt-floor cellar, and stooped under a low-hanging doorframe to the cell. Brother Mahan stood to his full height as they entered.

"Good morning, friends," Brother Mahan greeted them. "Blessed is the day that the Lord has made."

"We shall rejoice and be glad in it," Thomas said. "It is good to see thee smiling this morning, Brother Mahan."

"I have no fear of what's to come. I've known from the beginning this is a case that must be seen through to its end. Once I am acquitted, it will prevent future cases of a similar nature."

"Still," Nathan said, "it has been a hardship for thee and thy family. And all because of lies. Lies men told after swearing before God to tell the truth."

There was no answer for that. It was well known that Brother Mahan's accusers had lied about him crossing into Kentucky in order to incite slaves to leave. Thomas placed one hand on Brother Mahan's shoulder and the other on his son's. "Let us pray."

The men stood, heads bowed, while each spoke to the Lord in silent prayer. Nathan's mind wandered from the jail cell back to the cabin where his wife waited. Thank goodness Susanna was safe with his family. She was so young and unaware of the dangers the Griffiths faced whenever they helped runaway slaves.

Nathan's heart eased as he pictured Susanna in their cabin. By now she'd be feeding the chickens or turning the horses out to pasture. She'd written to him of her daily visits with his mother. Surely his mother had come to realize what a treasure Susanna was, despite that she'd not yet decided to become a member of the Society of Friends.

Susanna was warmth and gentleness and all things good and kind. Nathan asked the Lord to protect his dear wife and the rest of his family, then hastened to the *Amen* when he heard voices outside the cell.

Chambers Baird, Mahan's attorney, was escorted into the room. "Morning, gentlemen," he said. The men exchanged handshakes. "Now if you will excuse us, I must prepare my client for today's proceedings."

"Of course," Thomas said. "We will be in the courtroom, Brother Mahan, and we will be waiting with a fresh horse to take thee home."

"I'll be ready," Mahan replied and smiled broadly.

❄

The cold had settled into the Ohio Valley like an unwanted houseguest. That afternoon Susanna dressed with extra care, layering bustling petticoats beneath her skirt, her jacket covering several blouses and sweaters. She would leave at three o'clock, driving a wagonload of hay. If stopped by the bounty hunters, she'd say she was taking the load to Friends. By saying that, she'd be spared from the sin of lying, just as Eli had sidestepped the issue when asked if he had a slave in his house.

"We consider every man free in God's eyes," Martha had explained. "Therefore we never consider our special guests to be slaves. Just as we did not lie when we introduced Mr. Simmons as our cousin, for we are all brothers and sisters in the family of our Lord."

Susanna walked the short distance to the Griffiths' house and found Phoebe seated at the kitchen table. One look at the petite girl, smothered in layers of clothing and wrapped in a wool blanket, made Susanna hide her smile behind her fingers.

Phoebe laughed with her. "I know, ma'am. I look like a pile of old clothes somebody threw in the rag pile. But Miss Miriam fixed me a special bed in the wagon, and while you're up top driving those horses in the cold, I'll be warm and snug."

Martha walked into the kitchen and took both of Susanna's hands in hers. "Now, Daughter." Her brows drew together in a serious frown. "I have a hundred things to say. Is thee ready to listen?"

A hundred things? Perhaps Susanna should write them down.

"First," Martha said, "do not put thy life in danger. I know thee to be a smart girl. Use the intelligence God gave thee if difficulties arise. Second, it will be dark in just a few hours, but Eli has hitched our best horses for the job. They are reliable and steadfast, and will keep going until thee has reached thy destination. Third, remember that the Lord sends angels with thee. Rely on them for protection. And fourth, take my cape and gloves. They are the warmest we have."

Susanna smiled at her mother-in-law. "That's only four, Mother Griffith. What about the other ninety-six?"

Martha squeezed Susanna's hands. "I will save them until thee returns. Now, is thee ready?"

Susanna had worried all day about her journey. What if the bounty hunters caught Phoebe? Susanna would undoubtedly be arrested for aiding a fugitive slave and perhaps thrown in jail. Although that possibility was remote, some women had been imprisoned as the slaveholders became more and more desperate to recover their lost property. Finally after a day spent chasing away the what-ifs as though they were pesky flies, it was time to set out. "Oh yes, I'm anxious to get started."

Eli entered the kitchen and stopped at the hearth long enough to warm his hands. "It's getting colder by the hour. I wish we didn't have to send thee right away."

Susanna flicked her gaze to Phoebe's abdomen. She wasn't one to judge, but surely Phoebe would deliver her child soon. "I'll be in the hands of Friends in a few hours. I'm sure we'll rest in warm beds tonight."

Martha gave Susanna's hands a final squeeze and picked up a large covered basket. "Everything is packed and ready for thee. I even put in some of the gingerbread thee loves so much."

"Thank you." Susanna took the basket. "Someday you'll have to teach me how to make it."

"When thee returns, Daughter."

Eli turned from the fireplace and addressed their special guest. "Are you ready, Phoebe?"

"Oh yes," Phoebe answered, her eyes sparkling. "I've been praying for this day for many years, and now it's finally come. Just think, I'll be with my husband tonight, and we'll both be free."

Eli stooped to help Phoebe, who rose with difficulty from her chair. "Not yet, baby." She patted her middle. "You just stay in there a few more days. Soon you can come out and say hello to your daddy. Just a little while more."

Susanna gave Martha one last hug then trailed Eli and Phoebe to the barnyard. The wagon, piled with hay, looked as ordinary as every other hay wagon she'd seen. Eli crouched under the wagon, removed a wooden slat, and revealed the cramped space where Phoebe would lie amid blankets. *It's barely bigger than a coffin*, Susanna thought then whisked the image out of her mind. She was going to bring Phoebe to safety. She was going to return to the Griffiths' farmhouse tomorrow. She wouldn't allow another doubt to slither into her mind.

Susanna watched the young girl step onto the mounting block Eli had supplied and slowly slide her body into the space.

Eli replaced the slat and redistributed the hay so that nothing looked out of place, then threw the pitchfork on top of the load. After handing Susanna up to the driver's bench, he smiled warmly. "Good journey. We'll see thee tomorrow."

Susanna tried to fill her smile with confidence. "Tomorrow," she promised. She turned her gaze forward, snapped the reins, and the horses plodded forward.

❄

The first snow of the season came just as Susanna crossed the bridge over Red Oak Creek. She wasn't alarmed. The flakes fell like gentle feathers and melted as they touched the ground. Even though her toes were numb and her cheeks stung from the cold, this type of snow was no threat.

It reminded her of the day Nathan had asked her to marry him. He'd courted her for nearly a year, and everyone in her family knew his intentions, yet he'd taken his time getting around to the asking. That February day, he asked her to go for a walk in the snow. Her mother began to object, but perhaps read something on Nathan's face and agreed to the outing. Susanna and Nathan walked down the lane, arm in arm, with only the whisper of snowflakes to disturb the winter silence.

They turned at the end of the lane to make their way back when he stopped and faced her. "Susanna?"

She waited for him to go on, but he only smiled down at her, his brown eyes shining with kindness and love.

"Susanna," he repeated.

"Yes, Nathan?"

"Thee knows I've been speaking with thy parents about my family's farm near Ripley," he said, his breath visible in the frosty air.

"Yes, Nathan. I know."

"And thee knows my family is Quaker."

"Yes, Nathan."

"Does thee object?"

"Object to your family being Quakers? Of course not. Why do you ask?"

He took her gloved hands in his and held them against his chest. "Because if thee agrees to be my wife, thee will live with me and my family. I don't require thee to become one of the Friends, Susanna. That decision is up to thee and thy soul. But it's my hope that thee will agree to become my wife and to raise our children in the Quaker way."

She laughed, but the look of confusion on Nathan's face quickly quelled her laughter. "Oh, Nathan," she said, covering her mouth with one hand. "I'm not laughing at your proposal. I'm laughing with relief."

"Relief?"

"Yes! Thank goodness, you finally asked!"

His frown vanished as he pulled her close and tilted her chin toward his face. "Does thee agree to marry me, Susanna?"

"Of course, Nathan. I've been waiting and waiting for you to ask."

His nose was cold, but his lips were warm when he kissed her. The first of many kisses.

She ran back to her house, bursting with the news. Her parents set the date for the second Saturday in June. She floated through the next months, preparing her wedding chest and dreaming of becoming Nathan's wife.

Although Susanna's father had sold many horses to Nathan's father through the years, she'd never met the women in his family. When Martha and Miriam, dressed in plain gray dresses and black bonnets, arrived the day before her wedding, Susanna was unsure how they would receive her. She knew his mother had been concerned about her not being a Quaker, but Nathan was resolute. "Susanna is the woman of my heart," he said. "She's willing to learn more about the Society of Friends, and that's good enough for me."

How his words warmed her heart and calmed her apprehension. Concern about earning her mother-in-law's approval dwindled in the face of her husband's love, and she married Nathan with confidence and pride.

The horses stopped, stirring Susanna from her pleasant memories. A broken tree limb lay across the road, snow lining its bare branches. She hadn't realized how thick the snow had gotten. She tied the reins to the bench, climbed down the wagon, and pulled the branches out of the way. Thank goodness none of them were too heavy for her to move. Eli hadn't sent an ax or hatchet with her.

She reseated herself on the bench, a gust of wind swirling her skirts about her. It was getting colder as the sun moved closer to the horizon, but still Susanna wasn't alarmed. Two horses could easily pull the wagon as long as she stayed on the road. Perhaps she should check on Phoebe before she drove farther, but anyone who saw her might deduce the hay was a ruse.

Susanna snapped the reins and gave a silent prayer of thanksgiving as the horses began to move. Just as Mother Griffith had promised, the team pulled with resolute determination, needing almost no guidance from Susanna. Evening transformed into night, and the wind intensified, blowing the snow in horizontal sheets across the road.

A gust of wind struck her head-on, the snow clinging to the tendrils of hair that had escaped her cap. Susanna gathered the reins in one gloved hand and used the other to adjust a scarf around her bonnet. There was one good thing about the stiff brims of the Quaker bonnet—it kept most of the snow out of her face. If only all the Quaker ways were as easy as changing her bonnet style. She still hadn't adopted the Griffiths' way of speaking. Nathan used what he called plain speech whenever he spoke with the Friends, but never when he was conducting business in town. How odd it had been when Nathan first addressed her as *thee*. Now she yearned to hear his voice, telling her of his love and approval. When he finally came home, she'd cook his favorite meal and then simply sit and watch him eat. Her eyes were hungry for the sight of her husband. Especially the sight of him in their cabin, safe and warm.

Did Phoebe feel the same way? All of Susanna's troubles seemed insignificant compared to those of the young woman who lay hidden under the wagon. Not only was Phoebe a fugitive from the law, but she was also heavy with child. She'd risked her life, and her child's life, to be reunited with her husband.

If a woman was willing to risk everything in order to escape, then slavery must be worse than Susanna had ever imagined. The river that separated free Ohio from slave Kentucky had seen its share of drowned men and women, each one willing to die rather than live as a slave. But why did the sins of others have to endanger her husband?

Because Nathan couldn't sit and do nothing. At least that's how he'd explained it to her. "Therefore all things whatsoever ye would that men should do to you, do ye even so to them," he'd quoted and then kissed her forehead as if to say *argument concluded*.

Susanna hadn't been able to stop herself from quarreling when Nathan announced his intentions to accompany his father to Kentucky. Wouldn't he be surprised to know she was helping a runaway? A few weeks earlier, she'd insisted that Brother Mahan's fight had nothing to do with the Griffiths. Now she would be counted among the abolitionists.

The wind changed direction and speed. It howled through the heavily laden evergreens and pummeled her body with frosty fists. When the frigid wind stung her face like tiny pins, she knew it could mean only one thing.

Ice.

If the snow mixed with ice, the road would quickly become too slick. She estimated she was still an hour away from the Quaker settlement, but in this weather, it might take longer. Would she make it there before ice turned the road into a frozen byway? She urged the horses to pick up speed, but they increased their pace for no more than a hundred yards before they returned to their slower gait. In the dark Susanna couldn't gauge the amount of ice collecting on the road, so perhaps it was wiser to let the horses set their own speed. They could feel the road beneath their hooves, and in the near-whiteout conditions of this storm, the horses were better judges than she.

If only she weren't out here alone. What had she been thinking, volunteering to take a runaway slave to safety? This had never been her fight. She should have waited for someone else to come for Phoebe. Someone who wouldn't have had to travel alone or someone who had a better hiding place for the runaway. Could she really withstand this storm for another hour? For more than an hour? As it was, someone would probably find her covered in ice, frozen to the bench like a human-sized icicle. But there was no place to stop. She'd never be able to build a fire in this wind, and surely Phoebe wouldn't survive a full night in that small compartment under the wagon.

Susanna took a deep breath and struggled to calm her fears. Yes, the weather was bad, but panic and fear wouldn't help. Her horses were still plodding forward, and as long as they continued to move, she and her charge would eventually get to their destination. The Quaker settlement was due north of her current position. All she had to do was keep going.

Just keep going.

The horses stopped again. One horse whinnied while the other looked back at her as if waiting for a decision. Susanna squinted at the road ahead but saw nothing except a wall of snow.

A thousand needles pricked her feet as she jumped the short distance from the wheel's hub to the ground, her limbs protesting the movement. She patted the withers of the horse on the left. "What is it?" she asked.

The horse swung its head toward the sound of her voice

and shifted its weight from one hoof to the other. Susanna walked a few feet ahead and saw what had stopped the horses. The bridge over Washburn Run was gone.

She recalled the map Eli had drawn for her. "I don't need a map," she'd protested. "I know the road very well." But now she regretted her words. Although she'd made the trip with her father, she'd never thought to ask about alternate routes.

Going forward wasn't an option. Even if the horses could swim the icy water, Phoebe would likely drown. Going back wasn't an option. She'd come two-thirds of the way and returning to the Griffiths wouldn't solve anything. But staying put wasn't an option either. No one who might offer help was likely to be on the road in this weather, and Eli had cautioned her against trusting strangers.

Susanna absentmindedly stroked the horse and closed her eyes. A new level of weariness settled in her bones. If only she were in her warm cabin, safely tucked under quilts while the earth froze outside. If only she could snuggle under the hay until the weather quieted. If she could just rest for a little while, close her eyes, and let the worries dissolve into dreams of sunny summer days. . . .

A sudden gust of wind swirled her skirt and petticoats, sending a frigid tendril into the last warm spot on her body. This was madness. She couldn't simply stay on the road like a pile of stones. There was nothing wrong with the wagon, and she had to find shelter for the horses. What had Mother Griffith said to her? Rely on her intelligence and on the Lord's help. Susanna lifted her gaze. Her intelligence seemed to be as frozen as the rest of her. "What should I do,

Lord?" she asked the dark sky. "Where should I go?"

No answer came.

Susanna sighed and rubbed her cold nose on the horse's warm neck. Then as if driven by an invisible hand, the horses pricked their ears and began to move. Was this like Balaam's donkey? Had they seen an angel Susanna could not see?

She stepped away from the wagon and watched the horses circle until they stopped, the wagon now headed in the opposite direction. "Fine with me," Susanna said to the animals. "If you've got an idea, I'm willing to go along with it."

She walked to the back of the wagon and raised her voice above the wind. "Everything's all right, Phoebe. We're just taking a different way." No response came from the secret compartment. Was Phoebe still alive? Had she frozen to death, despite the extra clothing and quilts?

Susanna's heart shuddered at the thought of little Phoebe lying dead in that cramped space. She lowered her face to the spot where she knew Phoebe's head was. "Phoebe?" she called again, unsuccessful at hiding the growing tension in her voice. No answer.

"Phoebe!" Susanna shouted, preparing to remove the wooden slat. Then she heard the faint knocking from beneath the hay, and relief warmed her frozen body. Phoebe was all right. Frightened perhaps, and undoubtedly cold, but still alive.

Susanna climbed up the wagon and resumed her perch on the bench. A quick flick of the reins was all the horses needed to resume their steady pace. But where were they going? Susanna knew that a tired horse would instinctively head for the barn, but they were too far from home. Then she saw a glimmer of hope.

A light shone through the blustering snow, a mere pin-point of illumination that glowed in the frigid gloom. As the wagon drew nearer, two dark shapes formed—a farmhouse and a barn. So that's what the horses had sensed.

Somebody else's barn.

Chapter 3

Susanna tucked the quilts around Phoebe and rubbed the young girl's fingers. "You must have been freezing in that wagon."

"Don't worry about me, ma'am." Phoebe smiled. "All I had to do was lie quiet. You're the one with the red nose and white lips."

"Oh I'm sure I look a sight," Susanna said. "After I get you settled, I'll see to the horses and bring up the basket of food."

A frown crossed Phoebe's brow. "Do you think we'll be at your friends' farm tomorrow?"

Susanna wanted to comfort the girl, and an empty reassurance popped into her mind, though there was no use promising what she couldn't guarantee. "The Friends' settlement is only an hour or so away, Phoebe. But we can't travel on the roads until this storm passes."

Phoebe's gaze swept the loft. "We'll be warm enough in here, don't you think? If it's warm enough for the animals, it'll be warm enough for us."

As long as no one finds us, Susanna thought. The farmer who owned this barn seemed to be tucked in his warm house for the night. Susanna had simply opened the doors, and the horses had pulled the wagon into the barn. Now that she'd seen to Phoebe's safety, it was time to unhitch the horses and let them rest for the night.

"I'll be back in a few minutes," Susanna promised. "Do you like gingerbread?"

"I don't know, ma'am," Phoebe answered. "Don't think I've ever tasted it before."

"Well then, you're in for a treat." Susanna smiled in what she hoped was a reassuring manner and descended the ladder. When her feet touched the packed dirt of the barn's floor, she sagged against the rungs. "Thank You, Lord," she whispered. "Thank You for this shelter and for keeping Phoebe safe."

One horse nickered softly, and an involuntary smile crossed Susanna's lips. "And, oh yes, Lord. Thank You for the wisdom of horses."

The horse is probably laughing at that, Susanna thought. She pushed herself away from the ladder and went to unfasten the harnesses. The barn was large with stalls for two horses and one milk cow. Since there were no empty stalls for her horses, she let them walk freely in the barn. One animal went to the back of the wagon and began eating the hay, while the other drank deeply from the water trough.

Satisfied that she could do nothing else for them, Susanna took the basket of food from the wagon and returned to Phoebe. "Now," she said, and sat next to the girl, "let's see what Mother Griffith packed for us."

"Granny makes butter cookies for the master's family. Sometimes she brings home a few for us."

Susanna passed a plate of cold chicken to Phoebe. "Is your grandmother the cook?"

"The baker," Phoebe answered, her mouth full of meat.

"Demetria is the cook. Master Hansen's so rich, he's got a big old kitchen that's always hopping. But Granny isn't my grandmother."

"She isn't?"

"No, ma'am. All I know is I was born in Tennessee. But Granny, she's been good to me. When Tom and me got married, Granny made me the prettiest little bouquet of white and blue flowers. I don't know where she got flowers in January, but I suspect the master's wife would've been mighty angry if she'd discovered some of her hothouse flowers were gone. What about you, ma'am? Did you have one of those big old weddings with a new dress and sweet cake?"

Susanna thought back to her wedding day. "I suppose I did. I got married last summer. My mother and I worked on my dress for a month."

"What color was it?"

"Yellow," Susanna said.

"Oh I've always been partial to yellow. And did you put flowers in your hair?"

"Not in my hair, but on my bonnet."

Phoebe frowned. "It's not for me to say, ma'am, but I'm not sure flowers would help much on that bonnet."

Susanna touched the brim of her Quaker bonnet. "Oh no, not this bonnet. This is my married bonnet. My wedding bonnet was yellow, just like my dress."

"They made you wear that black bonnet after you got married?"

"No. I mean, nobody made me wear it. I chose to wear it, to show I was part of a Quaker family."

As though sensing she was stepping into dangerous territory, Phoebe changed the subject. "What else is in that basket, ma'am?"

"What? Oh, sorry." Susanna's attention returned to the basket where she found boiled potatoes. How could she have gone on and on about her wedding when Phoebe was probably starving?

"Tomorrow we'll have us a hot breakfast, I reckon," Phoebe said.

"If the storm blows itself out in time. Not even our know-it-all horses could find the road in this blizzard."

"Know-it-all horses?" Phoebe repeated. "What do you mean by—"

A man's voice stopped Phoebe's question. "Who's there?" he yelled.

The cold potato solidified in Susanna's mouth. She'd been talking so much she hadn't heard the door open. She glanced at Phoebe's round, frightened eyes and put a finger to her lips. Phoebe nodded her understanding.

"Who's there?" the man bellowed. "You didn't drive a hay wagon into my barn, unhitch your team, and leave. I know you're here."

Susanna covered Phoebe's face with a quilt. If the farmer found them, perhaps he'd believe Susanna was alone, that she'd been on the road, been caught by the storm, and had made a pallet in the shelter of his barn. It was the truth, after all. Just not the complete truth.

"This is the last time I'm asking before I get my new Kentucky rifle," he yelled menacingly. "Who's there?" He was losing whatever patience he had.

Susanna forced her voice out of her throat. "I am."

The sound of a woman's voice must have caught the farmer by surprise because her answer was met by silence. But a few seconds later, she heard footsteps on the rungs of the ladder. A flat-brimmed hat dusted with snow came into view, quickly followed by a white-bearded face.

The farmer lifted his lantern above his head, casting weak light on Susanna's seated form. He frowned at her for several tense seconds then lowered the lantern and descended the ladder.

When she heard the barn door close, Susanna let out the breath she'd been unconsciously holding. He'd seen she was alone, drawn the conclusion she'd hoped for, and had let her be. She laid a hand on top of the quilt. "It's all right," she whispered to the inert form. "I think he's going to let us stay. We won't have to face the snow until tomorrow morning."

Phoebe uncovered her face and struggled to sit up. "Granny said that after I make it to the Quaker settlement, the people there will help me and Tom move all the way to Canada. She said it's mighty cold in Canada. Colder even than Ohio. I guess I'd better get used to being cold."

"Canada can't be cold year round." Susanna searched the basket for the gingerbread. "I bet the spring and summer are beautiful there. I saw a drawing once of a giant waterfall in Canada. It was like a whole river falling off the side of a mountain, and at the bottom plumes of mist rose higher than the trees on the bank."

"That must be a sight to see." Phoebe bit into the sweet bread.

The two women ate in silence, allowing Susanna to hear clearly the sound of the barn door opening. Alarm shot through her heart. Why had the farmer come back? Susanna hastily re-covered Phoebe's head and turned to face the ladder.

It wasn't a scowling, bearded face that rose above the loft, but rather an older woman's soft countenance. She placed a lantern on the floor and smiled at Susanna. "Now then," she said softly. "What's this all about?"

Susanna swallowed hard and blurted out her story. The woman listened intently, nodding her head while Susanna explained her journey to the Quaker settlement in Bear Valley, and clucking her tongue in sympathy as Susanna described the blinding storm.

"You poor thing," the woman said. "But what about your companion? My husband said two people needed our help."

Susanna tried to hide her surprise. How had that farmer made out Phoebe's form in the dark loft? "Two people?" she repeated.

The farmer's wife stepped off the ladder and into the loft. "Two plates," she explained, pointing to the pile of bones. "You may have eaten all that chicken by yourself, but you wouldn't have used two plates to do it."

Susanna felt her face redden with mortification. What if her oversight had ruined all of Phoebe's hopes? She got to her feet and forced herself to meet the older woman's eyes.

The farmer's wife touched Susanna's arm. "I see by your bonnet that you're a Quaker."

"My husband's family are Friends," Susanna answered. "I

wear the bonnet out of respect for them."

The older woman's eyebrows drew together in a look of confusion. "You're not a Quaker? Is that what you're saying?"

"Yes, but. . . I mean, no. I'm. . ." No one had ever challenged Susanna in this manner. Only those who knew her and the Griffiths knew that Susanna had yet to petition the committee for membership in the Society of Friends.

The farmer's wife patted Susanna's arm. "No matter. I only ask because the fact that you're going to the settlement at Bear Valley with a person you want to keep hidden makes me wonder if you've got a runaway slave hidden beneath those quilts."

Susanna felt her stomach drop to her knees. Had she really made it this far, come so close to delivering Phoebe to safety, only to fail?

"And that bonnet says Quaker whether you deny it or not," the older woman continued. "We know the Quakers at Bear Valley have helped many a runaway before. Plus, a woman needing help would have come straight to the house, not tried to hide in our barn."

Susanna fisted her hands near her heart. She was at the mercy of this woman and her husband. "What are you going to do?"

"Help you inside and bed you down near the fireplace. If the storm has blown itself out by daybreak, my husband and I will put you back on the road."

Unbidden tears sprang into Susanna's eyes. "Oh, thank you," she whispered.

"We are Samuel and Elizabeth Miller, and you are safe

with us tonight. Once morning comes, you and your companion will have to be on your way. Alone."

"Yes, thank you," Susanna agreed. A new surge of energy strengthened her legs as she turned to help Phoebe to her feet. Mrs. Miller might think she'd be alone, but Susanna had learned one thing in the last few hours. The Lord was most certainly with her.

❄

Daybreak found Susanna sitting across the kitchen table from Samuel Miller. She'd greeted him cheerfully, even offered to help prepare breakfast, but the farmer continued to glower at her under his white bushy eyebrows.

"There are quite a few snowdrifts on my fields," he said, "and I can't say if the road will be any better. But I dare not allow that runaway to remain on my property much longer."

"I understand," Susanna answered. "We'll be on our way. Can you direct me to another road that will take us to the Quaker settlement?"

"*Humph*," he said. "It's not much of a road, but it's the only way. There's a network of trails the farmers around here use to drive livestock to market. That'll have to do." He pushed back from the table and reached for his hat and jacket. "Come to the barn when you're ready, and I'll show you the way. My wife and your companion are already there."

"Thank you," Susanna said, but the farmer was gone. *Strange man*, she thought. He'd been willing to let her and Phoebe stay in his house; now he wanted nothing to do with them.

Susanna put on the final layers of her clothing and

stepped outside. Pristine snow lay on the ground, and deep drifts bordered the house and barn, but the wind had finally stilled. Glints of sunlight bounced off the crystalline flakes, filling Susanna with a renewed sense of purpose. At least there'd be no storm to fight.

In the barn she found the team hitched to the wagon. Phoebe sat on a nearby bench, smiling. "Today's the day," she announced. "Today I see my Tom. Are you rested and ready to go?"

Susanna's heart warmed at Phoebe's cheerfulness. "I'm ready. But sorry to say you'll have to go back into the hiding spot."

"I know," Phoebe replied. "That don't matter to me. Just give me a hand, and I'll squeeze myself right in."

"Let me help you," Mrs. Miller said, rounding the wagon. "Susanna, I refilled your basket with a few things to eat on the road."

Susanna reached for Mrs. Miller. "Thank you for everything." She squeezed the older woman's hands. "If ever I can repay you—"

"Just take care of yourself," Mrs. Miller interrupted. "There wasn't anyone on the road during last night's storm, but today will be different."

Susanna climbed up the wagon and took her place on the bench. Mr. Miller rode up on a large roan gelding. "I'll go ahead of you. Follow my tracks. If I see anyone who may give you trouble, I'll come back to make sure you're all right. Otherwise it'd be better for me and Mrs. Miller if no one suspected we traveled together."

He was going to guide her? That was more than she'd expected. Perhaps his stern face masked a gentle heart. "Thank you, Mr. Miller. I appreciate all your kindness."

The farmer gave no response, only darkened his countenance and prodded his horse to move. Susanna looked back to where Mrs. Miller stood alone. The farmer's wife gave a nod, signaling that Phoebe was situated. After lifting her hand in farewell, Susanna drove the horses through the open barn door.

"Thank You for the Millers, Lord," she said as the wagon rumbled along the snow-covered ground. "Thank You for opening their hearts to us."

Chapter 4

Nathan and his father squeezed into the small courtroom on the second floor of the courthouse. Spectators spilled out onto the building's wide porch and to the lawn. Atop the courthouse, a bell tolled eleven times as the judge took his seat and called the court to order. Despite the crowd, the room was silent.

Witnesses and lawyers took turns giving evidence and arguing legal points, but Nathan's mind was on the other side of the Ohio River. If all went well, he'd go home to Susanna soon. How he missed her smile and her warm softness. He couldn't wait to sit by the evening fire and tell her about all he'd seen and done in Kentucky.

"Does thee see how calm Brother Mahan is?" Thomas whispered. "How strong he is in the Lord?"

Nathan refocused his attention on the lawyers. How eloquently they spoke against a citizen of Ohio being tried by a court in Kentucky. Yet their persuasive words did not hide the biggest threat to Nathan's family. If Brother Mahan were found guilty, the Griffiths and all the other abolitionists who helped runaway slaves could be identified and dragged out of the Free States for trials in the South.

Fraudulent trials no doubt, just like this one. Nathan thought of Brother Mahan's wife, Polly. She and the children had also suffered. What if Nathan had to make a decision between what his conscience told him was right and his duty as a husband to protect Susanna? Would he make the right choice?

As so often happened, a Bible verse floated into his mind. "*Take therefore no thought for the morrow: for the morrow shall take thought for the things of itself.*" Nathan gave silent thanks for the Holy Spirit's comfort. Yes, he'd see this trial through. He'd stand at his father's side, and then go home to his wife.

His lovely wife, safe at home.

Susanna followed the gelding's tracks into the rising sun. Why had the Millers been so cautious about letting her and Phoebe stay with them? She knew runaways could sometimes bring huge bounties to the hunters who tracked them, but neither the farmer nor his wife had said a word about fear of discovery.

Of course when Susanna had asked about Phoebe's whereabouts, Mrs. Miller had indicated that the girl was "safe in an upstairs room." Maybe the Millers had a hiding place. That would mean they were part of the network of people who helped runaway slaves and, other than their kindness to two strangers caught in a blizzard, the Millers had given no hint of their involvement.

Susanna turned her face to warm in the winter sunlight. God's creation never ceased to amaze her. A few hours earlier, she'd been fighting freezing wind and biting snow. Now she crossed the placid landscape at an untroubled pace. The route wound through fenced fields that lay under untouched mantles of snow, and although there were high drifts against the fences, the snow on the trail was only a few inches deep. Scattered along the way, heavily laden evergreens huddled in tight groups. On any other day, when she wasn't worried about a runaway slave, Susanna would've enjoyed the drive.

Mr. Miller had ridden so far ahead of her she'd never actually seen him, but his tracks made the course easy to follow. She scanned the trail he'd set for her. His horse's tracks showed a clear route, but a few yards later, she pulled her team to a stop.

There was a troubling disturbance in the immaculate snow. Hoof prints led from the tree line to the trail, stomping the snow into violet slush where Mr. Miller's horse had halted. Then what had happened? Susanna urged the horses on a few yards until she saw the single horse's tracks leading away from the slush.

"*Whoa,*" she called to the horses, pulling on the reins. The obedient team halted as Susanna pondered the situation. Evidently Mr. Miller had been stopped on the road, perhaps hailed by other travelers. He'd gone on, apparently alone. But if that were the case, where were the other travelers?

There were no other tracks. Either the other horses had evaporated into the sky or returned to the tree line from whence they'd come. That meant they were probably still there. A sharp pain darted through Susanna's head, and she rubbed her gloved hand against her forehead. Hadn't Mr. Miller said he'd come back if she were in trouble? Did the fact that he'd ridden ahead mean there was no danger?

Susanna's head dropped to her chest. What should she do? Hadn't she been through enough already? She'd nearly frozen to death the night before, and now just when the way seemed clear, she was forced to make another decision. Go ahead into possible danger, or turn back?

Turn back to where? Not to the Millers' farm. They'd made it clear they weren't willing to risk anything more.

Perhaps she could unhitch one of the horses and ride it to the settlement. She'd be faster on horseback, perhaps fast enough to outrun whatever trouble pursued her. And once she was among the Friends, one or more of them could return with her to the wagon.

But that would mean leaving Phoebe alone. Besides, she had no saddle for the horse, and she hadn't ridden bareback since she'd been a little girl. Images of galloping past villainous bounty hunters faded as reality took hold. If Susanna tried to outrace any pursuers, she'd end up on her bottom in the snow.

Susanna examined the single horse's tracks that led away from the slushy mess. Her imagination was running away with her. Obviously Mr. Miller had been stopped by someone and then ridden on alone. That he hadn't returned to warn her could mean only one thing: she had nothing to worry about.

Susanna flicked the reins across the horses' backs, and the wagon pulled ahead. They'd only traversed a few yards when two riders dashed from the tree line, their horses sending white plumes into the air as hooves crunched on snow. The lead rider blocked the trail, forcing Susanna's horses to stop while the other man paused beside the wagon.

He was a heavyset man dressed in a blue duster. He

touched the brim of his hat in greeting. "Morning, ma'am. How are you this fine morning?"

His friendly tone didn't fool Susanna. While one hand held his horse's reins, the other rested on the rifle laid across his saddle.

The second rider, a lean man with a sweat-stained hat, moved to the opposite side of the wagon. "Seems as though she don't much want to talk to you, Baxter."

The first rider smiled again. "Is that right, ma'am? You don't want to talk to me?"

It was one thing to be stopped by these men, but another to be toyed with—like a cat with its prey. "What do you want?" Susanna asked.

"So you do have a voice," Baxter said, a tobacco-stained smile crossing his face. "See there, Jamison? She ain't scared of me."

Jamison moved his jacket so that Susanna could see the pistol he'd shoved into his waistband. "I guess she's not," he replied.

Were they thieves? Bounty hunters? Only men determined to cause trouble carried pistols. Susanna put iron into her voice. "I repeat. What do you want?"

Baxter stood in his stirrups and leaned toward her. "I'll tell you what we want." His words were ripe with menace. "We want to know what you've got in that wagon."

Susanna adopted a casual air and looked over her shoulder, then frowned at Baxter in a pretense of confusion. "Hay, of course."

Jamison laughed loudly. "Guess she told you." He threw

his voice into a falsetto and imitated her. "Hay, of course."

Baxter wasn't amused. "I see by your bonnet that you're a Quaker. Bet you're on your way to that Quaker settlement in Bear Valley."

Susanna bristled at his intimidation. "What business is it of yours?"

Jamison let out another bark of laughter. "You've got yourself a hot one there, Baxter. Maybe *you* should be scared of *her*."

Baxter ignored his partner's outburst. "It's what's under the hay that interests me, ma'am. You see, we know Quakers like to hide runaway slaves any way they can. And a wagon big as this one, loaded with all that hay. . . Why, I'm thinking there could be at least four or five grown men hidden in there."

Susanna straightened, preparing herself to take on whatever trouble these men hurled. "No men are hidden in that hay," she asserted.

Baxter scratched the back of his head, pushing his hat low across his forehead. "I've heard that Quakers consider it a sin to tell a lie, but I don't think I quite believe you. It's awfully strange for a woman to be driving a hay wagon all by herself. Where's your man?"

Although she'd been trying to deny her fear, dread settled in the pit of Susanna's stomach. These men were bounty hunters. If they found Phoebe, who knew where they'd stop in their desire to punish those who aided the runaways?

"No answer, eh?" Baxter sneered at her. "Jamison, you awake over there?"

"Yes, boss."

"Go to the back, and light that hay on fire. Then we'll just sit back and wait for the slaves to jump out."

Fire? Alarm joined the dread in Susanna's belly. The fire could easily destroy the wagon and the hay. The thought of Phoebe trapped in the smoke and flames, burned alive or suffocated by the smoke, gave rise to a new level of terror.

Jamison dismounted and walked to the back of the wagon. Although Susanna couldn't see him, she heard the flint striking steel and knew she had only seconds to act. What should she do?

Drive ahead? No. There was no way her heavy wagon could outrun these men's horses. Where was Mr. Miller? Why hadn't he come back to help?

Baxter moved his horse to the rear of the wagon. "What's wrong?" he asked the other bounty hunter. "Don't tell me you can't light a fire."

"You know I can," Jamison answered. "But it's not so easy with wet hay."

Baxter climbed off his horse. "Give me that," he ordered. "I'll do it."

This is my chance, Susanna thought. With both men on the ground, she'd have a few moments to act before they could remount and chase her. The sickening smell of smoke wafted from the back of the wagon. How could she protect Phoebe?

She scanned the trail, desperately seeking a solution.

Then she saw the answer.

Susanna yelled and snapped the reins hard, forcing the

team to pull quickly. The horses whinnied and flattened their ears as smoke reached their noses, but they obeyed her command.

It would be difficult to convince the team to do what she wanted, but perhaps the smoke would confuse them enough to go against their natural instincts. She snapped the reins harder, and the animals picked up speed.

Behind her, she heard the men cursing and undoubtedly struggling to mount. She dared not look back. With another sharp snap of the reins, she drove the horses straight into a snowdrift.

The horses struggled to pull away but Susanna held the reins. "Whoa," she called. "Easy, now. Easy." She tied the reins to the bench and peered down the side of the wagon. *Yes!* She'd buried the secret compartment in the snow. That should protect Phoebe from both fire and smoke.

Without a second's hesitation, Susanna crawled over the bench to the top of the hay mound. She grabbed the pitchfork and tossed the burning clumps of hay onto the surrounding snow. *Hold on, Phoebe*, she pleaded silently. *Just hold on.*

Baxter and Jamison rode toward the wagon, the leaner man laughing and slapping his hat on his thigh. "What do you think you're doing, you crazy Quaker?" Baxter yelled. "You're going to get yourself burnt to a crisp."

Susanna ignored the men. From her spot on top of the load, she could see what the bounty hunters couldn't. The hay, still damp from the previous night's snow, was smoking more than burning, and the dry hay near the wagon's floor was packed too tightly to get enough air to burn. If she could remove the few patches of smoldering hay, she'd reduce the possibility of Phoebe taking in too much smoke.

Baxter used his rifle to nudge Jamison. "Get up there and help her."

Jamison stopped laughing. "What? Have you lost your mind, too?"

"You heard me," the heavyset man said. "Since the hay's too wet to burn good, get up there and help her throw it all out."

"I ain't no farm hand," Jamison argued. A look passed between the men. Then Jamison dismounted and, muttering beneath his breath, climbed to the top of the mound. He snatched the pitchfork from Susanna's hands. "Get down," he commanded. "Get out of here, so I can find the runaways you're trying so hard to save."

She hesitated. Should she cooperate or stand up to the bounty hunter? If he emptied the wagon, he'd prove there were no slaves beneath the hay. Then perhaps the two men would let her go on her way.

Jamison lowered his head to within an inch of hers and snarled, "Get off this wagon right now, or I'll throw you off."

She should be frightened. Any woman who knew what was good for her would be trembling by now. But other than her fear for Phoebe's survival, the only thing Susanna felt was anger.

Gathering her dignity around her like an invisible cloak, Susanna turned her back on the scoundrel and climbed down the wagon. When she was out of the way, Baxter took her place and began throwing armfuls of hay onto the snow. What would the bounty hunters do when they discovered there were no runaways in her wagon? Would they simply leave, or would they take out their disappointment on her?

Susanna stood by the horses as hay spurted from the wagon like water from a spring. There was only one thing left to do.

She knelt in the snow, closed her eyes, and folded her hands in front of her chest. "Dear Lord," she prayed, "I've been taught that every man is illuminated by the divine Light of Christ. Use that Light, O Lord, to help Mr. Baxter and Mr. Jamison look into their consciences. Give them the strength to overcome the darkness that prods them to do these wicked deeds. Help them to know the grace of God, which can bring salvation to their lives, no matter the depth of their sins."

Susanna opened her eyes. Both men stared down at her.

Baxter removed his hat and scowled at her. "Are you praying?"

"I am," Susanna said firmly.

"Are you praying for us?"

"Yes," she said.

Baxter climbed down the wagon and yanked Susanna to her feet. "Stop it! I don't need nobody praying for me. Nobody!"

Susanna met his scowl with a patient gaze.

Baxter pivoted and called up to the other man. "Can you touch the bottom with that pitchfork?"

Jamison stuck the tool through the hay in several spots

then repeated the action down the length of the wagon. "Seems as though she was telling the truth, boss. Nothing in this wagon but hay."

Baxter glared at Susanna. "Burn it. No Quaker's going to pray for me and get away with it." He strode to his horse.

Susanna returned to her knees.

"Did you hear me?" Baxter yelled. "Burn it!"

Jamison climbed down and mounted his horse. "No."

Baxter's face darkened. "Why, you worthless skunk. I knew you'd be no good when the going got tough. Get out of my way, and I'll burn it."

"No, boss. Nobody's going to burn this lady's wagon. And nobody's going to harm one hair on her head. What we've got here is a fine Christian lady who's done nothing wrong. She told us there weren't any slaves under the hay, and there aren't. So now we're going to go back to the tree where we tied that farmer then go on about our business."

Mr. Miller! The bounty hunters had ambushed him.

Baxter cursed loudly and spurred his horse. "This is quits for us," he yelled over his shoulder as he rode away.

"Good riddance!" Jamison shouted.

Susanna watched the bounty hunter's blue duster disappear into the dense forest.

Jamison walked toward Susanna, the pitchfork resting on his shoulder. "My momma used to pray for me. 'Course, it didn't do any good, but. . ."

Susanna stood. "If she could see you now, Mr. Jamison, I believe she'd be proud."

The man ducked his head, his face flooding with color.

"I don't know about that, ma'am." He walked toward the wagon, stopped, and turned back to Susanna. "Let's get this wagon out of the snow and the hay reloaded. We've got a farmer to rescue. I don't imagine his horse went far without him. He'll probably need a ride."

The sun was straight above Susanna's head by the time she arrived at the settlement. It didn't take long for her to identify the meetinghouse. Following Eli's instructions, she stopped the wagon in front of the building and waited for someone to come.

A trio of men approached. "Good day, Friend," they called.

"Good day, Friends," Susanna said. "I'm looking for Mr. Freeman. Can you help me?"

The men exchanged gazes, and the oldest of the three came closer. "If thee will allow me to join thee on the bench, I would be glad to drive thy wagon to Friend Freeman's barn."

This was the reply she'd been expecting. Eli had told her of the secret signal for communicating the presence of a runaway slave needing help. Once she'd uttered the name *Freeman*, the men of the settlement knew of her precious cargo. "Of course." She moved to allow room for the man to join her.

"I am Abner Larson." He took the reins and guided the horses away from the cluster of houses.

"My name is Susanna Griffith. My brother-in-law, Eli Wilson, sent me here."

Mr. Larson's shoulders visibly relaxd. "Oh yes. Eli. He has been here many times. Usually Brother Eli comes with Nathan Griffith. Be you Nathan's wife?"

Susanna felt her spirit lift at the mention of Nathan. "I am."

"How long has thee been on the road, Sister?"

"One night. Do you know Samuel Miller, a farmer who lives about two hours west of here?"

"I know him. He used to help many a poor soul seeking shelter. His son was badly injured by those who would keep the slave in shackles, and the Millers declined to help any longer."

That explained it. When he'd seen the settlement buildings, Mr. Miller had bid her farewell and turned his horse toward home.

"Why does thee ask about the Millers?" Mr. Larson asked.

"They helped me last night when I was caught in the blizzard."

"Thee was out in that terrible storm? Many a good man has been lost in blinding snow like that. Thank the Lord the Millers helped thee. Was the rest of thy journey smooth?"

Susanna almost laughed. *Smooth* wasn't a word she'd use to describe her encounter with the bounty hunters.

Mr. Larson listened as she told of the scoundrels who had tried to burn the hay. "Sister Griffith!" he exclaimed when she finished. "That was certainly quick thinking on thy part. As it says in the book of James, 'the prayer of the righteous is powerful and effective.' Seems as though the Lord used thee to remind the rogue of Christ's goodness that lives in us all. But why does thee travel alone? Could not Brother Eli or Brother Nathan make the trip?"

Susanna explained the circumstances of her solitary journey. When she told Mr. Larson about Phoebe's imminent delivery, he blanched and prodded the horses to move faster. Soon they arrived at a farmhouse surrounded by tall spruce trees. The wagon wheels had barely stopped moving when a group of men and women hurried from the house and nearby barn.

How good it was to be among Friends again. The women's white caps and the men's broad-brimmed black hats convinced Susanna she'd finally arrived safely. But what about Phoebe? Susanna hadn't dared to stop and check on the girl for fear that other bounty hunters could be spying on her.

A pair of strong arms lifted Susanna off the wagon, and she hurried to the back. Two men had removed the partition and were helping Phoebe slide out of the compartment. Susanna rushed to her side. "We made it, Phoebe. We're here at last. Are you all right?"

Tears streamed down Phoebe's face. "Am I free?" she whispered hoarsely. "Am I free?"

"Yes, Phoebe. You're free."

Phoebe wrapped her arms around her abdomen. "Oh, Lord! Thank You, Lord. Thank You, Jesus. My baby will never be a slave. Thank You, Lord."

Susanna's vision blurred as tears filled her eyes. She'd be willing to endure much more than a blizzard to feel the way she did at that moment.

"Where's my Tom?" Phoebe asked. "Do any of you know my husband, Tom? He came from the Hansen farm in Bracken County, Kentucky. Please, where's my Tom?"

Heads turned as the Friends muttered among themselves. When the conversation abated, Mr. Larson spoke for the group. "Is thy husband a tall man with a scar across his right cheek?"

"Yes," Phoebe answered. "Where is he? Where's my husband?"

"He is on a neighboring farm, only a few miles away. We will send for him." Mr. Larson gestured to a petite woman in a blue dress. "This is my wife. She will take care of thee."

Mrs. Larson came to Phoebe's side. "I fear that thy pains have already started. Am I right?"

Pains? Had Phoebe been in the first stages of delivering her child while she'd been stuffed in that stifling compartment?

"Yes, ma'am." Phoebe took a few steps and bent at the waist, her hands on her knees. "I didn't know the pains would be so strong. Granny told me the first hours of childbearing were the easiest."

"Come into the house," Mrs. Larson said, "and we will make thee comfortable. And do not worry about a thing. Many a baby has been born on this farm."

A look of uncertainty shadowed Phoebe's face, and she looked questioningly at Susanna. "It's all right," Susanna said reassuringly. "No one's going to hurt you or your baby. And your husband will be here soon."

Phoebe looked at the surrounding women then turned pleading eyes to Susanna. "Will you stay with me, ma'am? At least until my Tom comes?"

The Griffiths were expecting Susanna to return that very day. If she left within the hour, she'd be home by late afternoon. Phoebe's hand lightly touched Susanna's. "Please, ma'am?"

The poor girl. After what she'd been through the last few days, who could blame Phoebe for needing someone she knew to stay close? Susanna covered Phoebe's hand with her own. "Of course," she replied.

Chapter 5

Nathan and his father slowed their horses to a walk. "We'll be home soon," Thomas said. "No need to work the horses into a lather just to get there a few minutes earlier."

"I know thee is right, but I long to be home."

"Perhaps thee is missing thy wife." Thomas grinned teasingly.

"I find no shame in admitting it. Letters have been small comfort."

"I believe we were right to go to Mason County. Once again we have witnessed the truth behind the Lord's words: 'All things work together for good to them that love God.' I will never forget the silence of the courtroom when the jury pronounced Brother Mahan not guilty. Not even Judge Reid had the temerity to issue one of his lengthy philosophical statements."

"And the way Reverend Mahan stood motionless and stared silently at the judge. He was like a prophet of old, daring the nonbeliever to deny the power of the Lord."

"Brother Mahan will be home soon. His health is not good, but a few weeks at home will surely cure him."

They pulled their horses to a stop at the top of the hill. From that spot Nathan could see the Griffiths' farm and house.

"Smoke is coming out of the chimney," he said, "and the

horses are in the pasture. Seems as though everything's right enough."

"Yes," Thomas said. "But does thee see that smoke rising from the woods to the west?"

Nathan squinted in the direction his father had indicated. "Someone's made camp."

"Someone who wants to keep an eye on us. It is just as Brother Jackson told us. Bounty hunters so brazen, they have trespassed onto our property."

Apprehension squeezed Nathan's heart. He'd been wrong to leave his wife alone with rascals camping two hundred yards away from their cabin. "I need to go on, Father. After I've checked on Susanna, I'll bring her to the house."

Thomas nodded, and Nathan turned his horse toward the sheltered spot where he'd built the cabin for his wife. The weeks he'd spent in Kentucky seemed like months. Now that Brother Mahan was finally free from the awful jail, perhaps Nathan's life could return to its normal routine.

Nathan spurred his horse into a trot, a pace that matched his own heartbeat. He'd done what he could to keep in touch with his family, but nothing could replace the feel of his wife in his arms. Once they were safely reunited, he'd hold Susanna until his arms ached from the pleasure of it.

When the cabin came into view, Nathan smiled broadly. One second later, the smile withered into a concerned frown. There was no smoke coming from the chimney. Even if Susanna had left for a few hours, he should be able to smell wood smoke from the banked coals. He scanned the meadow where his horses grazed during fair-weather days; it was empty. Even the barnyard was bare, devoid of the ever-present chickens that spent the day scratching for bugs and seeds.

The cabin was a lifeless shell. A pain shot through Nathan's jaw as he realized something was seriously wrong. He fought the dreadful images that besieged his mind, holding panic at bay while he dismounted and ran into the cabin.

The cabin's single room was neat. The bed linens were arranged perfectly, and clean dishes had been placed on the shelves. Susanna's clothes hung from the pegs he'd driven into the wall, but her jacket, cape, and bonnet were missing.

Nathan forced air into his lungs. The orderliness of the cabin told him no one had broken in, and the absence of Susanna's outer garments pointed to the fact that she'd simply left.

Where was she?

Gradually Nathan's breath slowed, and his heartbeat resumed a normal rate. As his body relaxd, logic reappeared in his troubled mind. Susanna had probably gone to stay with his mother and sister in his absence. It was too much to expect a young woman, married for only five months, to live alone for three weeks.

Nathan stepped outside and started down the trail that led to his parents' house. Halfway there, his mother met him.

"Praise the Lord, thee has returned safely." Martha threw her arms around his neck.

"It's good to see thee, Mother." Nathan stepped back from her embrace and scanned the trail. "Where's Susanna? Isn't she with thee?"

Martha squeezed Nathan's hand in hers. "I have something to tell thee, Son."

❆

Nathan paced back and forth in front of the kitchen fireplace while his family watched. "I can't believe thee let her go," he said through clenched teeth. "Especially thee, Eli. Thee knows what could happen to Susanna if she's discovered."

Miriam stood to face her brother. "We've explained the circumstances of Susanna's journey. She was the only one of us who could go. Thee must not blame my husband."

When his wife was safely home, Nathan would apologize to whomever he'd offended. For the moment, he had no patience for politeness. "I'll be leaving within the hour. I need to change horses and pack provisions."

"Leaving?" Martha asked. "Where is thee going?"

"After Susanna, of course. There's only one road to the Friends' settlement in Bear Valley. I'm sure to meet her on the way."

"That would not be wise," Thomas said.

Nathan spun on his heel, ready to dispute his father's words. "Now thee speaks of wisdom? No one considered what was wise when they sent my wife on a perilous journey."

Thomas's eyebrows rose, and Nathan knew his tone had been impertinent. His father answered with calm deliberation. "I agree that thee should go. Not only for Susanna's sake but for thy own. I advise thee to wait until darkness falls. If the bounty hunters see thee leave, they are likely to follow. And that would put Susanna in greater jeopardy. We cannot know for sure that Susanna has delivered her special guest."

Nathan's shoulders slumped. Although he was anxious to find his wife and bring her back to the safety of their cabin, he knew his father was right. His hands fisted at his side. "This is my fault." His jaw tightened.

"No, Son. Susanna chose to make this trip, and we must honor the call she heard."

"I thought I could keep Susanna away from the danger. If anything happens to her—" Nathan covered his face with his hand and turned away from his family. He fought to maintain his composure, but his mother's gentle hand on his shoulder almost undid him.

"We have been in constant prayer for Susanna since she drove away," she said soothingly. "We will continue, without ceasing, until she returns."

Nathan's body longed to move, to mount a fresh horse and search for his wife. The muscles in his jaw clenched and unclenched as his good sense battled against his instincts. He'd pledged to protect Susanna. Was prayer really the only thing he could do? He looked at the earnest, placid faces of his sister and parents. They'd found comfort in the Lord, but Nathan's fretfulness would not allow him to be still.

"I'll pray," Nathan said. "But it will be outside where I can watch for the first sight of my wife."

Susanna sat by Phoebe's bed, wiping beads of perspiration from the girl's face and counting the minutes until Tom arrived. Susanna couldn't listen anymore to Phoebe's moans. Susanna had helped with births before, but nothing in her experience had prepared her for Phoebe's screams.

The midwife took no heed of Phoebe's distress. "It's a big baby and a little mother," she explained. "But there's no need to worry. Everything's moving right on schedule."

Phoebe blew out a long breath and relaxd her grip on the bedclothes. "I guess it won't be much longer before I'll be seeing my son."

Realizing the girl must be in between pains, Susanna refilled a cup with cool water. "You think it's a boy?"

"Must be. The way he's been kicking, and the fight he's putting up just to get out and see the world... Why, it must be a boy."

"What will you name him?"

Phoebe drained the cup and returned it to Susanna. "Tom, of course, after his daddy."

"And if it's a girl?"

Phoebe raised her eyebrows. "A girl? I hadn't much thought about girl names."

"Children are often named after grandparents. What is your mother's name?"

"Oh, ma'am, I don't know that. For as long as I can remember, there's just been Granny. She says my momma was sold shortly after I was weaned, and nobody knows who my daddy was. Granny took me in."

The image of a slave woman forced to abandon her child burned into Susanna's mind. That explained why Phoebe had risked her life and her baby's life to reach freedom. No one would separate Phoebe from her baby the way a cow was separated from a calf.

The midwife returned with clean linen. "There's someone here to see you," she said, smiling broadly.

For a second Susanna didn't know if the woman addressed her or Phoebe, but when a tall, dark man rushed into the room, Phoebe gave a shout of joy.

"Tom! Oh, Tom!" They embraced, and tears of joy streamed down the young girl's cheeks. "I made it, Tom," Phoebe said, between chortles of laughter. "I made it just in time."

Tom did not respond, only tightened his hold on his wife.

Susanna took the opportunity to slip away and search for the Larsons. She found the farmer with another man, emptying the Griffiths' hay wagon. Mrs. Larson stood nearby.

"How fares our guest?" the man asked.

"The midwife says the baby will come soon. I didn't know you had need of the hay."

"Yes, Sister Griffith. That's the way thy husband and I have arranged the passage. Those who watch the roads see a load of hay headed north and an empty wagon headed south. I sell the hay for thy family. In fact when thee returns tomorrow, I have a bag of coins to send with thee."

"Thank you, but I wish to begin my journey now. My responsibility to Phoebe has been discharged, and my husband's family expects me today."

"No, Sister. Stay thee the night. Tomorrow morning Friend Jacobson and his son will escort thee to your home."

"I'd rather go while the good weather holds. It's only four hours to the Griffiths' farm. If I leave now, I'll be home just after dark."

Mrs. Larson spoke for the first time. "'Tis not wise to

travel the roads at night, Sister. I know thee undertook the journey in the dark, but that could not be helped. Thy way home will be much safer."

"Besides," Mr. Larson added, "Brother Jacobson and his son cannot leave until morning. Although we could not offer thee our protection yesterday, we most certainly will tomorrow."

There was no way they could force her to stay. If she had to, she could hitch the horses to the wagon by herself and make the journey on her own.

Mrs. Larson laid a hand on Susanna's arm, startling her from her thoughts. "Thy mind is easy to read, Sister. Thy face shows quite clearly what thee is considering. And thee is correct. My husband and I will not force thee to stay. But thee risked so much to come, why prolong that risk by returning tonight?"

"My husband's family will be worried if I don't return tonight."

"Better a sleepless night followed by a morning of rejoicing than months of grief, should any harm come to thee."

While Susanna paused to consider her options, Mrs. Larson guided her out of the barn and toward the house. Susanna tossed one last look over her shoulder at the Griffiths' hay wagon. Although the Larsons' persuasion had been gentle, they'd made the decision for her. She'd be going home the next morning.

❄

A band of pale peach light rose above the trees, changing the black sky to violet when Susanna knocked softly at Phoebe's door. She knew the girl must be exhausted, yet she craved one last look at the beautiful baby born in the wee hours of the morning.

"Come in," Phoebe said.

"I don't want to disturb you," Susanna said, entering the room. "I wanted to say good-bye."

Phoebe held out a hand, and Susanna sat on the edge of the bed. "Oh, ma'am. How am I ever going to finish saying thank you? Because of you, my baby was born free. She'll never be a slave. I'll never have to watch her being carted away to another farm far away from me." Phoebe patted the child cradled in her arms.

Susanna used her finger to lift the baby's tiny, fisted hand. "She's so beautiful. Have you and Tom thought of a name yet?"

"We came up with the best name in the world for this little girl. We're going to call her Liberty Susanna."

Susanna felt the warmth as it rushed into her cheeks and knew she must be blushing. "Oh, Phoebe. You didn't name her. . .I mean, you didn't call her Susanna because. . ."

"Of course we did, ma'am. My baby and I owe everything to you. Our lives, our freedom, our whole future. Tom says that once I'm able to travel, we'll be on the road to Canada. He says your friends have a town there where the freed slaves live and work. It'll just be wonderful, don't you think? Me and Tom and Libby?"

Susanna raised the baby's hand to her lips and kissed it. "Hello, Libby. You're a lucky little girl to have such a brave momma."

"I don't know about that, ma'am. From what you told me, sounds like you had to face some mighty big wolves along the way. All I had to do was lie quietly in the bottom of a wagon."

"But my adventure's over." Susanna tucked the baby's hand under its blanket. "I'll be back home in a few hours." The rumble of men's voices carried up the stairs. "In fact that's probably my escort. Two Friends are going to accompany me this morning."

Phoebe squeezed Susanna's hand. "I hope I get to see you again someday, ma'am. I hope you'll get to see Libby when she's all grown up and beautiful. Won't that be the day? When my little girl can go anywhere she wants and not be afraid of slavers trying to catch her?"

"I pray that day comes soon."

Heavy footsteps trod up the stairs and stopped at Phoebe's door. "Susanna?" Mrs. Larson called. "Are you there?"

"Yes. Come in."

The door swung open, and Susanna's heart bounded for joy. There, in the doorway, stood her husband. "Nathan!" She shot off the bed and into his arms.

Nathan's arms tightened around her, and his lips brushed her hair. Tears filled Susanna's eyes as she lifted silent thanks for his safe return.

"*Shh.*" Nathan wiped away her tears with his thumb. "No need to cry. Everything's all right now."

"I know," Susanna whispered, her throat tight. "I know." She breathed deeply, inhaling the scent of her husband, and her worries evaporated. Nathan was safe and well.

His work-hardened hands cupped her face, lifting her gaze to his. "What's this I hear about a blizzard, two bounty hunters, a fire, and a runaway?"

Susanna ducked her head in embarrassment. Was Nathan angry? How did he know everything?

"Friend Larson told me all about thy trip when I found him at the meetinghouse," Nathan said. "I believe thee will have quite a story to tell on the way home."

Was that a smile Susanna heard in her husband's voice? Susanna glanced at Nathan's face and saw love and approval beaming from his eyes. She laid her head on his chest and rejoiced to feel his arms tighten around her once again.

The whimper of a baby caused Nathan to ease back from Susanna. "May I meet our special guest?"

Susanna took his hand and led him to the bed. "Nathan, this is Phoebe and her daughter, Liberty."

"Liberty Susanna." Phoebe moved the blanket away from the baby's face.

Nathan smiled down at his wife. "Good name."

❄

The piercing crow of the rooster woke Susanna, but she didn't have to wonder where her husband was. His arm held her tightly against him under the quilts. After an evening of celebrating her safe return with Nathan's family, the exhausted couple had returned to their cabin and stumbled into bed.

Nathan's lips on her head let Susanna know he no longer slept. "Good morning, wife," he said, yawning. "Did thee sleep well?"

"Very well. It's good to have you home again."

"It's good to be home."

A noise caused Susanna to rise up on one elbow. "Someone's in the barnyard."

"Is there?" Nathan yawned again.

"You know there is." Susanna narrowed her eyes. "Why aren't you concerned?"

"It's only Eli. He agreed to tend the stock one more day so we could rest. Lie down again so I may talk to thee."

Susanna nestled her head on her husband's shoulder. "You were mighty quiet yesterday when I told you everything that happened on the way to Bear Valley. Now that you've had time to think about it, I'm afraid of what you have to say."

"Afraid, Susanna? Of me?"

"No, Nathan. Never. But I fear you will chastise me for the risk I took, and if truth be told, I can't wait to do it again."

Nathan's fingers stroked Susanna's hair, the seconds ticking away in silence. Susanna had pledged to obey her husband, and if he forbade her from helping the runaways, she'd have no choice but to abide by his decision. Yet her experience with Phoebe had given her a purpose she'd never imagined. She could no longer simply look the other way.

Nathan's fingers stilled. "Thee would risk thy life again to help another runaway?"

Susanna rose to one elbow and looked into her husband's dark eyes. "Don't you risk your life when you go?"

"Not as much as thee did. A woman traveling alone can

be a lure for evil men. Does thee know what losing thee would mean to me? My heart would never heal from such a loss."

Susanna's heart warmed at her husband's words. "Nor would mine if I lost you. The weeks without you were the loneliest of my life. I've come to love your mother and sister as though they were my own family, but they were no substitute for you."

Nathan sat up and frowned at Susanna. "As your husband, I have the right to forbid thee from helping the runaways."

The very words Susanna had dreaded. But her husband's serious expression didn't deter her. "Don't the Friends believe that men and women are created equal in the eyes of God?"

"Thee speaks of the testimony of equality, and I do my best to be a witness to that belief. But how can I fulfill my pledge to protect thee if thee refuses to keep thyself away from danger?"

"It wouldn't always be as dangerous as it was with Phoebe. Eli and your father both said Phoebe's situation was unusual. And your sister told me runaways sometimes stay several days until suitable passage can be arranged."

"That's true."

"So it's unlikely that I'll ever be in such a dangerous circumstance again."

"Perhaps," Nathan muttered between clenched teeth.

Susanna rose to her knees and faced her husband. "I want to be your equal, Nathan. Knowing that I helped Phoebe and her baby made me feel as though I could fly. Don't ask me to give up such a wonderful mission. Until slavery is banished from this country, I want to be at your side, fighting it every step of the way."

Nathan took Susanna's hands in his and spoke in a soft tone. "Thee speaks more like a Friend every day. Has thee thought more about petitioning the committee for admittance?"

"I know your mother wants me to join. I've adopted the bonnet, and I enjoy going to First Day Meetings. But you said you'd give me all the time I needed."

"And I intend to keep my word. Now that thee wishes to enlist in the Quaker struggle against slavery, I thought that perhaps thee was ready to join."

"I love your family, Nathan, and I love you. But taking that last step. . .throwing off my family's traditions and taking up yours. . .oh, I don't know what's holding me back."

Susanna looked away from her husband's piercing gaze. He wanted her to join his faith. Was that so awful? If she did take that last step, if she did take up the title of Quaker, would he allow her to aid the runaways who came to the Griffiths for help?

"Nathan." Her words struggled past the lump in her throat. "Do you want me to become a Quaker?"

"That is a question that only thee and thy soul can answer, Susanna. If the Holy Spirit moves thee to join the Society, then I will be glad."

She swallowed and looked at her husband. "And if I never join?"

"Then we will continue as we are. Surely thee knows my

love does not hinge on thee becoming a Friend."

Susanna blew out a breath. How good Nathan was. How blessed she was to have a husband who loved the Lord and who loved her. Yet the question remained unanswered. "If I petition the committee for admittance, then will you allow me to help you when the runaways come?"

Nathan laid his cheek in his hand and studied her. After a long silence, he finally spoke. "I will not prevent thee from helping, Susanna. If thee feels moved to do something to help the runaways or to put an end to the abomination of slavery, I will not forbid it. But Susanna, thee must allow me to guide thee in these matters. My family has helped in this cause for many years. Tread softly, wife, and take the counsel of those who know the dangers."

Susanna threw her arms around her husband's neck, and he fell back on the pillows, his laughter ringing through the cabin. "Hold on there, wife, or thee will send us both to the cold floor!"

Susanna snuggled against him, returning her head to his shoulder. "Thank you, Nathan."

Nathan's arms surrounded her. "I do not believe that thee is the same wife I left three weeks ago."

"Of course I am. Who else would I be?"

"'Tis true thy name is still Susanna Griffith, but thee is not the girl I left. I know thee chafed at being left alone. Yet I returned to find a woman prepared to take on the worst atrocity known to mankind. Mother says thee has grown up."

Susanna recalled her pouting and sulking. Had it been only a few days ago that she'd been tempted to brood in the

347

mire of self-pity? She felt her face flush with embarrassment and covered her face with the sheet. "I hope Mother Griffith will forgive me."

"Worry not," Nathan said. "In fact, while thee was telling everyone about thy adventure last night, Mother told me that she and Father have decided they will celebrate Christmas."

Susanna's head popped back up. "Really? Won't they get in trouble?"

"Of course not. Our Meeting leaves matters such as these to each person's conscience. Mother says we will exchange gifts and have a family dinner. Is there more we should do?"

"No! I mean, that would be wonderful. My family goes to church on Christmas morning, and there are traditional songs—"

"I can't promise any singing, Susanna. Thee knows how the Friends feel about music. But if thee wants to sing. . ."

"No! I mean. . . It doesn't matter. If I feel a Christmas carol coming on I'll go to the barn and sing to the animals. How about that?"

Nathan held her chin in his fingers. "Would thee sing to the animals and not to me? Let me know of thy intention, and I'll escort thee to the lucky animals that get to hear thy voice lifted in song."

Laughter bubbled up from her heart. Helping Phoebe had tested Susanna, and she'd passed the test. All of her fears and worries had been for naught. Phoebe was on her way to safety, Nathan was home, and she could continue to help the fugitive slaves. "Oh, Nathan." Susanna flung her arms around his neck. "Thee is so good to me."

After many years of writing and publishing in the nonfiction world of academia, Claire Sanders turned her energy, humor, and creativity toward the production of compelling romantic fiction. Claire lives in the greater Houston area with her daughter and two well-loved dogs. When she isn't writing, you'll find her cooking, gardening, and dreaming of places to travel.

Recipe for Gingerbread Cookies
(from Colonial Williamsburg, Virginia)

INGREDIENTS:

1 cup sugar
2 teaspoons ginger
1 teaspoon nutmeg
1 teaspoon cinnamon
1½ teaspoons baking soda
½ teaspoon salt
1 cup melted margarine
½ cup evaporated milk

1 cup unsulfured molasses
¾ teaspoon vanilla extract
¾ teaspoon lemon extract
4 cups stone-ground or unbleached flour, unsifted

INSTRUCTIONS: Combine sugar, ginger, nutmeg, cinnamon, baking soda, and salt. Mix well. Add melted margarine, evaporated milk, and molasses. Add extracts. Mix well. Add flour 1 cup at a time, stirring constantly. Dough should be stiff enough to handle without sticking to fingers. Knead dough for a smoother texture. Add up to ½ cup additional flour if necessary to prevent sticking. When dough is smooth, roll it out ¼-inch thick on floured surface and cut into cookies. Bake on floured or greased cookie sheets in preheated 375 degree oven for 10 to 12 minutes. Gingerbread cookies are done when they spring back when touched.

A Letter to Our Readers

Dear Readers:

In order that we might better contribute to your reading enjoyment, we would appreciate you taking a few minutes to respond to the following questions. When completed, please return to the following: Fiction Editor, Barbour Publishing, Inc., P.O. Box 719, Uhrichsville, OH 44683.

1. Did you enjoy reading *A Quaker Christmas* by Lauralee Bliss, Ramona Cecil, Rachael Phillips, and Claire Sanders?
   - ❑ Very much. I would like to see more books like this.
   - ❑ Moderately—I would have enjoyed it more if _____
   _____
   _____

2. What influenced your decision to purchase this book?
   (Check those that apply.)
   - ❑ Cover
   - ❑ Back cover copy
   - ❑ Title
   - ❑ Price
   - ❑ Friends
   - ❑ Publicity
   - ❑ Other

3. Which story was your favorite?
   - ❑ *A Crossroad to Love*
   - ❑ *Pirate of My Heart*
   - ❑ *Simple Gifts*
   - ❑ *Equally Yoked*

4. Please check your age range:
   - ❑ Under 18
   - ❑ 18–24
   - ❑ 25–34
   - ❑ 35–45
   - ❑ 46–55
   - ❑ Over 55

5. How many hours per week do you read? _____

Name _____

Occupation _____

Address _____

City_____ State _____ Zip _____

E-mail _____